Marissa de Luna

Marissa is a passionate autho
twenties. After spending her
Marissa returned to England to complete her education.

With a keen passion for travelling, Marissa later took a career break and travelled around the globe for ten months. On returning home she spent time with her family in Goa, and it was this period in which Marissa, inspired by the Goan culture and lifestyle, decided to put pen to paper and started writing her first book.

Her previous books include *Goa Traffic*, *The Bittersweet Vine*, and *Under the Coconut Tree.*

Visit her website: www.marissadeluna.com

Poison in the Water

Lies, deceit and a love story that must be told

Marissa de Luna

Lost Button Publishing

For Anna

Prologue

Barnet, North London

'We've talked about this before.'

'It's just…'

'It'll help you.' Elaine sat down on the red chair. She motioned for her to sit opposite. 'Shall we do this?'

Celeste looked towards the door and back at Elaine.

'I want to know why you did it.'

She caught her reflection in the glass. Why was she even here?

It's unhealthy, Celeste. You have to let go. Her mother had said it and so had Alicia. But she couldn't let go. It wasn't that easy. Sometimes you had to pretend though. Pretend that everything was fine even though you were a mess underneath it all. And that last meeting with Rachel; it had been a mistake.

Something in Elaine's hand caught her eye. It looked familiar.

'You remember this picture?' Elaine placed a photograph on the desk beside them.

'Where did you get that? It's mine.'

'Okay, take it.'

She stared at the picture, before reaching out to it and gently touching it with the tips of her trembling fingers. The expression of the woman in the photograph was vacant, her grey eyes sunken and empty, her hair lifeless – any happiness had been sucked out of her.

'Take it away.' She could push as forcefully as he had. Perhaps not then, when she was… when she was raw with pain and grief, but now... now she was strong. One shove would do. Would that make it right?

'When was the picture taken?'

She clutched the gold bumblebee pendant that hung from her neck. 'About two years ago.'

'That would be around the time you –'

Celeste cut Elaine off. 'I wasn't in a good place then.'

'It's odd that someone would take a picture of you when you were in that condition.'

'Back then I couldn't tell the difference between what was normal and what wasn't.'

'How does it make you feel when you see that picture?'

'Angry. I should never have let things go that far. But I didn't know a person could change so much. I didn't realise what he was capable of.'

'What things are you referring to?'

Could she trust Elaine? Her mind drifted. One push, one bullet, one cut. Is that all it would take? Would the pain disappear then? Would she be able to forget?

Elaine leaned back in her chair. 'Can you explain to me how the woman in this picture feels?'

Celeste tucked a strand of her hair behind her ear. Her hair was shoulder length and dark brown now, the colour of a chestnut. Back to her natural colour after years of cropping it and dying it black – the way he liked it. Her cheeks were filling out too. She no longer carried that gaunt expression that made her mother pile more potatoes onto her plate. The blusher she had applied went some way to make her look alive. Alive. She was lucky to be alive.

She could feel the tears pricking the back of her eyes. The lump in her throat made it difficult for her to breathe, but she had promised herself no more tears. Swallowing hard, she bit the inside of her cheek until the metallic taste of blood stopped her. Then, closing her eyes, she tried to steady her breathing.

'Things were not always that bad.' She looked at the woman sitting in front of her. Elaine was safe in her floaty skirt and unoffending beige T-shirt, but Celeste knew she had made bad judgements before. That's why she was here, wasn't she? Elaine could be a little direct at times, but she had a way of making her say things she wouldn't normally. 'Okay,' she said eventually. Celeste looked at the clock on the wall. It was late. 'You want to know why I did it. Fine. I'll tell you my story.'

Part I

1

10th – 12th April 2007
Phuket, Thailand

'Ow!' Celeste yelped. She clutched her grazed ankle at the baggage carousel and looked up. A tall man wearing black and red board shorts and a white linen shirt smiled down at her apologetically as she crouched down, tending to her leg.

'My fault, sorry.' The man lifted up her heavy backpack as if it were a sack of feathers. He smiled an infectious smile, making her blush.

She noticed his backpack propped against the scuffed airport wall. A shark's tooth hung from a cord around his tanned neck. 'Traveller?'

He nodded.

She hobbled towards the wall and slumped against it. It was hot. Other travellers had said April was a bad time to visit Thailand, but she had tired of New Zealand. She wanted to experience a different culture and she knew Thailand was the best place for that. She looked over the man in front of her. There was something irresistible about his smile, which made her wonder how many girls he had bedded across the globe in shared hostel rooms.

'I'm Alex,' he said, dropping her bag to the floor and holding out his hand. He looked at her, really looked at her. Men often gave her a second glance, did a double take at a party commenting on her unique grey eyes and petite frame, but this was different. It was like he saw something he wanted in her. She found herself irrationally worrying about her appearance: did she have sleep in her eyes, had she stained her top from the burrito she had eaten mid-flight? Her cheeks burned as Alex studied her eyes.

Celeste took his hand and introduced herself.

'Pretty name.'

'Heavenly.'

He broke his gaze and blinked. 'I grabbed my bag off the carousel in haste and swiped your leg in the process. I didn't mean it and I apologised, there's no need for sarcasm.' Alex lifted his backpack onto his shoulders and Celeste watched his muscles flex under his shirt. He turned and walked towards the exit leaving behind the faint scent of sandalwood as he headed towards a group of taxi drivers shouting for his attention.

Celeste picked her bag up and put it on a chair nearby; she squatted with her back towards it so that the shoulder straps were at the same height as her neck. Gently, she lowered the bag on to her back. It had taken her three months of travel to figure out the perfect way of picking up fifty-five litres of possessions. Now she had it down to a tee.

*

Within two days she had grown tired of Phuket with its bright lights and trashy tourists. It wasn't the Thailand she had in mind. Thumbing through her guidebook, she stopped at Koh

Phi Phi. Almost every traveller she had met in the last forty-eight hours had been reading *The Beach*. The book seemed to be the travellers' bible, and dog-eared copies littered hostel common rooms. Hungry backpackers were keen to experience the same utopian lifestyle that Leonardo Di Caprio had stumbled upon in that movie set on the island. She considered it and was certain that it would be overrun by tourists, but it would be a stepping stone to the other islands. She would take a boat out there for a day or two and then move on to the lesser known Koh Lanta or Koh Tao.

The tuk-tuk pulled up alongside the ferry terminal near Phuket's marina where backpackers in flip flops walked along the rickety deck towards a white and blue boat. Celeste stepped down and paid the tuk-tuk driver ten baht. She was sure she had been ripped off, but she was too tired to argue. A strong stench of rotting fish and diesel made her retch. She steadied herself, trying to ignore the smell and then made her way, in the fake *Havaianas*, which she had picked up in the Phuket market, towards the front of the boat. She purchased her ticket and found a seat. A small barefoot boy, in a pair of shorts, sat precariously on the upper deck throwing rice into the water. Hundreds of silver fish, glimmering in the midday sun, swam up to eat his offerings. She looked out in amazement, momentarily distracted from her surroundings. It was unbearably hot in the cabin, and, with heavy luggage being thrown into the bowels of the ferry, it had started to rock. She felt a wave of nausea rising up within her.

'Ginger?' she heard a familiar voice and looked up.

It was Alex.

'No thanks,' she said, trying to think about not being sick in front of him. She wasn't sure if her eyes were playing games with her, but he looked more attractive now than he had done at the airport. He had a layer of stubble around his jaw and wore loose khaki linen trousers and a white T-shirt. He smelled of soap and sandalwood.

'It'll take that nauseated feeling away. Make you feel much better.' Alex thrust the bag of ginger lozenges at her. She took one and placed it in her mouth, sucking on it as hard as she could. After a few minutes the queasy feeling began to subside.

'So you're following me then?' He flashed her a smile, making her cheeks go pink.

'You sat down next to me,' she retorted. There was something arrogant in his manner that both attracted and repelled her. 'I need some air,' she said, reaching up to the window. Alex immediately sprang to his feet and tried to help her with the handle; his hand touched hers and an electric spark ran through her. Her heart rate quickened and she turned to him with the sudden urge to feel his lips on hers. His face was only a few centimetres away as he stood behind her. She noticed his brilliant blue eyes and his smooth lips. He grinned, and after pushing the window open, sat back down.

She stood up, filled her lungs with sea air then sat down again, avoiding his eyes. Could he sense that she wanted to kiss him? When she finally looked up, he winked at her, then pulled out his iPod and shoved the earpieces in.

How odd and rude of him to come and talk to her and then, like at the airport, just ignore her and do his own thing. She retrieved her bright pink iPod Nano from her bag, which had been a parting gift from work. Crosby in the Marketing team had even pre-loaded some music for her, which was a bonus, as she would never have got around to doing it herself. Technology was not her forte. Her mother always said she was too artistic for that.

As they pulled out of the Marina, she noticed the yachts that sparkled in the sun amidst the cool blue ocean. She watched carefully as their ferry passed a white yacht called *Principessa*. What would it be like to travel on one of those? To be able to have your crew bring you a club soda with ice or a cold flute of *Bollinger* on a hot day such as this. As a bead of sweat trickled down her back, she saw a woman in a large sun hat and oversized sun glasses appear on the back of the *Principessa* carrying a glass of something. She imagined it to be an ice-cold gin and tonic – something she could have done with right now. The woman wore an orange and black kaftan; a gold pendant hung low near her belly button and glimmered in the sunlight. She was talking animatedly on a mobile phone. A sliver of envy ran through Celeste. What she would give to travel to Koh Phi Phi on her own yacht rather than a ferry full of travellers.

'I'm going to own one of those some day,' Alex said, as if reading her mind. She noticed he too was looking at the *Principessa*. He pulled his earphones out and motioned for her to do the same. Celeste turned away and pretended she hadn't heard him, but he was persistent. Eventually he pulled her earphones out for her. 'If you owned a boat like that what would you call it?'

She often dreamed of all the things she would buy if and when she won the lottery, but she had never before thought of what she would call her yacht.

'Heavenly,' he suggested. 'That's what your name means, doesn't it?'

Celeste smiled. 'So you got it, eventually.'

'If I had a yacht I'd call it after the lady in my life,' Alex said.

'And what if she left you for someone better-off and better looking?'

'Ha! That would never happen.'

She rolled her eyes. 'So what do you do when you're not injuring people or being arrogant?'

'I'm a stripper'

He had her attention now. She pursed her lips unsure of what to say. 'So people pay to see *that*?' she said, pointing to his chest. She gave a mock look of surprise to hide the fact that she too was keen to see what was underneath his t-shirt.

'Ouch! I'm kidding. I work in Fleet Street back home. Finance. I wear a pinstripe but I never take it off for money. Actually, I've never been offered, but then I wouldn't kiss and tell even if I had.'

Celeste rolled her eyes again.

'So what do you do then when you're not hurting people with your wit?'

'I was a designer for *Cross* boutiques. Do you know them?'

Do I know them? 'Course I do. Spent most of my childhood there. Being dragged into one of those shops by my mother when she needed whatever you women need. I don't hold *Cross* in high regard. As a child those shops caused me many hours of suffering.'

She smiled. Most people she had met travelling had either not heard of *Cross* or thought she was posh for working for such a store. Finally, someone knew about its status in the fashion world. She felt elevated. 'Your mother must have good taste.'

'She did, but then I'm biased.'

'Did?'

'I lost her some time ago.'

'I'm sorry.'

Alex looked away from her. She wanted to reach out and comfort him, but held back reminding herself that she had only just met him.

He cleared his throat, 'Sounds like you're missing work. Like you want to pack in travelling and head back to the bright lights of London.'

Celeste tucked a strand of hair behind her ear. She missed her best friends – Bonnie and Alicia. She missed the late night phone calls and the movie marathons huddled in their pyjamas on Alicia's sofa. She missed *Cross* too – the flamboyant fuchsia carpet, the gold throne in the corner of her design studio, and the mannequins draped in organzas and silks, all securely fastened with the *Cross* signature gold bumblebee pins. And Celeste's boss, Maryanne, had become like a second mother to her. She had welcomed her into *Cross* when no one else would take a chance on a graduate designer.

Before she had left, Maryanne had said to her, in her Texan drawl, 'Go do what you have to do, darlin.' She had taken her jaw in her hand, her vibrant red nails digging into her soft cheeks. 'I remember the first time you walked in here. Spillin' tea all over my beautiful designs. I said to myself, "What the hell have I hired?" But you stayed late that day, kid, and re-sketched from memory what you'd seen. I knew then that you had something. When you come back, call me. We may… no we *will* have something for you.'

'I guess I do miss my life back home. But I'm not done yet,' she said, her eyes lighting up. 'There's so much to see and do here. I've only just started in Asia. Are you going back to your old job?'

'I'll have to muscle my way back in, but I'm good at what I do.'

She smiled. Why was she always attracted to arrogant, alpha males?

'So where are you heading next?' She heard Alex say.

'I'll stay out here for as long as I can, but I don't have much cash left.'

'Maybe we could travel on together.'

She looked at Alex out of the corner of her eye. 'Maybe.'

2

13th – 14th April 2007
Koh Phi Phi, Thailand

Celeste woke up to the noisy whirring of the fan in the far left corner of her room. It was stiflingly hot. Sweat trickled down from beneath her hairline towards her nose and cheeks. She wiped it away with the back of her hand.

Outside, a child was playing with something that sounded like a toy drum. She could hear chickens clucking. She glanced over to the lilac leather travel alarm clock that Alicia had given her for her last birthday. It was from an expensive store on Bond Street and she had deliberated whether to bring it with her. 'Take nothing of value,' a friend had said. 'The last thing you want to do is have it nicked.' The lilac reminded her of the lavender that hung in Alicia's bathroom. She wished for a bit of luxury now.

A gecko caught her eye as it scurried out from behind the curtain towards the bathroom. Before she had time to follow it there was a sharp rap on the door. Celeste wrapped the bed sheet around her and rose to her feet, stepping over a line of black ants.

'Wake up, wake up,' said a voice from behind the door, now half ajar.

She looked at the open door, her mouth gaping open. 'What the hell? You can't just come into my room.'

A woman appeared from behind the door.

She took in the woman's shabby appearance and dishevelled hair. She wore a pale blue dress, which blended perfectly with the patchily decorated walls and worn door of the room.

'Gud, gud you alone. That man is nat here with you-la. Engleesh girls always bring back men with them.'

Celeste couldn't place her accent. It didn't sound Thai. 'What man?'

'Tall one, blue eyes. Blue eyes means gud times,' the woman said winking at Celeste.

She rubbed her eyes with one hand, her other hand still holding the sheet around her. Looking around the room she remembered that she had bumped into Alex in one of the beach shacks last night. They had been drinking together, and he had walked her to her door. But that was it. She was certain that he hadn't come in.

'Don't go to bed just yet!' Alex had said to her in front of a group of travellers they had only just befriended. She had though. The alcohol had gone straight to her head and for once she didn't feel like getting drunk. If she had had another cocktail, she would have done something crazy like skinny-dipping and sleeping under the stars, like she had done in Fiji. Or worse still, she may have ended up in Alex's bed. She didn't want that, not yet. She had to play it cool if she wanted him to stick around, although she wasn't sure if she really wanted that either.

'You only paid for one night, remember?' The woman in front of her said, bringing Celeste back into the present. 'I booked this room already-la.' The lady behind the door opened it fully now to show a mop and bucket and a pile of sheets on a trolley behind her.

'But I need the room for another night, at least,' Celeste pleaded. Now she recalled that she had only enough money for one night's stay when she had checked in. She had to go to a bank on the island after that so she had money to get her through the next couple of days.

'Then you pay. No pay, no stay-la.'

Celeste scanned the room for her handbag. An orange and red striped cloth bag had now replaced the leather one she had started her trip with. She was careful where she put it – when it got wet the colours bled everywhere. Most of the T-shirts she had stored in there were now shades of orange or pink.

She spotted the colourful cloth behind the fan and walked over to it, careful to cover her body with the off-white bed-sheet. She had never slept naked before, but it was just so hot – there was no way she would have had a wink of sleep if she hadn't stripped bare last night.

'Three hundred baht' the woman said, looking at her from the doorway.

'I only paid two-fifty for last night,' Celeste protested.

'Look, lady, you find someplace else. It's Saturday night-la. Overflows from Koh Pha Ngan are coming here for full moon,' she said, pointing to the ceiling.

Celeste weighed up her options and then handed over the money. The woman greedily counted the notes before stuffing them into her bra and exiting the room.

Closing the door, Celeste lay back onto the hard mattress. She could hear the same routine happen a few doors down, but despite having parted with what little cash she had left, Celeste was happy. She was in Thailand. The sun was beaming through the thin fabric of the pink curtains that hung over the window and it made her smile.

Another sharp bang on the door woke her a couple of hours later. Again, she wrapped the sheets around her and opened the door to see Alex, fresh and bright eyed.

'Hey Mai Tai, you ready to go to Monkey Island?'

'What? Stop calling me that,' she said. He had started calling her that last night, possibly because they had been drinking Mai Tais at the time.

'Last night it was your idea. Wild monkeys taking over an island – could be like *Planet of the Apes*, you said.'

Celeste got back into bed feeling self-conscious in her flimsy sheet. It *had* been her idea – it was always her idea. After all, life was for living.

'Look, heavenly one, I'm going. The boat leaves in an hour. I'll see you down at the *Plantain Shack*. I need a bowl of conjee to get rid of this stinking hangover. That *Samsom* whiskey is a killer. It was a top night after you went to bed. Should've stayed out.' And with that he was gone, slamming the fragile blue door behind him, making the walls shudder.

Celeste smiled, twisted herself of the bed, letting the sheet drop, and followed the trail of ants into the bathroom.

*

Monkey Island was just as she imagined – a sand island with chattering monkeys swinging from every tree. The guides held out bananas and the monkeys sauntered over to eat from their hands. She had enjoyed their picnic lunch and chasing sand crabs with Alex, but, just as they were about to board the tourist boat home, a small child with pink sun block on her nose started shrieking as a monkey approached her. The child's mother started screaming in French and simultaneously a monkey bit the child's father who had reached down to rescue the little girl. There was pandemonium after that as people started to jump on to the boat, and she was sure it was going to capsize.

Alex just grinned. 'Typical,' he had said, as he casually put his arm around her. At first she had flinched, but after a moment his hand felt reassuring there.

She put her key in the lock to the door of her room then she heard a noise – a grunting noise – then another sound as if the furniture in her room was being moved about. She turned the key and carefully opened the door, her heart racing. She looked directly at her dresser. Apart from a low wooden bed and a chair, it was the only other piece of furniture in the room. A naked Thai lady was perched on the edge of the dresser. The woman's straight black hair only partially covered her breasts. A tubby English man in his late fifties with a thick, white beard stood stark naked in between the spread legs of the Thai woman. He hadn't noticed Celeste open the door and was still thrusting himself into the young woman as Celeste gaped in shock.

'Get *aaaat*!' A shrill noise came out of the woman's mouth and her eyes pierced through Celeste. She immediately looked at the floor only to find a pair of pink satin and black lace knickers. Her eyes scanned the floor and only stopped when they hit a leather mask with straps. Immediately, Celeste averted her gaze to the ceiling. She thought about leaving, but this was her room. What the hell were they doing in her room? The man, red and sweaty from his exertion, turned and looked at Celeste.

'Well don't just stand there, get out,' he said, amidst his heavy breathing. Droplets of sweat ran down the sides of his face. He showed no shame and didn't even attempt to cover himself or the woman.

'Er…' Celeste stuttered. 'Th-this is my room. I've paid for it.'

'I don't think so,' said the man releasing the young woman's thighs and turning his whole body towards Celeste, showing her more than she wanted to see. 'See here, this is our honeymoon.' He pointed to the flower petals on the bed and the basket of fruit in the corner, which she had failed to see.

She glanced around and noticed that all of her belongings were gone. Peering her head back around the door she checked the number. It was definitely her room.

'Get *aaat*, get *aaat*!' the bride was shrieking, still perched on the dresser.

'Fine. I'll go and find the manager and sort this mess out.' As she closed the door behind her, despite her own predicament, she couldn't help but feel sorry for the bride, married to a slob and honeymooning in a backpackers' resort. She eventually found the manager, but she was not in the least bit helpful. She opened her grubby A4 notebook and ran her finger down the list of names. 'Bloady, Bloady,' she said, shaking her head from side to side.

'No, B-R-O-A-D-Y. Broady,' Celeste corrected her. 'My name is Celeste Broady.'

'Ah, ah, Okay. Bloady.' The lady looked up and smiled before looking back down at the register. 'So hot,' she said. 'Bad weather's coming.' The manager sniffed the air as if she could smell the monsoon approaching.

Celeste drummed her fingers on the counter. 'Yesterday, I checked-in yesterday. And I paid for tonight this morning.

Three hundred baht to a lady in a blue dress.'

'Fifty baht, too much. Rooms here only two-fifty baht.' The lady behind the counter looked at Celeste intently. 'You only pay for one night. It says so in the book. We no send people round in morning. That woman no employee of *Best Value Phi Phi*.'

'What the hell?' Celeste clenched her fist into a ball. 'Where's my stuff then? How could someone just do that? Don't you have any security? I want my money back.'

The receptionist peered into the doorway behind her, ignoring Celeste's rant. 'We have it,' she said triumphantly, like she had done Celeste a favour by not throwing out her worldly possessions. She shifted on her feet and then disappeared into the back room appearing a minute later with her backpack and a plastic bag. 'You stuff,' she said, handing Celeste both items. 'But you no getting money back. Not our fault you gave money to anyone.'

Celeste gritted her teeth. After a deep breath she asked, 'Have you got any other rooms available for tonight?' It was far too hot to be traipsing around the island of Phi Phi looking for accommodation during the full moon.

'Try *Chiki's Tours* on Phi Phi Beach. They have big yellow sign and '*Chiki's Tours*' in red on the front. I know Chiki. She my friend. Tell her I sent you.' The landlord scribbled something in Thai on a small piece of paper and handed it over to Celeste, who had already lifted her backpack onto her shoulders.

After having no luck at *Chiki's*, Celeste started to walk around the island. After three pineapple juices and an hour spent walking into resorts, hotels and hostels only to be told they had no rooms available, Celeste realised she only had one option left.

3

19th June 2007
Krabi, Thailand

The house in Krabi had been built into the side of a hill, overlooking a turquoise sea, but close enough to walk down to the beach and the bustling strip of restaurants and bars. Yet the house, with its pagoda style roof was high up enough not to get caught in the mayhem of touristville. Even though it was the wet season it didn't seem to bother the busloads of day-trippers. Krabi was always packed.

'For you,' Alex said, holding out a single pink damask rose.

Celeste narrowed her eyes. 'What have you done now?' She walked over to him, took the rose and allowed him to wrap his arms around her.

'I was walking past Aawut's stall. This just caught my eye and reminded me of you. You had a pink flower in your hair the day you came to my hotel in Phi Phi.'

'My beautiful brown hair, that you convinced me to chop off and dye black. I look like a pixie.'

'You look sexy. I like it short and spiky like that, and black sets off those eyes of yours.'

Celeste made a face, but Alex had been right. She had been chatted up more than usual since she had it cut and she couldn't deny that she loved it when Alex put a protective arm around her, warning all other men away.

He looked at her closely. 'I've never met anyone with grey eyes before. It was those eyes that made me say yes when you were begging to sleep in my bed. I knew then you were going to be all mine.'

'I said I'd take the floor. You suggested the bed.'

'I'm glad that old man was banging the Thai girl in your bedroom. If that had never happened you wouldn't have agreed to come to Krabi with me.'

'I suppose I wouldn't have.' Before Celeste met Alex she had had her fair share of boyfriends. It was hard not to in the world of fashion. There was always a show or a party to go to where drink was free flowing and male models were looking for a good time. But she had never dated a man like Alex before – someone who didn't play mind games, someone who treated her so well. He had confessed to her one rainy evening over a *Chang* beer that he used to be a player. But he had also confessed after a few more beers that there was something about Celeste that kept him keen. 'Something,' he said, 'that satisfies my hunger. You, heavenly one, have set the bar high.' She had laughed away his comments, but inside she was ecstatic.

Part of her was desperate to get back home to show off her new trophy. Alex was not only a gentleman, but he was beyond good looking. She had noticed the way other travellers turned to look at him when they were out shopping or in a bar. And she couldn't help but revel when he pulled her close to whisper something in her ear or put his arm around her like he owned her. There was something very sexy about the way he did it, especially when they were in front of other people. If she had been called a feminist before, she certainly wasn't one now. There was something about Alex that made Celeste want to turn back time and go back to the days of being a kept woman. If Alex wanted to own Celeste, then she would be his.

'Come on, get ready. I want to take you out to dinner. And wear that red dress.'

Celeste obeyed.

4

24th – 25th June 2007
Krabi, Thailand

'Why you no clean that table?'

'Dai,' Celeste said with pleading eyes. 'The man is out of order. He can't order me around like that!'

'He is paying customer. Stop being lazy and go clean table. You are waitress or no?'

'Urghh!' Celeste said, gritting her teeth and narrowing her eyes at Dai. Sweat trickled down her back. It was hot in the kitchens where hundreds of live crabs were thrown into large vats of boiling water every day. She pushed open the door to the restaurant and looked towards the table she had to clean. She tilted her head. The sweaty bald man who had been perving on her had left. Another man was sitting at the table. She smiled.

'What are you doing here?' she asked.

'Saving you,' Alex said.

Celeste playfully hit him with her tea towel. 'Seriously, Alex! I can't just leave. Good job in getting rid of that fat slob though.'

Alex grinned. 'Come on, let's get out of here,' he said, putting his arm around her and pulling her close.

'I can't.'

'I've had a word with Dai. It's fine. Seriously. He's given you the afternoon off.'

Of course Alex hadn't spoken to Dai. She hated it when he lied like this just to get his own way. She wouldn't get paid for her afternoon lounging around with Alex, drinking Mai Tais and Cosmopolitans that tasted nothing like they should. Alex would end up paying the rent again and she couldn't let that happen.

'I can't.'

Alex put his hands around her wrists, then tightened his grip.

'Alex,' Celeste said. She looked down at his hands on hers.

Immediately, he let go. Then he looked at her with puppy dog eyes. 'One afternoon,' he said with a wink.

She hesitated.

'Go on.'

'Alex Renshaw, you're naughty!' She pulled off her cloth apron and left it on the dirty table as she left with Alex's arm around her as they set off to *The Conch Shell*.

'One more my good man!' Alex said to Joe, the barman at their favourite watering hole.

'When you two gonna go home? You're like locals now, you been here so long. You even let your good lady work at that good-for-nothing's shack. Come on Alex, you need to be looking after your woman,' Joe said.

Celeste rested her head on her outstretched arms, which were flat against the wooden table. 'It's not like that in our culture,' she said to Joe. The afternoon drinking was already making her feel sleepy.

Joe let out a deep laugh. 'Culture, culture. I know about

cultures, miss. Believe me, we have working girls in our culture too,' Joe said. He winked at Alex before disappearing into the back room.

Alex frowned.

'He's joking. Don't worry.'

'*The Crab Shack* is pretty bad though. Come on Celeste. I'm sure working at *Cross* was a million miles from the squalor at that place.'

She raised her head and lifted a bottle of beer to her lips. She drained its contents and put it back down on the table. 'What do you mean, squalor? We used to eat there nearly every Friday till I started working there.'

'It's filthy in the kitchen. You said so yourself.'

'I'm sure the *McDonalds* up the road is filthy too if you went into its kitchens,' Celeste stood up.

'You're missing the point.' Alex rose to his feet and stroked her hair.

'What exactly is your point?'

'You hate it there. I said I could support us till we get back home.'

'And when are we going home?'

'Yesterday, you said you were done with England. It didn't have the buzz, apparently, that Asia had. Today, you're ready to go back? Why the sudden change of heart?'

She frowned. She *had* said that yesterday. Now she wasn't sure where that outburst had come from. Alex was right. Dai's was a pit. She hated working there. Why was she putting herself through it? And why was she arguing with Alex, when he had just saved her from that hellhole?

'Where you going?' Joe asked from the bar. 'I got your beers here.'

Alex took out cash from his pocket and put it on the table. 'We don't need the beers.' Taking Celeste by the hand he led her out of the bar.

'I just need some fresh air. We don't have to leave,' Celeste said. A tear ran down her face but she wasn't sure why she was crying. She had wanted to work. Working made her feel alive. It wasn't fair that Alex had a job he loved at the dive centre, which was clean and friendly and was a nice little top up to his savings that he was still managing to live off. The issue was all hers. She couldn't just give up her shitty job and continue sponging off Alex for the rest of their time in Thailand. 'I hate my job. And I hate having no money.'

Alex held her. 'I told you not to worry.' For a moment Celeste wanted her thoughts to stop spiralling. She wanted to believe him. She could forget her money worries and live off Alex. A life with him would be idyllic. She rested her head on his chest. Her body relaxed and she let him lead the way home.

*

Celeste sat back in her chair, twirling her pen in her hand. She thought about her old life – the black tie events she had attended on behalf of *Cross*, the early evening cocktails with the girls, the working lunches and networking breakfasts. She missed those days. She imagined Alicia and Bonnie with their boutique, rubbing shoulders with ladies who lunched, and she felt a sliver of envy run through her.

For a split second she felt greedy. Like her nine-year-old self who refused to smile until she got those red shoes she wanted. Only years later did she realise her parents couldn't afford them, but had dipped into their savings to buy them just to make her happy. She pushed away that thought. It wasn't good to dwell on things she couldn't change. And this was different. So what if she wanted to have it all. Why not?

She turned back to her postcard. *You'll be glad to know we're thinking of making our way back home*, she wrote. She heard their front door open and close. She quickly signed her postcard to Alicia and slipped it in the drawer.

'So you quit?' Alex said, as he walked towards her.

She got up from her chair and jumped into his arms.

'I shouldn't say this, but you look better for it.'

She blushed. His smile still gave her butterflies. She squeezed his waist with her legs and kissed him on the lips. 'You were right. This morning when you were at the dive school I went in and quit before Dai could fire me for walking out. It *is* filthy in there.'

'And this is new?' Alex asked, letting the fabric of her green kaftan slip between his fingers.

Celeste closed an eye. 'Last pay cheque. I know I shouldn't have… but,'

Alex laughed as she released her grip and slid to the floor. 'You wanted to cheer yourself up? You women are all the same.' He walked towards the bathroom.

His statement was throwaway. It shouldn't have hurt but it did. Celeste retrieved her postcard. Her jealousy made her consider how she felt about Alex. But recently she had spoken to her best friend, Alicia and she too thought it was more than a holiday romance.

'Maybe this is real,' Alicia said when she had called her friend.

‘I don’t know,’ Celeste had said, holding the receiver in one hand and chewing her fingernails of the other.

‘You’ve been living together. You talk about him every time you call. You can’t help yourself. Bonnie’s going out with a married man and you haven’t even asked about her. It’s unlike you. I was just saying to Rachel the other day that – ’

‘Who’s Rachel?’ Celeste felt a prick of jealousy.

‘A friend. Gorgeous. You’d like her. I met her through Sophia.’

‘Sophia?’ Celeste’s heart sank a little further.

‘You know, the half Indian, half Iranian girl. She’s a member at *The Emerald Rooms*. I’ll introduce you when you’re back. Apparently it’s the place to be seen these days. It’s where all the young hot bachelors hang out. Anyway, I was saying, I said to Rachel that it must be love. You must be in love!’

5

Barnet, North London

'So was it love with Alex?' Elaine asked.

Celeste nodded. 'I wouldn't have dyed my hair black for just anyone. But he liked it that way. Said it complemented my grey eyes and naturally red lips. I've never needed much lipstick. And I wore red, because that's what he liked, and bikinis because he preferred them to a one-piece. At the time I thought all couples did things like that, and I suppose they do at the start of a new relationship. But I always had that desire to please Alex, even at the very end.'

'But you don't want to please him now?'

Celeste flinched. Her eyes darted around the room. 'It's difficult.' Why was everyone so concerned with how she felt about Alex now? It was hard enough letting go of the memories, without constantly being reminded of him. Thoughts of him making her breakfast in bed on a lazy Saturday and giving her foot-rubs when she had had a long day were always entering her mind when she least expected. He had always been there for her, making sure her needs were met. In Krabi, he had said 'no' to a once-in-a-lifetime night dive experience just because she had come down with the flu. And he had looked after her throughout her five-day illness, buying in fresh chicken soup and an armful of flu remedies. Alex had always made time for her back then. He had deserved her unconditional love. But she had to recognise that he had changed. By the end he was no longer the man she had met in Thailand. That love they shared had turned into something else.

It's unhealthy to think that way, her mother had said. It was because of her mother that she was here, in this room, speaking to Elaine. Elaine, with her curly blond hair and her floaty skirt. But there was no harm in telling Elaine her secrets. Elaine wouldn't judger her.

'I still…' she started.

Elaine tilted her head and looked at her.

'I still have a lot more to say before we get to the present day. We're still in Thailand, in 2007.'

6

6th November 2007
Krabi, Thailand

'Hey, you're up,' Celeste whispered in Alex's ear. She kissed him as he gently opened his eyes. The morning sun flooded their room through the cracks in the wooden shutters.

'What time is it?'

'Nine. You don't have work till later.'

Sitting up, Alex leaned over to his side table and lifted a bottle of water to his lips.

She watched as he drank the half litre without stopping. 'Why do you always do that?'

'Do what?'

'Drink so much water before you even get out of bed.'

'Because I'm thirsty.'

'The alcohol and the heat?'

'Nah, I've always done it. Every day, since I was about thirteen. My mother used to say you lose water in your sleep, so you should always wake up and drink some for your brain to function efficiently. I guess it became a habit. Can't do without it now.'

Celeste grinned.

'Explains why you're so clever then.'

Alex put the empty water bottle down. 'It's true.' He leaned over to kiss her, before heading for the shower.

'Wait, I need to talk to you.'

'You said that last night,' Alex said with a wink. 'I like your kind of talking.'

She felt her cheeks flush. 'I tried talking to you last night. You got distracted.'

'Did we not talk, last night?'

'I want to go back home.' She looked at Alex. She expected a frown or a twitch of his lips, but there was nothing. She spoke to fill the silence. 'I'm done with travelling. I'm done with wearing the same clothes day in and day out. I wanna go home. Part of me thought that travelling would satisfy my desire for life. I thought the feeling of constantly wanting more would disappear. But the opposite has happened. I want my old life back.'

Alex smiled.

'I've so much more to achieve. I still want to travel and see the world, but I want to do it wearing pretty shoes and expensive dresses.' She put her face in her hands. 'God, that sounds awful, materialistic.' She looked at Alex and then closed her eyes waiting for his reaction.

Alex laughed. 'I love you, Celeste Broady.'

Her eyes opened and her jaw dropped. Alex had never said those three words to her before. Thoughts of going home suddenly vanished. Hadn't Alex only recently confessed, after too much *Sangsom*, that he had never said 'I love you' to anyone. Or had she made it up in one of her daydreams? She shook her head. What was she thinking? Alex Renshaw had just told her that he loved her! A smile spread across her face.

'You're not greedy, you're passionate. You love life. You have ambition coming out of your pores. I've seen you sketching designs in that leather-wrapped journal of yours. You're desperate to get back to what you love doing. We're kindred spirits, you and I,' Alex said as he made his way downstairs. Moments later he arrived back upstairs with two glasses and the bottle of champagne. He popped the cork and some of the liquid spilled onto the bed.

'Don't waste it! If I didn't know you better I'd say you were trying to distract me with all this talk of love!' She wrapped the bed sheets around her. 'You've ignored my question about going home and completely side-tracked me.'

Alex filled the glasses and raised his to hers. 'To our future as soulmates.'

Celeste took a glass and chinked his. She took a sip. 'Is it wrong for this to taste good at nine in the morning?'

'See, kindred.'

'I'm not letting you get out of this conversation.'

Alex turned away. 'I'm not sure if I am ready to go back and face the music.'

'What do you mean?' she asked, her enthusiasm dipping.

'Nothing.' Alex sat back down on the bed.

'Soulmates tell each other everything.'

'If you want to go back now then…'

Celeste looked around their living space. She couldn't stay here much longer. She wanted a home, her own home. 'I don't think I could last another month out here.'

'If you need to go…'

She didn't want to lose Alex and she had already ruined this precious moment because she wanted more. Damn it. Why couldn't she just let things be, for once? The thought of moving away from him made her feel weak inside. But she had dreams, dreams which wouldn't come true if they remained in her head. She hadn't gotten out of East Row by sitting around and waiting for things to happen. If she wanted something, she had to make it happen. But now Alex was a part of her dreams. She wouldn't go without him. Would he stay on without her? Or was he testing her? It wouldn't be the first time he wanted Celeste to prove her love, like when he asked her to travel to Krabi with him when she had already made plans to go to Koh Lanta. Alex could be cruel when he wanted.

'I don't want to leave you, but,' Celeste hesitated, 'I have to go back.'

'Will you always put everything else ahead of me?'

'I get the impression you'll never want to leave this place.'

Alex tilted his head. He seemed to be considering it. 'Give me a week,'

Celeste nodded, but she had already made up her mind, and for once she wasn't going to let Alex change it.

7

2nd December 2007
Mayfair, London

'I'm back!' Celeste called, as she opened the shop door to Alicia and Bonnie's boutique.

'You're here.' Alicia looked at her watch. 'I wasn't expecting you for at least an hour. What time did your train get in?' She put down her pen and rushed over to embrace Celeste.

'You look fantastic, as ever. I've missed you so much.'

'And look at you. Look at *your* hair!'

'It was Alex's idea. Your hair is still as red as ever, beautiful.'

'Oh my mop is as bad as it's always been.'

Alicia's hair was anything but a mop. Her thick red curls glistened like she had just walked out of a salon. 'A black pixie cut, I would never have thought you would do something like that. You look a little bit like Bonnie. But it suits you. Suits those luscious grey eyes of yours. Love is doing you good,' Alicia touched the back of Celeste's head. 'I so wanted to pick you up from the station. I had pink peonies and everything.' Alicia pointed to the bunch of flowers on the counter. Bonnie should be here shortly. Did I tell you she sold her share in the boutique and has moved to Edinburgh?'

Celeste pouted. 'So much has happened whilst I've been

away. She walked over to the flowers and lifted them to her nose. 'My favourite. I had to come back before you replaced me with one of those other girls you've been hanging round with – Rachel and Sophia.'

'Oh never mind them. We want to hear all about this Alex guy.'

'That's why I'm early. He surprised me at Bristol station. He was waiting outside because he said it was more comfortable to be driven than to take the train. And he wanted to see me.' Celeste felt a warmth rise to her cheeks.

'Do men like that still exist?'

'Men like what?' Bonnie said from the doorway.

*

'I just fell in love,' Bonnie said, half way through their lunch, when Alicia had gone to the ladies.

Celeste eyed her friend. Alicia was right, her dark hair was similar to Bonnie's, although Bonnie's hair had grown to just below her shoulders. It suited her and she looked stunning, as always. She had noticed the way the waiter looked at her a second longer when he served them earlier. Bonnie could have had any man she wanted – with long hair or short hair. It was a shame she wanted a married man.

'I didn't know he was married at the time and now it's too late. I'm in love. He's going to leave his wife though. I know it sounds clichéd, but he is waiting for the right moment. You see, the stupid cow suffers from depression. So he has to find the right time.'

Celeste played with the remainder of her eggs Benedict. 'I'm not going to judge you. You can't help who you fall in love with.'

Bonnie put her hand on her forearm. 'I was worried about what you'd think. I couldn't have both you and Alicia against me. That would be terrible.'

'Alicia's only trying to help. She cares for you. She doesn't want to see you as the other woman your whole life. She's experienced it, remember?'

'Oh yes. She hasn't let me forget about her sister's episode.'

'Episode! It was more like a life sentence. Portia spent four years waiting in the wings for a man, who let's face it, never loved her.'

'I'm not Portia. I know what I'm doing.'

'What are you two gossiping about?' Alicia said, returning to their table.

Celeste looked up at Alicia as she squeezed past the wooden pillar back into her seat. 'I was telling her about the Alex Renshaw.'

'You didn't mention his surname before. I don't suppose he's an actual Renshaw, is he?'

Celeste nodded. When she had told her parents about Alex her father had claimed to have heard of the family. She had been stunned into silence when her father said that Warwick Renshaw, Alex's dad, was frequently in the papers as one of Britain's richest men.

'Explains why he's such a gentleman,' said Alicia.

'So you know about the Renshaws?'

'I've heard about them. I'm sure Mummy and Daddy used to go to the Renshaws' for their annual summer ball. They used to have the most extravagant parties until his mother died. Poor woman. Now his father has someone half his age. Warwick has quite a reputation, and they say that Alex...' Alicia trailed off. 'So you're meeting his dad tonight, you said?'

‘What do they say?’ Celeste asked.

‘Oh nothing.’ Alicia shot Bonnie a curious look that didn’t go unnoticed by Celeste.

‘What do they say about Alex?’ Celeste asked. Her pulse quickened. She didn’t like that her friends knew something that she didn’t about the man she was in love with.

‘I heard that he takes after his father,’ Alicia said softly. ‘But you know how people gossip and make up the most ghastly rumours. Which reminds me, I must introduce you to Rachel and Sophia. They are horribly attracted to gossip. It’s quite terrible, but quite interesting too. I try and avoid their club though, Bonnie’s a member….’

‘Was a member,’ Bonnie said.

‘It’s full of wannabes and I don’t want to be tarnished with the same brush. Instead I just meet the girls for coffee and a catch up, but they can’t go too long without something alcoholic.’

‘Alex’s been quite honest about his past. I know he wasn’t a saint,’ Celeste said, ignoring Alicia’s diversion. She couldn’t help but think of the phrase *like father, like son*.

‘A saint he was not,’ Bonnie said. ‘But… no… I mean it was all such a long time ago. And I’m sure not all of it’s true.’

‘He’s told you about his past. That’s a first for any man,’ Alicia said.

Celeste twisted the stem of her wine glass in her fingers. She looked up at Bonnie and felt envious. Her naturally dark hair, almond shaped eyes and quick wit made her stand out in a crowd. Alex’s wealth had been news to her when her father had told her what he knew, and something had changed between them. Alex was the same, but she felt a little inadequate, like she wasn’t good enough for him. She was sure that someone like Bonnie would be someone Alex would consider as marriage material. She could perhaps compete in the looks department, but she could never compete with a private-school upbringing. 'I didn't know anything about the Renshaws when I met him, and he never spoke of money.'

'Well, would it have changed things if he had?' Alicia asked.

'I guess not.'

'Is he going to work for his father? I've heard Warwick's very astute when it comes to business. He doesn't take any prisoners. Although I'm not sure if that applies to his sons.'

'Alex's taking a job with his dad till he finds his feet. He's not happy about it, but it'll get him started.'

'If your parents can help you out a little, you should take advantage of it. Alicia and I wouldn't be where we are without the bank of mum and dad.'

'I guess not,' Celeste said with a smile. She could never borrow from her parents. They had less than her. Her mind started to drift. 'There is something about Alex that does bother me though.'

'What's that?' Bonnie said, leaning forward.

'When we were in Thailand we used to go to this club on the beach, get drunk on *Sangsom* and dance the night away.'

'Nothing wrong with that!'

'It's not that. It was just this one time a guy started dancing next to me, you know – up close. Alex had gone to the bar and I was drunk. I didn't even notice the creep behind me. Before I knew it, Alex had returned and had punched the guy, right in his face. I mean, I'm sure that guy didn't mean any harm. You know what guys are like in nightclubs.'

Bonnie made a face. 'Did you ask Alex why he did it?'

'He said the guy was trying to rub up against me and was

trying to put his hand up my skirt. I was drunk, but not that drunk. I would have known if some stranger was trying to touch me. Later, he confessed that he wasn't sure. But he likes being in control. The anger of not being in control of the situation took over, I guess, and he just saw red. He hit him before he knew it.'

'Some men are like that. They get all territorial and possessive. You should be flattered by his jealousy. You don't think he would harm you?' Bonnie asked.

Celeste shook her head.

'Well, that's fine then. We all have our flaws. As long as he doesn't make it a habit.'

Celeste shrugged. The look on Bonnie's face betrayed her words, and Celeste felt a little resentment for having told her. She could be so righteous sometimes. She decided not to tell her friends that with just a single punch Alex had knocked the man out cold. She didn't want them to judge him before they met him. So she dropped the subject and asked Bonnie what shade of lipstick she was wearing. She didn't listen to the answer. All this talk of money, the wandering eye of Warwick Renshaw and this dark side of Alex was making her feel quite uneasy.

8

5th December 2007
Mayfair, London

'Rachel, you made it. How divine. Come and sit next to me.' Sophia patted the purple velvet sofa next to where she was seated. 'How've you been? Is that *Fendi*?' She asked pointing to Rachel's handbag. She didn't wait for an answer. 'You must tell me about Positano. Is it worth a visit? I haven't been to Italy in ages.'

Rachel scanned the room and then sat down. 'It was beautiful. I could have spent another couple of nights there.'

'Oh, then you should have luvvie, you should have. You stayed in Luca's villa?'

'It was fantastic.'

'I was just saying to a friend that he must go there too...'

'You talking about me, Soph?' A tall man in a navy suit and crisp white shirt, clutching a glass of champagne walked up to where they were seated.

'William?' Sophia asked, raising her eyebrows.

'Of course, darling,' he replied.

She stood up and kissed him on both cheeks. 'You must meet my dear friend Rach. She's one of us,' Sophia said with a wink. 'Willy's been on a long holiday too.'

‘Let’s get you a drink then.’ He clicked his fingers in the air and a waiter arrived to take his order of champagne, which arrived moments later. Sophia took a glass, made her excuses and stepped away. Rachel nervously leaned back on the plush sofa and accepted the drink, clinking glasses with the handsome man. She had heard that *The Emerald Rooms* was the place to meet someone. She didn’t realise it would happen so soon though. She took a sip of the champagne, letting the bubbles effervesce at the back of her mouth. It was presumptuous of him ordering her a drink without even asking what she had wanted, but she liked it. She ran her fingers through her hair and leaned in closer to hear what he was saying.

‘This club’s pretty exclusive. Best in London. I’ve lived here for a good part of my life. I’ve seen the inside of some of these so-called exclusive clubs. Bloody hell some of them are no better than a glorified *Butlins,* and some are so far up themselves it’s untrue. But *The Emerald Rooms*, this club has the right amount of everything.’ He placed his hand on her shoulder making the hairs on her arms stand on end. As she knocked back her drink she noticed Sophia looking over at them from the bar. Her cheeks coloured and her friend looked away. Sophia was a mysterious woman she had met through a work colleague. She had immediately taken her under her wing, even though they didn’t know each other well. Sophia had got her into this club straight away, bypassing the six month waiting list and Rachel supposed she had to be thankful to her for that, but there was something almost sinister in the way that Sophia looked at her sometimes. She had broached the subject with Alicia, but Alicia accused her of watching too many episodes of *Gossip Girl* – typical of Alicia, ever the diplomat.

She caught Sophia's eye and then looked away feeling a pang of guilt. Sophia had been kind enough to get her into the club. Plus, she was one of the only single friends she had left. She looked around the room. William was right. *The Emerald Rooms* was a perfect members' club. It was glamorous yet comfortable and only a little pretentious. And it was cosy. The room they were in was only small, with space for about fifty people. The dim light from the chandeliers ensured privacy for people at the edge of the room. She could understand why so many celebrities were members.

'Where do all these doors lead?' Rachel asked. She had only been to the club a handful of times and they had never strayed from the main bar.

'That door there leads to the stairs to the bathrooms and the restaurant,' William said, pointing towards the door directly in front of her. 'The room over there is the *Onyx* bar. It's a decent sort of place. Good for a drink after work, before this room really gets going.'

'What's through that door there?' Rachel turned and pointed to a silver door at the back of the room.

'Ah, that door,' William squeezed her shoulder. 'I'm sure we'll come to that later. There's another bar upstairs, a library and a day room, done up like your nan's living room. Not worth the trip. This is the room you need to be in.'

Rachel took a sip of her drink. The champagne was good, but she really needed something to take the edge off. The women in this club were all dripping in diamonds, sipping champagne and dressed in varying lengths of black. They stood about laughing with men Rachel could only imagine were not their husbands. The men wore suits with white shirts. Their top shirt buttons open signifying the end of the day. Rachel smiled. Diamonds and white shirts – the uniform of the wealthy. 'I don't suppose you have something a little stronger?' Rachel asked briefly touching her finger to her nose. She took another sip of the pale liquid in her glass and looked at William out of the corner of her eye.

William grinned. 'Know our Soph well?'

'She got me my membership here.'

'Well, I'm sure we can get something for you then. After all she did say you were one of us.'

'You're not joining me?'

William stood up and Rachel followed. Placing his hand on the small of her back he guided her towards the silver door. She felt her spine tingle as his hand moved up her back.

He stopped at the door and turned to her. 'You're terribly sexy,' he whispered.

She felt her face flush. William punched in a code and turned the handle. 'Welcome to paradise.'

9

Barnet, North London

'I moved in with Alex. It was a mews in Mayfair. A house the Renshaws happened to have lying empty. I think a member of staff was staying there before Alex booted him out. He blindfolded me when he took me to see the place. Wouldn't let me open my eyes till he put the key in my hand outside. The house was perfect.'

'Did you have fun decorating it together?'

Celeste narrowed her eyes at Elaine. 'What have they been telling you?'

Elaine held up her hands, then she dropped them and picked up her pen.

'I don't want you to write this down.'

'I'm only making notes for myself, Celeste. No one else will see them.'

Celeste crossed her arms over her chest. She looked away. 'I didn't decorate the house. Alex's father, Warwick, had a personal assistant, Kealana, who used to do things like that. She decorated the house before we moved in. She was always flitting in and out of our lives. I knew when she had been in our house because she always left a vase of fresh white lilies on the console table and removed pictures of Alex and I, placing them in our bedroom – something or the other about Feng Shui. I once told Alex it was ludicrous. But he said that since Kealana had been about *Renshaw* had been going from strength to strength. You couldn't argue with that. She had a thing about keeping the entrances of each house clutter free as well. I found it odd that she had the freedom to do as she pleased. She had keys to all the *Renshaw* properties around the world. She flew around the globe like she was a Renshaw herself. It unnerved me a little. But I soon learned I had to get used to staff being around all the time.'

'Perhaps Kealana was the mother figure the Renshaws were missing. And by having a key, she made their lives easier.'

Celeste looked into the distance. 'Hmm, I suppose. I misjudged her though. But then I misjudged a lot of things.' She looked back to Elaine and smiled.

'So you were living your dream?'

'Thought I had it all. I had come from nothing and things just kept getting better and better. I didn't question anything for fear of losing it, and I really had no reason to.'

'You believe that you came from nothing?'

'Back then I did.'

'Did you ever talk about your up-bringing with Alex?'

She shook her head. 'Not then.'

'How did you feel about having come from the East Row council estate?'

'There was a time in my life when I couldn't bear to think about it. Someone only had to ask me what my favourite cereal was as a child and I would break out into a cold sweat. As if when I told them they would be able to glimpse into my past. But I finally got over that at university. I realised we all come from different walks of life. I'm proud of where I've come from. Plus, it gave me the drive to make me achieve. I wanted success and I made it happen. I'm determined.'

'Do you always get what you want?'

Celeste uncrossed her arms. She fiddled with the hem of her cardigan. 'I studied hard. Well, I can't say I was great with academic subjects, but I knew I had a talent for design so I put all my effort into that. I wanted a well-paid job in London and I knew I'd have to work hard to get it. Once I got it, though, I wasn't satisfied. My dream shifted. I wanted to see the world – eat street food in Bangkok, climb a glacier in New Zealand, dance till dawn at a beach party in Fiji. And I did just that. I remember sitting on that aeroplane flying out of London thinking I was the luckiest girl in the world. Then when I had done all that, I wanted my job back. I wanted to buy fancy things. Alex called it passion for life – perhaps it was just greed.'

Elaine made a note in her book. 'Over time our dreams change. Wanting to give up the travelling lifestyle after a year of living that way is more natural than living a nomadic lifestyle. You wanted routine.'

'At this point I knew Alex and I were going to be together. I – ' Celeste stopped herself. Had she said too much? She eyed Elaine who was busy scribbling something. What was she writing? She had hoped that the feeling, the *unhealthy* feeling would have passed. But those feelings were still there, bubbling underneath. When she closed her eyes at night and when she opened them in the morning those feelings made themselves known, nagging at her, bringing her down. She looked at the clock. Did they have enough time? Celeste waited for Elaine to say something – something to excuse how she had felt about Alex.

Eventually, she nodded.

How had she lost the ability to read people without a physical nod or shake of the head? She could do it so well before. Before what? No, she didn't want to think of that right now. The blood loss had been so severe, the trauma intense. But it wasn't that one incident that had changed the way her mind functioned. It had been a slow process. Orchestrated perfectly over years and years, and *he* had been behind it.

'Celeste?'

'I was tired of living out of a backpack on a meagre existence, sponging off Alex. Although that didn't change when we got back to London. I insisted on paying the bills because he wouldn't let me pay him any rent. Don't get me wrong, the gas bill alone did some damage. Heating a house with single pane sash windows doesn't come cheap. But it was nowhere near the rent I should have been paying. Alex said he could afford it, and after a while I stopped complaining. I couldn't complain. My time with him, in London, was perfect. Like I said, things just got better and better. You could say it was the rise before the fall.'

10

5th December 2007
Mayfair, London

Rachel stepped out of the room and closed the silver door behind her.

'There you are,' Sophia said.

'Oh, I was just…'

Sophia narrowed her eyes and smiled. 'I can see what you were doing, Rach.'

'Ladies,' William said, with a grin as he opened the door Rachel had just closed. He disappeared down the corridor.

'I don't know what to…' Rachel looked at the floor hoping Sophia wouldn't notice her flushed cheeks. She touched the underside of her nose worried that some residue was left behind. She felt foolish carrying on with William in *The Emerald Rooms* like a teenager. Somehow he had managed to bring out a side to her that she didn't know existed.

'There's no need to be embarrassed. We're all adults here. Although most of the members here don't act like it,' William had said to her just over an hour ago. But she was anxious. She had heard rumours that Sophia and William had been lovers. She knew no more than that. The uncertainty of why their affair ended made her feel uneasy, but at least she could understand why Sophia was here sniffing around, wanting to know how things were going between her and William. She didn't really want to think of Sophia and William together. But supposedly, the club members of *Emerald Rooms* all seemed to have some kind of history with one another.

Did all rich people behave like this? Rachel was a member, but her bank balance made her feel like an imposter. She earned well, with a banking job in the city, but her salary was incomparable to... well to whom? William certainly had money. Most of the men at *The Emerald Rooms* did, or so it appeared from their frivolous lifestyles. They came from wealth you could just tell – the way they addressed their female acquaintances with over-the-top cries of 'darrrling', and their limitless tabs behind the bar. But Rachel wondered where Sophia's money came from? She never talked about a job. Had she married money at some point in her life? Or was she born into it? Then again, did it matter? The women were all there for the same reason as Rachel – they were all just trying to get a boyfriend in a city where single women outnumbered men.

'No need to be apologetic,' Sophia said, waking Rachel from her thoughts. But Sophia's face betrayed her words. 'I can see Willy has a soft spot for you, and I can hardly mind that.'

11

10th December 2007
Mayfair, London

'London's changed since you left, fashions have changed. You have the East producing higher quality garments and new designers are opening boutiques left, right and centre. And the department stores, *oof!* Don't get me started. They're going to be the end of us.' Maryanne fixed her eyes on Celeste. 'But I must be crazy because I still want to expand. I don't have children. My shops are my babies and I want to open that final store in Hong Kong. That's where people are shopping these days. Look at the figures.' Maryanne pulled a folder out of her drawer and placed it on the table in front of her.

Celeste perused the contents. She didn't have a head for numbers, but she could tell the market in Hong Kong was more buoyant than the retail market in London just by looking at the colourful pie chart.

'I need an investor to make Hong Kong a reality. I have a couple of bigwigs in the retail world lined up to view our next collection. But I need a designer. Someone who can make sure *Cross* stays ahead of the game. Your replacement was a waste of time. Cost me more money than she was worth – designed a terrible spring collection.'

Celeste supressed a smile. Maryanne was a tough boss to please and she didn't put up with second best.

'Tell me, kid, do you still have an eye for what's going to be in fashion three seasons before it actually happens?'

'I can tell you that *Marc Jacobs* will re-launch tweed for his next fall collection and bags are going to be structured. Low waist jeans are not here to stay and the colour of the season will be plum – a deep purple. Chunky knits will also be making a comeback and I have a beautiful design in mind for a classic cashmere wrap, which is guaranteed to be a wardrobe staple – perhaps part of a capsule collection.'

'You remind me so much of myself when I was your age. You want it all don't you? Life better make way for you. I don't blame you, kid. And if things go well, we can talk about you investing into *Cross* – being part of it. God knows there's no one else to carry on my legacy. Maryanne leaned back in her chair. 'Truth be told, I rather you have your own money than marry into it. That causes all sorts of problems.'

'How did…'

'London's not as big as you think darlin'. You can't be dating one of London's most eligible bachelors and expect it to stay under wraps.'

'I've only been back a week or so.'

'I expected you to meet someone. You're a good-looking gal, striking even, with that new hair of yours. Plus, you've got determination and a bit of oomph. That's attractive in itself. But a Renshaw! Who would have guessed?'

Was Maryanne implying that she was punching above her weight?

'You be careful. The rich like to play games. And the Renshaws, they certainly know how to play the game.'

'You know them?' Last night she had cancelled plans to meet Alicia's new friends, Rachel and Sophia, to meet Alex's father. She had heard so much about Rachel and Sophia, she was worried they were taking her place in Alicia's life. Sophia sounded like a bitch, but Rachel sounded like someone she would get along with. She was keen to meet them, but she couldn't resist Alex's offer when he said he wanted to introduce her to his dad.

Warwick Renshaw had been charming but sharp. He had questioned her in depth about *Cross* and spoke to her with a keen fascination in the retail industry. A sector he said was far too risky for *Renshaw* to ever dabble in. She had laughed, a nervous laugh, not knowing whether he was joking or being serious.

'I knew Warwick once,' Maryanne said with distant look that said it all.

So Alicia was right, Celeste mused. Warwick had been a player in his time. Was he already married when he had met Maryanne? Or had it been just a passing fling? Celeste could see the attraction of the older man. His neat attire and Tom Selleck deep-set eyes. He exuded charisma, wealth and power.

'I could use your help with this, kid. If you thought I worked you hard before you went off on your trip well that was nothing. I need 110% from you.'

Celeste had forgotten just how demanding Maryanne could be. But at the same time this offer had lit a fire inside her. She leaned back in her chair and bit the inside of her cheek to stop herself from smiling. Alex's parting words as she left him this morning came back to her. 'Poker face,' he had said. 'Don't give away your hand too soon.'

'Unlike the Renshaws I'm not going to play games. We both

know each other far too well for that. I can offer you this,' Maryanne said, tapping a calculator with a fuchsia painted fingernail. She turned the calculator around, showed the screen to Celeste. 'It's a good opportunity. Take it or leave it.' Maryanne looked at her rose-gold and silver *Rolex*, which was far too big on her delicate wrist.

'I'll take it,' Celeste said without hesitation. Forget Alex's advice to never accept the first offer. She hadn't listened to him when he told her to document all her conversations with Maryanne, she reasoned, so she didn't have to follow his advice on salary negotiation. She was too creative for all that. And the way Alex thought wasn't healthy. Sometimes, the way he spoke about his business affairs was bordering on paranoia. She worried if his mistrust and compulsive need to keep records of everything would spill into his personal life too. Just today, whilst she was eating her cereal, she saw him rearrange the apples in the fruit bowl in order of size. She had never noticed him do that before.

Maryanne picked up a gold bumblebee pin on her desk and twisted it between her thumb and forefinger. 'As a child, someone once told me that bees represent the realisation of one's desire. When I started *Cross* I chose the bee as my signature emblem because I had finally satisfied that. The Paris store has been a success from day one. This is my final chapter, Celeste. I *will* open a store in Hong Kong. The bumblebee never fails me.' Maryanne stood up and walked with Celeste to the door. '*Cross* boutiques are all I have left. Now,' she said, opening the door, 'get out of my office, and I'll see you bright and early next Monday.'

12

20th July 2008
Mayfair, London

Celeste had been back at *Cross* for seven months now and she and Maryanne had found a rhythm to their work. She found she worked best designing in the afternoon, the mornings always seemed to be taken up with selecting colours and fabrics, styling models and fitting samples. Then when Maryanne knocked on her door later in the day they would go through the new designs, making changes to a cuff here and a collar there before she went home. Lately she was lucky if she went home before eight. Today she was told she needed to stay 'as long as it takes' to finalise the new collection. All these long hours were beginning to tire her and weren't something she was used to after months of travel. She tried to remember if the hours at *Cross* were this long before her career break. She didn't think so. Something was going on with Maryanne but she couldn't quite figure out what it was. She looked up at her boss and helped herself to another spring roll. Whatever it was, she liked Maryanne. She would go so far as to call her a friend. A good friend. 'I could understand if it was love, but I don't think it is,' Celeste said.

'Bonnie just wants what she can't have. She's always been

like that. Alicia once bought this red *Gucci* bag, the last in the store. Bonnie wanted it – whined about it so much that Alicia ended up giving it to her' Celeste said.

'Did she ever steal one of your boyfriends when y'all were in university?'

'No. But I'm sure my boyfriends thought about it. Men find her irresistible. I think it's her flawless skin.'

'Maybe she wants a different kind of connection. One without the day in and day out of a committed relationship.'

'Or she has no morals.' Immediately Celeste had touched her fingers to her lips. 'I shouldn't have said that. I don't think that of Bonnie.' Celeste looked into a box of cold dumplings wondering why she had repeated what Alex had said the night before. Alex didn't know Bonnie like she did, but she supposed he had reason to say what he had. Alex had only recently confided that his father, the dashing Warwick Renshaw, had been a serial philanderer and had cheated on his mother so many times that he had lost count, confirming what her friends had said. 'Even when she was sick,' Alex had said, making Celeste reach out to him. She had to hold on to moments like that. It wasn't often that Alex bared his soul.

'If it's bothering you so much, kid, why don't you speak to her about it?'

Celeste put down her chopsticks. 'She's up in Edinburgh now. Alicia and I don't see much of her anymore.' But it wasn't just that and she knew it. No matter where in the world she was, she always spoke to Alicia. They would call or *Skype* each other every other day without fail. With Bonnie it was different. She wanted to call her, but Alex had only recently planted a seed of doubt in her mind about her friend after hearing of her affair, casually assassinating Bonnie's character.

'Who wrecks a marriage like that?' he asked as he dried himself after his shower. 'She probably can't get a man herself. So she has to take something that isn't hers.' She had argued back – telling him that Bonnie and Matt were meant to be, trying to defend her friend. They had ended up raising their voices at each other until Alex accused her of not believing in the sanctity of marriage, after which he had slammed the front door and walked away. As usual she ended up apologising – Alex was never wrong, or so he believed. And she had hoped that he would have changed his mind about her friend when they met. She had noticed how his eyes widened when he saw her. She couldn't blame him. Bonnie was tall and skinny and had a natural beauty in an Angelina Jolie sort of way.

'And you have Alex,' Maryanne said, bringing Celeste out of her thoughts.

'He complains that I spend more time here than I do with him.'

'Make sure you give your other-half time. It's important. I know this is rich coming from me when I'm the one keeping you imprisoned here. But I know what men can be like. Leave them alone too much and who knows what could happen. After this collection is finished and the investors have had a look, y'all should take some time out.'

'What do you mean?'

'Take a holiday with your man. Paris is beautiful at this time of year.'

13

22nd July 2008
Mayfair, London

'And I thought my father was the slave driver,' Alex said. He was sitting on their white leather sofa drinking a glass of Burgundy. The sofa had been Celeste's idea. They had bought it from *Natuzzi* in the sales on Boxing Day last year. Every time she looked at it she felt a small triumph over Kealana. She expected Kealana to be aghast when she saw it, but she had taken it well, barely batted an eyelid. It was childish, but it was one of the few items she had bought for the house.

Celeste closed the door behind her. 'I'm learning about the ins and outs of how a boutique like *Cross* operates. Everything, Alex. It's not just designing. Maryanne is teaching me so much. I'm even learning about marketing. It's intense and it takes time. But I love it.'

'You do realise she's giving you her dirty work, don't you? In the nineties, they called it job enrichment. It's all the same – more work, less pay.'

'You said I was on a good wage. Don't you think that Maryanne is gearing me up to take over one day? She has no heir.'

Alex laughed. He stood up and walked up to Celeste. Then he kissed her on her lips. 'Or she just wants you to think that.

She sounds pretty shrewd to me. I worry about you. It's ten o'clock and you'll be up and out by six tomorrow.'

'A couple of investors came in to view our new collection yesterday. Maryanne said they were making the right noises. They asked the right questions.'

'But look at how tired you are. You deserve better than this. And I spend most evenings alone or at Bill's. This isn't what I signed up to when I asked you to move in with me.'

'How is Bill?' Celeste asked, trying to change the topic. She didn't want to talk about *Cross*. Not today. Not after what she had found out. Bill was neutral territory – Alex's best friend. She had met him several times since they had got back from travelling and she liked him. He was loud and a bit brash, but he had a charming personality. When you spoke to him he gave you his full attention as if no one else in the room existed. It was rare these days to talk with someone who actually listened.

'Bill's fussing after Angela and her baby bump. But this is not about Bill. It's about your work getting in the way of our relationship and your health.'

Celeste bit her lip. Alex was right. She felt shattered. 'I have to do this,' she said, walking towards the kitchen. She took out a bowl from the cupboard and filled it with cornflakes. Maryanne needs me, she trusts me. I can't let her down. Hong Kong is going to happen.'

'How many hours does Maryanne work?'

Celeste frowned. 'Don't start. She's old.'

'You're smarter than that.'

Celeste turned and narrowed her eyes at Alex.

'I didn't mean it like that. Listen honey, what I meant to say was that if this means so much to her she should be staying late too. She isn't that old. She's in her fifties.'

'How do you know how old she is?'

'She sounds like she's in her fifties.'

Celeste filled her cereal bowl with milk and sprinkled some sugar on the top. 'Late fifties, could be sixties.' Celeste thought about the dark circles under her boss' eyes and her frail, trembling hands when she picked up a pencil to sketch earlier.

'She's in her fifties,' Alex said confidently. He walked up to Celeste and removed the bowl of cereal from her hand. He drained the contents in the sink and put the remainder in the bin.

'I was eating that.'

'You can't go to bed on just cereal. I bet you didn't have any lunch either. Let me make you something.'

'What time did you get back?' Celeste said, seating herself on a barstool. She watched as Alex poured her a glass of red.

'Been back about an hour. I had a big lunch. One of those pointless business affairs.' Alex put a pan of water on the hob, adding some pasta to it.

'And how was work?'

'Busy. Too boring to talk about.'

'I'm always going on about *Cross*. The world of finance can't be that boring.'

'Graham is not pulling his weight at the moment.'

'I thought he was the apple of your father's eye.'

'Seems he's not the efficient elder brother I thought he was.'

'Tell me more.'

'I don't want to talk about it. Not now. It's depressing.'

Celeste stood up, took a large sip of her wine and wrapped her arms around Alex's waist, burying her face in his back.

'What's wrong?' Alex asked. 'I can tell something isn't right.

Remember we promised each other – no secrets.'

She smiled. It was true. Just two days after she had moved in with him, he had made her make that promise. She was kind of glad that he did. It made her feel secure, like when he put his arm around her on that rickety boat in Thailand. 'I did something I shouldn't have. I took a look at the accounts for *Cross* London today. Maryanne was in a meeting. I was searching for a design for a lounge pant I had created before I left to go travelling. I couldn't find it anywhere,' she blurted out trying to justify her actions, although she never had to with Alex. He always knew what was going on in her mind.

'And?'

'Her computer was open. It was left unlocked.'

'Ah, so you went snooping,' Alex said with a grin. 'I'll remember to put a password on mine.'

'She's normally careful with locking her computer. I thought I would look for a scanned image of the design. Maryanne is better than me at keeping copies. I wasn't looking for accounts. The page was just left open though. It's like she wanted me to find them or something.' Celeste felt guilty as the words left her mouth – she knew what Alex was going to say after she told him what she had found. Maryanne wasn't just her boss she was her friend too.

'What did you find out?' Alex asked.

'I found out that my computer literacy is improving as are my maths skills. Basically, *Cross* is screwed.' Celeste released Alex and sat back on her stool. 'We're breaking our backs on this new collection, but I think we need to sort out the finances of the London store first. I think Maryanne is having difficulty paying back some of the company's loans this year. Surely investors will look at that sort of thing.'

'From what I hear *Cross* has good accountants. Sometimes you can hide that sort of thing. Did you ask her about it?'

Celeste shook her head. Alex added frozen peas to the boiling pasta. 'I'm no business graduate, but it looks like the company is in a fair amount of debt. Her dreams of opening a store in Hong Kong are completely unrealistic. I feel like I have to say something. But Maryanne's so stubborn. She's going to bury herself with this.'

'Happens with all businesses. You have to continually evolve. Keep your ideas fresh and new or you stagnate and die. Sounds like her advisors are not doing their job.' Alex sieved the pasta and peas and opened a jar of pesto. He stirred a tablespoon into the pasta and poured it into a bowl. He handed it to Celeste with a fork.

'My saviour.' She took a mouthful of food.

Alex scratched his chin. 'If a ship is sinking, don't you think you should jump?'

'I could've got it wrong.' She stopped herself from saying that she wanted to be there for Maryanne, no matter what. Alex would never understand mixing emotion with business. It was all cut-throat in the world of trading and financial investment.

'Your gut's been telling you something's not been right for some time. Now you know.'

Celeste scrunched her nose, regretting having told Alex. 'I suppose,' she said, putting her fork down. 'But I still can't leave. I made a promise to Maryanne and I'm sticking by it.'

'You should at least take a break.'

Maryanne had told her the same thing, suggesting Paris. She did need a holiday, but Celeste had a better idea. She had never made it to Hong Kong when they had been travelling.

And if she wanted to get an idea of what designs would sell there, she had to visit. Alex had been asking her to go with him there for some time now. He had started to travel to Asia regularly on business. His brother, Graham was taking a back seat. He had a work trip coming up. It would be ideal.

'Maybe,' Celeste said with a smile. 'Maybe I could come with you to Hong Kong next month.'

Alex scooped her up in his arms and kissed her.

14

17th – 23rd August 2008
Central District, Hong Kong

'The humidity's oppressive,' Celeste said as they entered the hotel lobby. She had enjoyed spending the day walking the narrow streets of Hong Kong. After a trip to the fashionable *Lane Crawford*, they had looked in fascination at the hawkers selling black century eggs and skewers of meat alongside live goldfish on Tung Choi Street. She had been enticed by the golden ducks hanging in restaurant windows, intoxicated by the mouth-watering smell of spices and plum sauce, and they had stopped for Pi Pa duck and rice mid-afternoon. But after a few hours of roaming the streets, Celeste's hair curled and her clothes clung to her damp skin. So she was only too happy when Alex suggested they go back to their hotel, to enter the world of cool air-conditioning and controlled humidity.

'Imagine if you had to catch a bus,' Alex said.

'I know, I sound like a spoilt brat.'

'It wasn't so long ago you were backpacking in Thailand. If I remember, the *Best Value Phi Phi* didn't have air-con.'

Celeste made a face.

'We were free then. Now, we're chained to our desks.' Alex called the elevator and then interlinked his hand in Celeste's, kissing her on her cheek, the way he always did. She breathed in his sandalwood cologne and pulled him in a little closer. 'Warwick's working me to the bone and it's not much better for you. All for a few creature comforts.'

They stepped into the elevator. Celeste tapped his watch with her polished, pink fingernail. 'Would you be able to give up your *Breitling*?' It had cost Alex more than her dad's car.

'You win.' Alex pressed the button for floor twenty-seven 'I'm glad you decided to come with me. If you didn't work, you could come away with me all the time.'

'Alex, we've been through this.'

He put his hands up. 'Okay, okay. I'll be busy with this new venture Warwick is considering in Hong Kong. Your support here is priceless. That's all I wanted to say.' The elevator arrived at their floor and they stepped out. Alex fumbled for the room key in his pocket.

'I wouldn't call all this priceless.' Celeste looked around. 'It must have set you back.' She was about to thank Alex for his generosity – again. After all, he hadn't yet let her spend a penny on this trip earlier in the day he had insisted on buying her an expensive dress. It turned out that Hong Kong was more on-trend than she had thought. But how many times could she say thank you? Her daily existence was turning in to one long thank you. *Renshaw Limited* had even paid for the flights, business class! 'It's a fourteen hour flight. We can't be cramped in economy for that long,' Alex had said.

'We did it when we were travelling,' Celeste had tried to reason, but Alex had rolled his eyes. 'We're not travelling now. It's a business trip. *Renshaw* is paying.' The conversation had ended there, with Alex kissing her on the forehead and telling her not to worry. But Celeste had worried. The tickets were more than double the price of an economy fare, and she had wanted to pay for the flights, because the hotel Alex had chosen was way out of her price range. She ended up letting Kealana book the flights and the hotel. Alex, of course, had got his way.

She had thanked him when they were in their luxurious aircraft seats and then again when they had checked into their plush, five-star suite. Thanking him now seemed a little over-the-top. As he had reminded her time and time again, they were a couple now – they shared everything. *But at what cost*? – she sometimes wondered. Alex usually got his way, not just because of his charm but because he was usually footing the bill. It was a destructive thought, one which could cause their relationship harm, so she didn't dwell on it too much.

Alex leaned forward and kissed her lips, and she felt a tingle as she usually did. This was the reason she chose as to why she could never say 'no' him. His brilliant blue eyes looking longingly at her were enough to sway her, even when she was at her most determined. Perhaps this was true love – the kind of love she read about. As Alex pulled the room key out of his wallet a business card fell on the floor. Celeste bent down to pick it up.

'You have got to be kidding me?' She dropped her shopping bags.

'What?' Alex's eyes followed hers towards the business card.

'Is this a card for *Asian Escorts*?' she said, picking it up.

Alex laughed. 'Yep.'

'Why would you have this?'

'You can't think that I would…'

'What do you expect me to think?' Her face reddened.

'The dinner I had last night with Mr Lau, who I might add is our biggest client in Hong Kong, gave me the card. Thought he was doing me a favour.'

'And you didn't think to tell him you had a girlfriend. You just slipped it in your wallet. Did you use it last night? You didn't come back to the hotel till gone midnight. Our first night in Hong Kong and I was left on my own.'

'We're not having this conversation.' Alex shook his head as he opened the door to their suite and walked inside.

Celeste followed with her shopping bags. 'Why not?'

'What time did I get back to the hotel yesterday?'

'I just said, around midnight.'

'And that gave me time for a five course meal and a visit from an escort?'

'Maybe it wasn't five courses. What else are you keeping from me?' She put her bags down and took off her coat.

'You don't trust me?'

'You had this in your pocket, not me. Don't turn this on me.' She waved the card in front of him. The shiny red lettering of *Asian Escorts* embossed on the card sent a shiver down her spine.

'Why would I beg you to come away with me if I wanted to use escorts? I've been to Hong Kong before without you.'

'And God knows what you got up to then.'

Alex walked over to Celeste. He took the card from her and ripped it up throwing the pieces onto the floor. Instinctively, she wanted to tidy them up but she was learning not to bother. A month ago Alex had hired a cleaner for their little mews. 'We can afford it,' he said and he was right. He, of course, paid for it. She had felt guilty at first and had only recently told her mother about it in hushed tones like she had committed a crime. Alicia had told her not to be so silly. But then Alicia had had staff around her from when she was in nappies. There would be a cleaner here too. After all, they were in a hotel. Why should she bother to pick up the pieces of paper?

'You know what it's like doing business in the East.'

She looked up from the ripped business card to Alex.

'I told Mr Lau that I had a girlfriend, to which he responded that he had many girlfriends. I then had to put it in my wallet as a sign of respect. I didn't want to offend him.' Alex put his arms around her.

She pursed her lips and tilted her head. 'I suppose,' she said, her shoulders dropping.

Alex smiled. 'You're terribly sexy when you're angry.' She tried to supress a smile, but she couldn't.

'That conversation couldn't have happened at a worse time though.' Alex said, looking behind her.

Celeste turned around. She hadn't noticed the bottle of *Krug* on ice and two champagne flutes. Rose petals had been scattered by the base of the cooler. She turned back to face Alex.

'For you,' he said, with those blue eyes and cheeky grin that made her melt.

She released herself from his grip, walked over to the panoramic window and looked past the multitude of skyscrapers towards Kowloon and Victoria harbour. The evening's Symphony of Lights was coming to an end.

'An apology for leaving you alone on your first night.'

Celeste made a face, feeling a little guilty. 'Sorry, I snapped. It was a bit of a shock to see that fall out of your wallet.'

'Hong Kong business men may stop pressuring me to use escorts and visit strip bars if I had someone permanent in my life.' Alex walked over to her. He popped the cork on the bottle of champagne and filled the glasses, passing Celeste one. 'Celeste Broady, believe it or not, I knew I loved you the minute I saw you. Even after a long and tiring flight, heaving around a backpack which weighed more than you, you took my breath away.' Alex pushed a lock of her black hair behind her ear. 'You're exactly what your name suggests – heavenly. Without you my life's incomplete. Now...' he said, putting his glass down. Bending on one knee, he took a small black velvet box out from his pocket. 'Marry me.'

*

Celeste looked at the diamond solitaire sitting proudly on her left hand. She estimated it at two carats at least. The stone was perfect, just like Alex. She fiddled with it so it caught the light. Her eyes followed the reflection on the curtains.

She looked over at Alex, sleeping next to her. The light was dim, dinner had just been served, and most of the other passengers in their cabin were preparing to sleep. Celeste pressed the button on her armrest as she adjusted her seat into a bed. Immediately an air hostess was at her side with a small bottle of mineral water asking her if she would need anything else before she turned in.

She politely declined. The flight out to Hong Kong, business class, had been a luxury. She had never before flown in such style. Not having to queue at immigration or having to wait long for her luggage. She couldn't help but think of her trip to Morocco earlier this year. She had taken the flight to make a quick visit to the trims market looking for a new buckle for the '*Cross*' bag Maryanne was designing. For the short three-hour flight she had been jammed between a grubby man who didn't quite fit in his seat and the world's loudest snorer. Alex had laughed at her. 'You went on business, surely they should send you business class,' he had said. But they had not. She should have known then that *Cross* had been in financial trouble, but she didn't think of it. She had just ignored it, not knowing any better. She took a deep breath. The nice thing about flying business class was that it was so quiet. No children crying for their mothers, no uneasy shifting or people straining to watch a movie on a single screen. Celeste lay down and pulled on her eye mask.

She couldn't sleep. Fidgeting in her seat for a few minutes, she eventually pulled off the mask and found her diary. She looked at the days ahead filled with meetings with various suppliers and designers and shook her head. Giddy with champagne and the thought of being Mrs Renshaw, she knew she was the luckiest woman alive. But yesterday Alex had asked her another question, which had swiftly brought her back to reality. And Celeste Broady had no idea how to answer it.

15

Barnet, North London

'The proposal was a shock?'

'Yes and no.'

'What do you mean by that?'

'Alex always got what he wanted. I suppose that's what attracted me to him. One time he wanted pistachio ice cream. But it was gone one in the morning and most of the ice cream shops in London were closed. We drove to Leicester Square and not a single store had any, so Alex telephoned the Maître D' of his favourite restaurant, which, of course, was closed. But they opened up just so he could get two scoops of pistachio ice cream. It was annoying as hell at the time. I said to Alex, "It's only dessert. Don't cause that man any bother." But I learned it wasn't the ice cream. It was the principle of the matter for Alex – and he tipped him handsomely for his efforts. Alex wanted people to go out of their way for him, to remind them that he mattered.'

'That didn't really answer my question.'

'I'm getting there. When Bill came on the scene, Alex felt a little threatened I guess. It forced his hand. I was to be his and his alone – I didn't know at the time it was the reason he proposed, but I see it now. Like the ice cream, Alex was just making a point.'

Elaine nodded. 'Okay, you're referring to Alex's best friend, Bill?'

Celeste eyed Elaine. Was she really trying to help? She had got more out of her in the last forty-five minutes than anyone else had in the past year. She wondered if, like others, Elaine thought she had a problem. Her mind started to drift. If Elaine talked, it could cause her problems. It wasn't as if she needed anyone paying closer attention to her, especially not now.

'Celeste?'

'Yes. Alex's best friend, Bill. It's funny they were so similar, Bill and Alex. Bill had the same confidence, which attracted the women. He was slightly shorter than Alex, but not by much. They both loved champagne, whiskey, fast cars, and as I later found out, yachts. But unlike Alex, Bill could laugh at himself. He loved doing accents and impressions. When I first met him I honestly thought he spoke like a West Country farmer. He kept the accent up for the first forty minutes over dinner. I didn't understand what everyone else at the table found so funny! He liked to make people laugh even if they were laughing at him. Alex didn't mind people laughing with him, never at him though.

And Bill, he lived in the moment. He'd call us up and say he had booked tickets to Vegas on the spur of the moment. You know, that sort of thing. Whereas Alex planned everything, calculated everything – liked order in his life. I used to tease him that he knew exactly what pants he was going to wear a week before he wore them.'

'Bill came between you and Alex?'

'Bill had a wife – has a wife. There have been times when

I thought Bill was going to leave her, but he hasn't yet. Her name's Angela and she's stunning. I think she used to be a model. She has beautiful long blond hair and high cheekbones. Alex introduced me to Bill soon after we got back from travelling. Unlike Alex, Bill flirted with everyone. He turned on the charm with me, and even though I'd heard Alex's stories about his friend being a womaniser I couldn't help but be taken in by his charm. I would never cross the line with Bill – I loved Alex too much, but I played along, as you do. A little bit of healthy flirting never hurt anyone, or so I thought.

'We were at an early summer garden party that year. Must have been in May. It was unusually hot. I was cooling down by the river at the bottom of the garden and Bill comes over to me. He starts telling me what a wonderful guy Alex is. Of course, I told him I already knew that. I was in love with Alex. I knew it then. I couldn't do anything back then without thinking of Alex. A song would play and I would think, "Oh Alex would like this." I would be out at lunch with the girls and think about his favourite dish. You know it's love if you have someone on your mind twenty-four hours a day. At least for me, that meant love. I never thought of other boyfriends in the same way before.

'Anyway, so I was talking to Bill about how amazing Alex is, and then he puts his arm around me, in a friendly way. I didn't think for a minute that he was coming on to me, but I'd be lying if I said I wasn't attracted to him in that moment. Before I knew it, Alex was at my side. He gave Bill a frosty look that said stay away, and I suppose I was flattered by the jealousy. A few nights later when Alex was out on a business dinner, Bill arrived at our door with the offer of taking me to a local Indian. I said yes. I texted Alex to let him know, but I guess I didn't realise just how jealous he was. We had barely touched our chicken tikka, when Alex turned up at our table saying his dinner had been cut short. But it felt like a cover up. Alex wanted to make sure Bill wasn't going to try anything on with me. That was the real Alex. He wanted me and that was that. Not long after that we went to Hong Kong and Alex proposed.'

'He didn't trust you?'

'I thought that at first. I was a bit funny with him when he turned up at our dinner. But he clearly said that it was Bill he had trust issues with. Apparently, Bill's wife had dated Alex when they were much younger – before Angela had started dating Bill. It wasn't anything serious, but Alex said Bill was trying to get even with him about it. So I understood why he felt insecure. And hearing about what his mother went through with Warwick made his story even more believable. At that time Alex and Bill had the kind of relationship where they were best of friends, but somehow also fiercely in competition with one another. Asking me to marry him was just Alex sticking two fingers up to Bill.'

'I can understand that, but I think you are putting yourself down.'

'Am I?'

'You said there was another decision Alex had asked you to make after his proposal.'

'Yes, one that would change my life forever.'

16

11th October 2008
Mayfair, London

Rachel held her new clutch under her arm making sure Sophia got a good look at the jewelled beetle clasp. The *Bottega Veneta* bag had been a gift from William. Sophia stared for a moment. 'You've been going out with Willy for, what, nearly a year now?'

Rachel nodded.

'Don't worry. He wasn't mine to keep.'

Rachel frowned. 'What do you mean?'

'That nonsense between us has been over for a long time.'

Rachel was silent. She hadn't told Sophia that she and William had been dating, but she had tried to keep it quiet. It had been William's idea and she was only too happy to go along with it. She knew just how catty girls at the club could be. Sophia was a prime example.

'Nothing ever stays under wraps here. You were here, weren't you, when Amanda was caught with her knickers down with that good-for-nothing CEO of *Greylings*? Who, rumour has it, has just lost his job. Undoubtedly, it's something fraudulent. Really, only one member saw the whole episode and they may as well have published it in the monthly newsletter.' Sophia let out a low chuckle. 'But listen, she wasn't the first and she certainly won't be the last. Ask Alicia the next time you see her, she isn't even a member here, but this club has a reputation, ask anyone. Come, walk with me to the gardens. I need a ciggie.' Sophia gently touched Rachel's arm directing her towards the back of the club.

They walked into the courtyard and stood under a patio heater whilst Sophia lit a cigarette. 'Willy will never really belong to any one person.'

Rachel shivered as she stood in the cold. She wanted to go back inside, but she was also desperate to know what Sophia had to say.

'He's a bit of a law unto himself. He's had his way with most of the attractive women in here. And he tips well. The waiters are like his personal assistants. They'll do anything to protect him.'

'Does he need protecting?'

'They've got his back. Whatever you do don't ever cause a scene here involving Willy. They'll kick you out. No question. He's as thick as thieves with the management. Wouldn't surprise me if he owned the place, or part of it. He has his fingers in a lot of pies and if he doesn't own something, he certainly knows people who do.'

'Why would I make a scene?'

Sophia laughed a deep laugh, sending a shiver down Rachel's spine. 'When Willy has had enough of you, he'll ignore you and reject your calls. You won't be able to contact him again; he'll see to that. He may even tell you some truths that will shock you to your core. Your little bubble will burst. Your emotions will be raw and unmanageable. The first time you see him again will be here, most probably, because you'll come here every day hoping to catch him. When you do see him you'll lash out and your membership will be terminated.'

It was Rachel's turn to laugh. Everyone at *The Emerald Rooms* was so dramatic, like they were in an episode of *Desperate Housewives*. 'Don't worry about me.'

Sophia shrugged her shoulders. 'I don't worry about anyone too much, luvvie. But I've been there, remember. I know what its like.'

'But you're friends with him now. It couldn't have been that bad.'

'Maybe I didn't fall for him that hard.' Sophia winked, but Rachel noticed there was something behind her smile. 'Pain? Hatred? Or just plain, old-fashioned jealousy? Rachel didn't speak her mind. Instead she just nodded, eager to find out what else Sophia knew about William.

When Rachel first started dating William she had been worried when he insisted on staying at a suite in *The Emerald Rooms* instead of taking her back to his place. Her friends joked that he had a wife and child at home, and she too had started to consider if there was any truth in that. Her mates certainly slept around with married men. Even, goodie-two-shoes Alicia had several tales of dating married men. Both her sister and her best friend, Bonnie, were at it. Bonnie was gorgeous. Could have anyone. Yet she had chosen a married man. Apparently you couldn't be too picky these days. It was the noughties and *de rigueur*, or so she had been told – the norm of the fractured society they lived in.

But then last night, after a couple of lines and two bottles of champagne, William had taken her to his apartment. Whilst he slept, she had walked around his home in a giddy state examining his possessions. Peeking though his wardrobes, she was relieved there were only men's clothes on hangers and only men's toiletries in the bathroom. It was a small apartment which could have just been his city bolt-hole, but Rachel didn't care. There were no pictures of a wife or another woman. She had even checked the drawers of the big mahogany desk that stood in the centre of his office before she had crept back under the duvet to be with him.

'When I was with him, and it wasn't for long,' Sophia said, 'Willy used to travel quite a bit. He was always going off to some far-flung destination. I was just a good shag when he called into port.' Sophia stubbed out her cigarette and lit another.

'He does travel quite a bit,' Rachel said, hesitantly. A week ago he had phoned her from Heathrow after a business trip. 'I'll be there in under an hour. Be ready,' was all he had said.

At the time Rachel had blushed. Happy that she was the first person he wanted to see. She had just enough time to shower, paint her nails and slip on a dress before he arrived. But now she wondered, was she just a plaything? A so-called booty call? Their relationship so far had been good. It suited them both. She didn't have to worry about being perfect for him every day, so when she did see him she made sure she looked her best – picking an outfit he loved to see her in, or lingerie he had bought her from a previous trip. The distance between them kept their relationship alive, she reasoned.

Rachel looked at Sophia with her red painted nails and lipstick to match. Sophia may have been just a casual sleeping partner to William, but then that was Sophia. She could be a high-class escort for all Rachel knew – she certainly spent like one. William didn't treat Rachel like a bit on the side. She wasn't just a companion for dinner, or a quick lay, they shared their dreams. That wasn't what you did with a mistress? Or was it? The rich seemed to have their own set of rules.

'I don't mean to disillusion you. You've been with him for longer than most,'

Rachel cheeks coloured as she stepped back into the doorway, her body seeking warmth.

Sophia blew smoke upwards towards the bedrooms of the club. 'Let me tell you two things. And I'm only doing this because I like you.'

Rachel managed a smile. If Sophia treated people she liked like this, she couldn't imagine what her enemies had to face. She could be a bitch sometimes.

'Firstly, if William doesn't want to take you away with him on one of his trips you're nothing but someone to screw on the weekends. He has only ever taken one other person away with him and you could say that was true love. Must have been.'

Rachel frowned. 'Who?'

'Now, if he takes you away it probably means something. But believe me it's bloody hard to make him take you. I asked him once. It was the beginning of the end for us.' Sophia stubbed out her cigarette and walked towards the door.

'Wait, you said two things. You said you were going to tell me two things.'

'Oh yes, the other thing.' Sophia stopped and looked at Rachel. 'It's not me that you have to be worried about. Nice bag by the way.' Sophia gave Rachel wry smile before she stepped inside the club and disappeared into the throng of people.

Rachel watched her go, unable to move. A raindrop hit her forehead. 'What the hell?' she said in to the cold night air, but nobody was there to hear her.

17

14th October 2008
Mayfair, London

'You like it?' William asked after taking a sip of his wine.

'It's beautiful,' she said, touching the *Dior* watch. 'I don't think I've ever owned something so exquisite.'

'Get used to it. I like spoiling you.' William took out his mobile phone from his pocket. It vibrated in his hand. He looked at the screen and smiled.

'A new watch and dinner at *Angelus*, I must be doing something right.'

'Then you'll forgive me for having to fly off to Paris on Saturday.' William took a sip of his wine, his lips were already stained by the tannins.

'Why Paris?' she asked. Her heart hammered in her chest as she considered asking if she could accompany him on this trip. She didn't want to suffer the same fate as Sophia.

'I'm looking at investing in a company out there. Need to see for myself if it's worth the investment.'

'Do you need to go on Saturday? What about Bella's party? You were going to meet my friends. They all want to see you. You never even let me take any pictures of you!' Rachel pouted.

'Sorry, Rachel,' William said, offering no other explanation.

'Can you not go just a day later?'

'I've a good friend in Saint-Germain. He's flying out tomorrow. I have to meet him. It would be rude otherwise.'

'Fine,' Rachel said. He was being rude by missing her best friend's birthday, and she had wanted him to meet some of her other friends. She had told Alicia all about him and vice versa. But he didn't seem too concerned and she didn't want to turn this into a fight. She held her tongue and took a breath. 'Do you need company?' she asked eventually, watching for a reaction. If the question bothered him, he certainly didn't show it. Either Sophia was lying or William had a good poker face.

He took a mouthful of his food. 'What about your friend's party? I thought you couldn't miss it,' he asked in between chewing. He signalled to the waiter and ordered another bottle of *Barolo*.

'She would understand,' Rachel said, even though she knew Bella wouldn't. But she would rather spend time in Paris with William than with her girlfriends.

'What about the weekend after? I was thinking we could get a cabin in the New Forest. There's a great hotel. A *Relais and Chateaux* – '

'What about Paris?' Her hands trembled under the table. She was determined to prove to Sophia that she wasn't just a bit on the side, she was the real deal.

William was silent.

'Why can't we just go away for a couple of nights? Paris would be perfect. Take me away with you just this once. Paris is so romantic.'

'I do care for you Rachel. But…'

His words made her bristle. She didn't want care she wanted

love, head over heels love.

He picked up his fork and cut a piece of pork tenderloin on his plate. 'You usually this whiney? Is this the true Rachel?'

Rachel's jaw dropped open. 'If you think I'm whiney then…' she trailed off, her confidence suddenly deserting her. She loved William even if he could be a bit obtuse sometimes. Going away with him was a sore point. Sophia had already pointed that out. Why had she riled him? William was the best of a bad bunch Rachel had dated. What else was out there? Her single girlfriends were proof that there were no decent men left in London. But it was time to find out how he truly felt about her before she fell deeper into the relationship and reached a point of no return. If he refused to take her to Paris, well then she would know she had been wasting her time.

'All I'm asking for is one trip.'

'I don't normally…'

'Is this just normal to you?'

He put down his knife and fork and gave her a look she had not seen before. A look that said, don't push me.

She leaned back in her chair, met his gaze and held it. Should she push him and lose him forever like Sophia had? Or should she drop it and try again another time? She looked away first as she realised William would always have the last say. 'Say you'll think about it at least,' she mumbled, eventually.

'I'll think about it,' William said, a smile returning to his face.

18

15th October 2008
Mayfair, London

'I need to give Warwick an answer soon,' Alex said, slipping his arms around Celeste.

'You've been flying here, there and everywhere. I haven't had time to talk to you properly.' Celeste released herself from Alex's grip and sat down on the sofa. Before leaving Hong Kong, Alex had told her about *Renshaw*'s planned expansion into Hong Kong. Apparently it was inevitable if they wanted to grow. And, of course, Alex would be heading up this new branch.

He had asked Celeste if she would leave *Cross* and go with him to Hong Kong and she had been taking her time to decide. It was a big decision for both of them, but it seemed that Alex had already made up his mind. He had cleverly asked her to marry him before he asked her to move country with him. Now she was in a dilemma, and it appeared he would go to Hong Kong no matter what she decided.

'I don't want to leave my job. I spoke to Maryanne today. The investors she had lined up have pulled out. If I don't help her now she could lose *Cross* forever. Maryanne's a good friend. She's even confessed about *Cross*'s financial situation.

It took her a lot of courage to do that. Did you know that a department store is trying to buy *Cross* out? That would devastate her.'

Alex was silent, his eyebrows knitted together. She hated seeing him like this: sullen and moody.

'Did you ask your father about Graham?' she asked.

'I told you before.'

'That Graham isn't capable.'

'And Sarah is pregnant now.'

'Oh,' Celeste said. 'I didn't know.' A sliver of envy pricked her but she shook it away. She and Alex had decided, soon after they moved to London, that they didn't want a family. To be honest, it had been more Alex's decision than hers, but she had happily agreed.

'They're keeping it quiet. Until the three months are up, or whatever.'

'So you're the only one that can go?' Celeste knew the answer, yet she had to ask the question. Alex wanted to head up *Renshaw* in Hong Kong. He wanted to be in control without Graham constantly nipping at his heels, or at least trying to.

'You said it yourself, it's a good opportunity. The money's good. You'll never want for anything.'

'Except a job. Plus, I promised Maryanne.'

'Since when have you become so sentimental? Do you think Maryanne would do the same for you if she had been offered an amazing life in Hong Kong?'

'Don't be like that. You go first, I'll follow. Let me just get *Cross* through the next collection and the next round of investors and I'll be there. I promised her one last collection to see what we can do.'

'I need your support.' Alex said.

'Kealana will get you set up. She knows you,' Celeste said, and for once she felt thankful for the woman. 'She has organised enough houses for the Renshaws. She can organise the kitchen better than I can – labels facing outwards, takeaway menus neatly filed by cuisine.'

'I earn more than enough for both of us. A new collection won't make a difference to *Cross*. The woman has no business acumen. She needs to close the store in Paris, concentrate on London and forget her dream of opening a third store. She's going senile.'

'Have you never wanted to follow your dreams?'

'This is my dream, Celeste. Us moving to Hong Kong, together.'

'What will I do in Hong Kong?'

'Do what you want. There's a huge network of wives I can introduce you to.'

'I've worked for as long as I can remember. Even growing up I had a newspaper round. I can't just give it up. I can't just sit around and do lunches at some club with a bunch of air-heads.'

Alex smiled. He sat at the breakfast bar and drummed his fingers on the granite. 'This is why I want to marry you. You're just like me – stubborn and ambitious. What do I have to do to make you come with me?'

'Solve all *Cross*'s problems so Maryanne can open a store in Hong Kong. I can be based at that store. It'll be perfect.' Celeste walked up to Alex and caressed his face in her hands.

'I could, you know…' he said eventually.

'Use Daddy's small change to buy out *Cross*?' Celeste asked. For a second she thought he was being serious, then she realised it was too far-fetched, even for the Renshaws.

'I wish I could set you up in Hong Kong,' Alex tucked a strand of her black hair behind Celeste's ear. 'Unfortunately, honey, *Renshaw* isn't into fancy women's clothing.' He narrowed his eyes. 'There are so many good jobs in retail in Hong Kong. I'm sure Mr Lau...'

'I don't want to know about Mr Lau.' Celeste imagined a fat, balding man who had a lecherous look in his eye and a handful of *Asian Escorts* cards.

'You're going to have to meet him when we are out there. You're going to have to be nice.'

'Bite me!' Celeste said with a smile. 'You've made your mind up, haven't you?'

'I have to go. I have no choice.'

'You could stay here with me.'

'Every day I delay this move, *Renshaw* is losing money.'

'We're working on the summer collection now. I'll finish it and I'll be there with bells on.'

'I'm going to worry about you.'

'I'll be with Maryanne most days and Alicia is just around the corner.'

'They're your family, whilst I'm disposable. What would you do without Alicia and Maryanne?'

'Don't be jealous. I've had to do something with my time whilst you've been swanning off all over the world for the benefit of *Renshaw*, not to mention those late business meetings. If I didn't know better I would say you were having an affair.'

Alex put his arms around Celeste. 'Listen, if you don't want to go to Hong Kong with me right now, there is one thing you can do for me before I leave.'

'What?'

'I'll show you,' Alex said with a mischievous smile.

19

Barnet, North London

'You let him go?' Elaine asked.

'Don't be ridiculous. I followed him. He was the love of my life. After he left, I felt this huge gap in my life. I realised that I wanted Alex more than a job. Before he went I don't think I appreciated what I really had with him.

'I mean I had it all, didn't I? An amazing boyfriend who sent me love notes for no apparent reason. He would also send my favourite sandwich to *Cross* when he knew I would be too busy at work to go and buy lunch. I had a job that I loved, and a boss whom I adored. Not many people can say that they had it all, but I did. London was good to us during that time. We were earning well. I'm sure I was earning more money than my entire set of school friends back in Bristol. I bet none of them ever thought that Celeste Broady, with her pig-tails and ill-fitting clothes, would ever be living that life.

'Alex was probably earning enough to support a small city. I didn't know that then.' Celeste made a face. 'I asked Alex, of course I did, but he was just so cagey about it. Growing up on a council estate, everyone talked about how little they were earning. I guessed with Alex's kind of wealth one just doesn't mention it. He said that once, that talking about money was vulgar.' She shrugged. "I earn enough, enough to not worry about spending," is what Alex said one time when I asked. So we spent without thinking too much. At least, I reminded myself not to think about it every time I pulled out my *Amex*. I knew Alex made a lot. He made even more in Hong Kong.'

'And you kept in touch with Bonnie and Alicia whilst you were in London?'

Everyone wanted to know about her friends; her so-called friends. Her mother had tried to get in touch with Bonnie. She should have never had. Bonnie and Alicia, friends forever. But friends are not supposed to hurt you.

'Celeste?'

'I met Alicia whenever I could and when we couldn't meet, we spoke on the phone. We went to the theatre together, on shopping trips and ate ice-cream in our pyjamas when Alex was away. You know, the usual girly stuff. She became the sister I never had. It can be difficult being an only child. Alicia practically lived with me when Alex was busy or away with work. And Alex didn't mind it because it kept me occupied. It was handy she lived close by.'

'And Bonnie?'

Bonnie, Bonnie, Bonnie. 'Like I said, she had moved to Edinburgh and I didn't bother keeping in touch. I felt I could cut her out of my life after… well we had an argument and we drifted apart. Alicia spoke to her often, and I got to know Bonnie's news through her. Alicia was good like that, always trying to keep the peace.'

Elaine wrote something in her journal. Celeste watched her hand move across the page and flinched. 'You mentioned two other girls before. Sophia and Rachel?'

'Sophia I never met. I rarely went to *The Emerald Rooms* where they all met regularly. Our paths just never crossed and I don't think Alicia kept up her friendship with them for long.'

'And Rachel?'

Celeste felt a shiver run down her spine. 'I can't say I was ever friends with her.'

'Alicia sounds like your rock.'

'Alex was my rock.'

Elaine nodded. 'Your friendship with Alicia remained strong throughout your marriage?'

Celeste touched her eyes. 'No,' she said in a whisper, before closing her eyes and turning away from Elaine.

'Friendships can be like that. One minute you are close as siblings. The next…'

'It wasn't like that,' Celeste snapped. 'Like most friends we had our ups and downs, but then we lost touch. First Bonnie, then Alicia. He saw to that.'

20

3rd – 4th November 2008
Mayfair, London

Three weeks earlier Celeste had agreed to bring their wedding forward. It was what Alex had wanted. 'If I can't go to Hong Kong with you then at least let me go as your husband,' he had said, giving her a card of the Renshaws' trusted events planner. She had agreed instantly. It made sense to bring the wedding forward. At least this way, when Alex went off to Hong Kong, they parted as man and wife.

Now, she was ready to tell the girls. She had flounced around all morning, in a fit of excitement after arranging to meet Alicia and Bonnie for lunch to share her news with them. Alex rolled his eyes after she tried on the fourth outfit.

'Black or navy tights?'

'We need to leave now or I'll get stuck in traffic after I drop you.'

'Okay okay,' Celeste said, selecting the navy tights from her drawer. 'I can't wait to see their faces when I tell them.'

'Bill was happy enough when I told him. Glad he has someone to join him in the married stakes.'

'He's a man. He just wants to know the date and time. Although I'm surprised he didn't warn you against marriage.'

Bill was an outrageous flirt and knew how to charm just about anything. Only last week he had made Alex's secretary blush at an after-work networking event. Celeste wasn't standing close enough to them to hear what Bill was saying to the married mother of two, but she could tell by the way he leaned towards his victim and gently touched her back that he was up to no good. She had caught Alex's eye and they had shared a look. You had to hand it to Bill, at least he knew how to liven up a boring works' event.

'Bill likes to flirt, but he'd never go beyond that. He'd never leave Angela.'

'Perhaps he doesn't tell you everything. We all know how you feel about cheating spouses.'

Alex assured her Bill's advances never went beyond a flirtation. Of course Alex had to say that – he held Bonnie's affair against her and it had become his mantra after what he had witnessed his mother go through. The countless evenings he had seen her crying in the kitchen when she thought Alex was in his study. But despite that, Celeste wanted to remind him how concerned he had been when he thought Bill was making a pass at her, but she didn't. She didn't want a fight, not now.

'He believes in the sanctity of marriage,' Alex said.

'So long as you don't join him in chasing after other women.'

'Celeste, honey, I only have eyes for you. Now hurry up. Why did you agree to East London? I hate East London. It's so –'

'Alternative.'

'I was going to say dirty.'

'Snob. I could get a cab.'

'I never see you. Soon you'll be getting cabs everywhere when I'm In Hong Kong. I'll drop you and I'll pick you up as well.'

'Don't you trust me, Alex? Think I'm meeting another man?'

Alex put his arms around her. 'I love you too much. That's the problem.'

'No one else gets the chauffer treatment these days from their other halves,' Celeste said, brushing away any worrying thoughts of Alex's need to be in control to one side.

'I keep telling you that you're one lucky gal,' Alex said, letting go of Celeste. 'Bill's looking at a new contract in the East – something to do with carbon credits. He may be a neighbour when we're in Hong Kong.'

'I didn't know he was into the environment.'

'You know Bill. He's a maverick.'

Celeste nodded. But she didn't know Bill, not that well and she had no interest in Bill's business affairs either. So she let the matter drop. The thought of Bill being in Hong Kong gave her some comfort, though. At least Alex would have someone to call on. And Alex was right, Bill may have flirted, but as far as she knew it never went any further than that. She grabbed her yellow scarf and handbag from the bed and headed downstairs after Alex.

*

Celeste gazed straight ahead. Rain hit the windscreen as the car sped towards W1. The sky was black. As she and Alex headed home in the pouring rain, she wished she had never organised to with meet Bonnie and Alicia in the first place. The lunch had ended abruptly and had irreparably damaged the friendship she had with the girls. A tear ran down her cheek as she replayed what had happened.

After they were seated and their drinks had arrived, Celeste had broken the news to Bonnie and Alicia. 'Oh Celeste,' Alicia cried embracing her best friend. 'How utterly romantic. I wish that would happen to me. I'll clear my diary and do whatever you need me to do. After all that's what a maid of honour is for.'

Bonnie had flashed Celeste a smile, but she could see by the way her lips were firmly pressed together that the smile wasn't genuine. 'You should take time to think about it. It's worrying that he wants to get married so quickly,' she said. She had picked up just a hint of a Scottish accent. It suited her and made her words sound less harsh than they were intended.

She took a deep breath. She hadn't seen much of Bonnie over the last year, but she expected her to trust her judgement, and at least be happy for her if nothing else.

'Oh Bonnie,' Alicia said, running her fingers through her fiery, red hair. 'It's because of Hong Kong, silly. See how happy Celeste is.'

Bonnie excused herself and went to the toilet.

'Take no notice of her, Celeste, she's having a tough time with Matt – he won't leave his wife. And look, she has practically finished her wine.' Alicia pointed to Bonnie's empty glass. 'She's terribly unhappy. I think she wants what you have. It's just envy.'

'It's mean what she said, without understanding what Alex and I have together.'

'Oh, do be kind to her. She's so fragile at the moment.'

Celeste sighed.

'I don't think I can make that weekend in any case,' Bonnie said, returning to the table. Her eyeliner had smudged below her right eye and she kept touching the tip of her nose with the back of her hand. 'I'll try my best. But it's the only weekend that Matt and I have got planned, and we booked a place in Ireland.'

'Hmm,' Celeste said. She glanced over at Alicia who was smiling brightly. She looked back at Bonnie. 'I know it's last minute, but it would mean the world to me if you could come. You two are the only friends I really want at my wedding. As it is, I have the Renshaws' events planner to deal with. She's as thin as a rake, wears skyscraper heels and her eyebrows twitch every time I make a suggestion. It's awful. If I'm not careful she'll ruin my wedding day. The old maid probably wants Alex for herself. I'm probably having the wedding she dreamed about as a child,' Celeste said, trying to lighten the mood, but when Bonnie didn't even attempt a smile she felt her body temperature creeping up.

'Bonnie, come on,' Alicia encouraged. 'You can't miss Celeste's wedding!'

'Why can't I? No one cares about Matt. None of you ever want to meet him.'

'So, this is why you are angry,' Celeste folded her arms. She remembered her conversation with Alex earlier – how adultery had ruined his mother. Before she could stop herself she blurted out his words. 'Matt's married. What you're doing, it's wrong.'

'What I have with Matt is real.'

'It's fake, Bonnie. Completely fake!'

'You would know about that, wouldn't you?' Bonnie said. She topped up her glass with the bottle of wine. Alicia put her face in her hands.

'What d'you mean by that?' Celeste asked.

'I know all about your little secret from Alicia,' Bonnie said with a smirk.

Celeste looked at Alicia and back at Bonnie. There were no secrets between them.

'Tell me, does Alex know that you grew up in a council estate? Or are you saving that for the wedding night? You say my relationship isn't real, but yours is built on lies. Pot calling the kettle black, wouldn't you say?'

Celeste looked at Bonnie her mouth ajar. She almost laughed. She turned to look at Alicia whose eyes were brimming. 'I have nothing to be ashamed about. You know about my upbringing and you have no idea what Alex knows about me. I don't know what Alicia has said to you, but even if she has told you a pack of lies, you can't compare my situation to yours. It's pathetic.'

'Celeste, I never meant to…' Alicia started.

Celeste stood up. Taking her coat from the chair she walked towards the front of the restaurant.

'Wait Celeste,' Alicia said as she tried to catch up with Celeste. 'Bonnie took everything I said out of context. I don't know why. She asked me what Alex thought of your childhood and I said we hadn't talked about it. I said that maybe you hadn't told him yet. But I didn't mean anything by that. It was just talk.'

Celeste stopped and turned to face Alicia. She let her eyes focus on her friend for a second, but she found she had nothing to say. She turned around and carried on walking until she was out of the restaurant. She had immediately called Alex and had waited in the rain until he arrived. They had found an eatery close by, and over a plate of Pad Thai and a bottle of *Gavi,* Celeste explained what had happened.

'Screw them. You don't need them.' Alex had wiped a tear

from her face. 'It doesn't matter where you grew up. Bonnie is just trying to drive a wedge between us. You gotta be careful. She can't even find a boyfriend who isn't already married. It doesn't matter where you grew up,' he said again. 'None of it matters.'

Celeste shrugged. 'And she is probably on coke too. She returned from the loo, desperately touching her nose.'

Alex raised his eyebrows. 'Well, you don't want to get involved with that.'

She had heard Alex previously snigger at where people grew up, and she knew Bill and Alex pigeonholed their friends into "old" and "new" money. She had told him before that he shouldn't be so judgemental, but he had laughed it off as a bit of fun. Was Alex being genuine or was there was some truth in what Bonnie had said? Perhaps there was some dishonesty in their relationship. But Celeste didn't want to think about that. She never felt inferior when she was with Alex. Now no one questioned her past because Alex had validated her in this new circle of friends – one where flash cars and second homes were just a part of everyday life.

*

Later that night she had spoken to Alex about East Row until her eyes had closed, and in the morning, when she woke, she felt like she could take on the world. She wanted to call Alicia and make things right. Alicia wasn't the sort to stir things up or talk badly of others. Back at university when they had met, Alicia hadn't even batted an eyelid when she told her about the regular car fires she had witnessed living on the East Row estate. In fact, Alicia had always been her champion, her voice of reason when she felt she just didn't fit in.

Bonnie too deserved a call. And she had been the one to snap at Bonnie first. Celeste walked over to the phone, but something held her back. Bonnie hadn't said what she had because she wanted to help her, she had said it because she wanted to hurt her, come between her and Alex. Even Alex had pointed that out last night. She crossed her arms over her chest and decided not to call either friend. As Alex had said to her yesterday, 'Let them call you.'

21

25th November 2008
Mayfair, London

'There you are,' Maryanne said as Celeste walked through the door.

Celeste checked her watch. 'It's seven. You're never in so early.'

'I need to talk to you.'

She took off her coat and hung it on the ornate gold stand in the corner of the room. She could feel Maryanne's eyes on her, watching her every move. 'What's the matter?' She asked noticing the dark circles around Maryanne's eyes and the grey roots of her hair. Maryanne had let her appearance slip over the past year. It wasn't surprising given the stress she was under. Maybe Alex was right, perhaps it was time for Maryanne to retire.

It was then that she realised what her boss was about to tell her. Her stomach turned. This was it. It was over for *Cross*. There would be no summer collection to finish. She was free to go. She felt the knot in her stomach tighten. Her feelings were mixed. *Cross* was her world, but at the same time she couldn't wait to be with Alex. She wasn't herself when he wasn't around, and he had been gone for four days now – an unavoidable trip before the wedding. It was only for a week, and she had become used to him flying here, there and everywhere. But this time with the wedding fast approaching, it felt like an eternity. More than anything, she missed his touch – the two kisses he gave her every morning before he left for work and the bear hugs he would spring on her when she was doing something mundane like sketching or chopping fruit. She didn't want him to move to Hong Kong without her. But *Cross*… *Cross* was part of her. It was her only form of independence.

Maryanne closed the office door and motioned for her to sit down and then took the seat opposite. She let out a sigh. 'I have news.'

Celeste leaned forward. She could feel her heart thumping in her chest.

'I've told you we are in a financial situation, but I haven't told you just how bad it is.'

Celeste didn't want to say that she had seen the damned spread-sheet for herself. Instead she remained silent and nodded for Maryanne to continue.

'I didn't want to do this just before your wedding, kid, but I've no choice. My hands are tied.'

'Is it over?' she asked. Her mouth was dry.

'I've been meeting with a Mr Harris recently. He's one of the investors that initially showed some interest, but then backed away. Then a few weeks ago he called with a whole host of new questions. I get the impression that he knows the trouble we're in.'

Celeste winced. It could easily happen. Alex had said so himself. A good accountant could cover up *Cross*'s mistakes but a better one could find them.

'He's had some retail experience, not much, but he's looking for a readymade brand to invest in. He sounds like a rich kid with some money to spend. He's not ideal. Ordinarily darlin' we wouldn't wanna get into bed with someone like this.'

'We,' Celeste thought, there probably was no 'we' anymore. She was planning to ask Maryanne today if she could do some freelance work for *Cross* from Hong Kong, but what was the point in asking now? A new investor was unlikely to work in her favour.

'He knows more about *Cross* than I've told him. I suppose he's done his homework.' Maryanne rested her head on the back of her hand. 'So they're getting a good deal. He's willing to purchase a fifty one per cent stake in *Cross Boutiques*.'

'That's a controlling share! He'll more or less own it.'

'I'll still have a lifetime job with *Cross*. And you…' She fiddled with the gold bumblebee broach on her lapel. 'You don't need to worry about the finer details. Your job is secure. Harris is polite and charmin' and he's someone we can both work with. Although I don't think we'll see much of him. He has this partner, a right-hand man, Toby Cain, who we'll deal with – or so he said.'

'But you're giving up so much. You started this label from scratch – on your own.'

Maryanne didn't meet her eyes. 'I'm old darlin' but I'm not stupid. I can't continue like this. Harris' proposal came in at the right time.'

'What about approaching other investors?'

Maryanne shook her head. 'You don't just put an ad in the paper for such an investor darlin'. It's all done through contacts and agents, and believe me I've spoken to people I know in the industry. Not many people are willing to invest with retail the way it is at the moment. I've been speaking with Mr Harris for sometime. We've finally reached an agreement. I'm sorry to have kept you in the dark. But the situation was…difficult.'

She looked up at Maryanne – the woman she admired and respected, the woman she had one day hoped to become. Maryanne looked tired. The determination in her eyes had vanished. She was no longer the bright-eyed, feisty woman she had met on the first day of the job. But Celeste couldn't hold what Maryanne had done against her. After all, it was her business. 'So that's it then.'

'You still want to work after you get married? You aren't tempted to be a lady of leisure? Alex Renshaw can certainly keep you,'

'I don't want to be a kept woman.'

'Good, kid, stay independent for as long as you can. I tried to do that with *Cross Boutiques*.'

'You did your best,' Celeste said, forcing the words from her mouth. She noticed then that Maryanne's eyes were moist and she realised she couldn't be angry with her. The decision must have been hard for her.

'I know that you want to go to Hong Kong with Alex after the wedding.'

'You do?' Celeste asked.

Maryanne nodded.

She really was as transparent as Alex said she was. She hadn't confided in Maryanne about Hong Kong yet.

'You needn't worry about looking for a job in Hong Kong though.'

'Why's that?'

'Part of my deal with Harris is that *Cross* opens a final boutique in Hong Kong. Turns out it works in his favour as well as mine. He already has dealings there and owns retail space on Causeway Bay on Hong Kong Island – Five hundred square feet. See, I told you he'd done his homework.'

'It sounds too good to be true.'

'Don't question it, kid,' Maryanne said, giving Celeste a steely look. 'It's good for you. That Alex of yours is a lucky charm.' Maryanne tried a smile. 'So, you'll be leaving me soon.'

'I could stay here for a while, if you need me.'

Her boss smiled. 'No darling', you must go. Harris has specifically requested that you head up the design team from the Hong Kong store. Hong Kong has some great opportunities. We'll resource our materials from there as well from now on.'

'How does Harris know me?'

Maryanne looked away. 'Word gets around in this industry, and you've come a long way since you started here.'

'Will you be there too?'

'I'll come up and down, but I'm needed here, and you're more than capable.'

'I don't know if I'll be able to manage on my own.'

'I won't leave you to the wolves.'

Celeste bit her lower lip. Maryanne was right, it was all going in her favour, but something about it just didn't feel right. Was it just the nerves of running her own team without her old boss? 'Do you have to do this?' she asked. The words were out before she could stop them. 'I spoke to Alex and he said we could get a specialist in. Consolidate our assets. Close the store in Paris and use the capital receipts from that to plough into *Cross* London.'

Maryanne laughed. 'Hell, this is a great opportunity for you, kid. Grab it with both hands. You get to stay at *Cross* and move to Hong Kong to be with your husband.'

Celeste swallowed hard. It was a win-win situation for her.

'So it is settled. After your honeymoon you'll report to me from Hong Kong.'

'So soon?'

'It's how Harris wants this to work.'

'I don't think I like the sound of him.'

'You'll get used to him. Now let's start the day. It's gone eight already.' Maryanne stood up and smoothed her skirt with her hands. 'Oh one other thing darlin', I'm sorry for the late notice but I won't be able to make Saturday.'

'Our wedding?'

'Sorry, family emergency.'

'Oh.' Maryanne had been the first to accept Celeste's invitation. If she remembered correctly, Maryanne said that she would have gate-crashed had she not been invited. Maryanne didn't even have family, as far as she knew. Alex's words came back to her, 'Maryanne's selfish,' he had said, when she told him about *Cross*'s financial ruin. 'You're sticking by her, but would she do the same for you?' Celeste had ignored him. She and Maryanne were not just colleagues – they were friends she had reasoned. Had it all been an act? Could Alex see what she couldn't?

She looked expectantly at Maryanne, but she didn't say another word on the matter. She just picked up the phone and organised her morning. Celeste swallowed back the lump in her throat.

22

Barnet, North London

'We never had a honeymoon.'

'They required you at *Cross* sooner than you expected?' Elaine asked.

'Please, I wasn't that important, just a pawn in their little game. I know that now. I blame myself about Maryanne.'

'Why's that?'

Celeste fiddled with the gold chain that hung around her neck. The gold bumblebee swung as she pulled at the necklace. 'I should have seen it coming.'

'What?'

'All of it – the investment, the sickness.'

Elaine looked at her notes. 'Celeste, you're losing me. What should you have seen? Who was sick?'

Celeste narrowed her eyes. 'Maryanne was sick. I found that out much later, when it was too late. She tried to save me.'

'How?'

She leaned back in her chair and looked out of the window. It was dark outside and eerily quiet. She looked at the ticking clock on the wall. 'We'll get there.'

'You were married weren't you, Elaine? Where did you go

on honeymoon?'

'Lake Como.'

'I hear it's beautiful.'

'It is.'

'How would you feel if your husband was too busy to go on honeymoon? Would you be angry?'

'I suppose I would.'

'At the time I wasn't angry. Not at all, but afterwards, I was angry.'

'You didn't mind at the time?'

'It all made sense then. The reasons as to why we couldn't go. Alex was heading up *Renshaw* in Hong Kong. Doing what exactly, I don't know. I tried asking him several times but he kept his business dealings to himself. Sometimes he would tell me about a difficult investor or a deal going wrong and words like *Nasdaq* and *Nikkei* and *SEHK* soon became familiar but no matter how much I tried to find out or learn about it, Alex shut me out. He was either too busy to explain or he lost his patience with me. I should have pushed him harder. But he always said that fashion and finance were worlds apart.

'We were off to Hong Kong. I had the world at my feet. Yet again things were going my way. Maryanne had been right – Alex Renshaw was my lucky charm. And I was a Renshaw now. I saw Hong Kong as one long honeymoon. And don't forget, I too was busy with the excitement of heading up my own design team. Hong Kong is at the cutting edge of fashion. They want everything there before it hits stores in Britain. I remember geometric cuts were huge over there when we moved. My first design was a plaid tunic cut on the angle. We sold out within a week.'

'A honeymoon is when newly-weds take time out to be on

their own. Get to know each other in private. It's a time when you shouldn't have to think about the daily stresses of life. Some people say it is the foundation of a successful marriage.'

Celeste laughed. 'Maybe, back in the day, when couples met for the first time at the altar. I knew everything about Alex by the time we got married.' She hesitated, 'On second thoughts, perhaps you're right.'

'Did the wedding go as planned?'

'You could say that.'

'Was it a grand affair?'

'You would think that, wouldn't you? That it would be grand. Hundreds of well-to-do people.'

'You didn't want a big, glamorous wedding?'

'In my mind, it was going to be alternative, edgy. I was thinking of an over-the-top cake from Chocccywoccydoo-dah, in tiers of white chocolate with a gold candelabra and maybe a skull – a little McQueen-esque. I am a designer after all. ' She looked at her tan brogues, khaki cardigan and black trousers. An outfit she would never have worn five years ago.

'Alex liked things a certain way, a skull on a wedding cake was out of the question. We stuck to a seven tier classic white cake.'

'Alex liked to keep things traditional.'

'Alex liked his way, and, more importantly, his way of life.'

'His way of life?'

'I eventually got used to it. Waiters were always tipped generously, so we always got the best table. We flew business class, first class sometimes. Taxis everywhere. He even had a chauffer pick me up when needed. Before we were married, I was reluctant to give in to this way of living, and in a way I was still getting used to the perks of dating a rich man. After marriage it became a way of life, and soon I didn't think of it as an extravagance anymore. To me the luxuries had become necessities, and living in Hong Kong we had more glitz and glamour than you could imagine. But when I was planning a wedding I was still a Broady. Having a big glamorous wedding at *Blenheim Palace,* as suggested by his father, seemed a bit fraudulent to me. I was scared. I guess I wasn't sure if I could pull it off.'

'Because you grew up with so little?'

'I suppose,' Celeste said, studying the floor.

'Alex asked me what kind of a wedding I had in mind when we decided to bring the date forward. Some girls dream of their wedding all their lives. They know exactly what they want. But I wasn't like that. It all happened so quickly, so I wasn't sure what I wanted. I had an idea of an art gallery wedding or something like that, but I knew the mention of that would set Alex's eyes rolling after the cake conversation. And the wedding was about us, not about me. So I ummed and aahed and ended the conversation. Later that day I bought ten wedding and bride magazines and confused myself so much that I nearly called the wedding off. I don't know why. I don't know what happened.'

'Pre-wedding nerves are natural.'

Celeste shrugged. 'I'm not sure it was that. Perhaps it was the fear of being swallowed alive into the *Renshaw* empire. It turned out to be a small wedding. Fifty guests. I suppose if I'd married any old Joe Bloggs, fifty guests would have seemed like a big wedding. It was elegant though – everything in blue and white. It sounds clinical, but it wasn't. My mother has a picture of the full wedding party and it looks like something out of a movie. Alex paid a fortune for some top London photographer, a Lawrence someone or the other. I think he shot the Royals at some stage in his career.' She let her mind drift. A smile formed on her lips. 'But I mustn't be bitter. Alicia once told me that I should cherish the memories.'

'Alicia's right. We can't look back on our lives with regret. We have to appreciate our past, it makes us what we are today. Just because your wedding didn't necessarily turn out how you had planned, doesn't mean that you have to make every memory that you have a bad one.'

'I often wonder this – if you have a perfect wedding, does that mean your marriage won't be perfect? On my parents' wedding day it didn't stop raining. They could only afford sausage rolls and egg salad, and the cake fell off the stand. They have one of the strongest marriages I know. Do you think statisticians have done some research on the correlation of a good wedding day to an unhappy marriage?'

'Your parents didn't enjoy their wedding?'

Celeste bit her lower lip. 'They loved it. My mother always says it was perfect.'

'There you go. I think you have your answer.'

'Very clever.'

'Did your wedding turn out how you had wanted?'

'I suppose. I worried that as the bride, my parents would have to foot this huge bill. Of course I would have paid, but…'

'Did Alex expect your parents to contribute?'

'Alex was a doll about the whole thing. A few nights after my fight with Bonnie and Alicia he took me out to dinner – a tiny little Italian in Soho – not pretentious or anything like he usually insisted on. Alex was so adorable and understanding then. I didn't have to say a word. Over a glass of *Sauvignon* he said that if I was fine with it, he would book the wedding planner who organised his brother's wedding, and she would sort out whatever needed doing. He also said that he was going to pay the entire bill. Not his father or his company. He was going to pay for it all. I think he knew I was worried what his father would think if they had to pay for it. Alex paying for it all meant that they would never have known. I felt hugely relieved.'

'Did you get on with his father and the rest of his family?'

'Alex was close to Warwick; and Graham, despite what he said about his inability to run *Renshaw*. If it's one thing the three of them agreed on it was food, so I got to know Graham and Warwick through that medium. They were often in London for *Renshaw* business so we all used to meet up. And Warwick hosted a boozy Sunday lunch most weekends. Graham and his wife Sarah would always be there. Warwick used to enjoy teasing Alex about the two cars he wrote off in his younger years and his one expulsion from school for smoking in the boys' loos. I got the impression that when they were growing up Alex was the naughty one of the two, a bit of a handful, but the golden boy as well – the son that couldn't do wrong.'

'And Graham, was he the inept older brother Alex made him out to be?'

'I could see Graham watching Warwick and Alex interacting with one another. His gaze would become intense. He used to be in a trance-like state watching them, until Sarah squeezed his leg and whispered something in his ear. It was clear that Warwick lavished Alex with attention and left him out in the cold. I guess Warwick saw himself in Alex – they both liked to work hard and play hard. Graham on the other hand was quiet and had been with his wife Sarah forever. He was the good son who probably wanted to pursue a career in IT, not the financial markets.'

'A disappointment to his father?'

Celeste frowned. 'I wouldn't say that. Occasionally, Warwick would talk to Graham about emerging markets and futures, complex things to do with *Renshaw* that went way over my head. Alex was often left out. It never bothered him though. I found out why later, much later. But to answer your question, I got on well with his family. Warwick was always kind to me. He always asked about *Cross* and really listened. His eyes didn't glaze over the way some do when I talk shop.'

'You mentioned the wedding planner before.'

'We had differing opinions. She had started her career in some *Renshaw* enterprise and was fiercely loyal to them. She dictated on the flowers and the colour scheme so it matched the Renshaw coat of arms. She belittled my ideas. Of course, she never said anything to me, but I could tell by the way her eyebrows twitched at my suggestions. "Fashion and weddings are two different things," she said to me once when I reminded her I was a designer. She was wrong. They're not that different at all.'

'Did you discuss this with Alex?'

'He was so busy with work and flying up and down to Hong Kong, I didn't want to bother him. Plus, with everything that was happening at *Cross* I was glad of the help and that it wasn't Kealana helping out.'

'Could your mother have helped?'

Celeste laughed. 'I love my mother, but our tastes are so different, and she would have had a heart-attack if she knew how much the flowers alone had cost. I didn't want to burden anyone, and Alex was paying for the wedding planner's services. God knows how much she charged. I overheard her say to the caterer that I was hard work. I should have told Alex then, but I didn't. And Alex liked the way she worked. He liked her attention to detail, her efficiency. Alex was the sort of person who wanted everything catalogued. All his socks were in one drawer, each pair in a separate compartment, his pants in another. He separated his white T-Shirts from the blue ones and the black ones. One year I gave him a label maker as a birthday present, he loved it. I knew a wedding planner would get everything perfect. Alex liked perfect. It was an easy solution. At the time I was happy to accommodate.'

'Did your friends and family attend?'

Celeste picked at an invisible piece of fluff on her cardigan and then looked at her watch. 'I didn't want Bonnie to be part of the wedding party after what had happened. I admit I said some horrible stuff to her too, but I couldn't forgive her for how she made me feel. I was unsure about Alicia. Plus, Maryanne had let me down. I decided against bridesmaids in the end.'

'How did you feel about Maryanne not attending?'

'I was so angry. I complained to Alex, but I could see that "what did you expect" look in his eye. He never liked Maryanne.'

'You forgave her?'

'I had to with the move to Hong Kong. I had so much going on and I needed her help.'

'Did you get to the bottom of why she didn't attend?'

Celeste held on to the gold bumblebee pendant. 'Eventually, when it was too late.'

'Do you want to expand on that?'

She shook her head.

'So did Alicia and Bonnie come to the wedding?'

'They came. I didn't speak to them much. Alicia was flirting with Bill. It annoyed me. Her new boyfriend, Tom, doted on her, but he couldn't make it. It was mean of her.'

'Why did it annoy you?'

Celeste shrugged. 'It just did. Bill left his wife at home because she was unwell. I had fought with Bonnie about her cheating with a married man, and here Alicia was flirting with Bill, who was also married. It didn't seem right.'

'Were you close to Bill?'

Her breathing quickened. 'I suppose. He was always at our house. We spent time together, Alex, Bill and I. We used to tease him, call him Alex's other woman. I resented it sometimes when they travelled together on a business endeavour and I couldn't go because of a work commitment. "Chasing money" is a term they used when they had to fly somewhere for business. Bill always used to check up on me when Alex was away, despite Alex's jealousy. That was nice of him. Of course, after Alex proposed he stopped flirting with me. Alex may have said something – or perhaps it was an unspoken rule between them.'

'Do you think you were upset that Alicia was flirting with your friend? Someone you were close to – someone Alex was once jealous of losing you to, as opposed to a moralistic issue with adultery?'

'What are you trying to say?'

'Was adultery the only reason you were annoyed?'

'No,' Celeste snapped. She took a deep breath. 'I suppose you are right. Bill was my friend, and she was taking his time. I made up with Alicia soon after the wedding though. She made that happen, and I was grateful to her for that. She called and texted until she was back in my life. She was persistent and she knew how to make me smile.'

Celeste leaned back in her chair. Despite her initial reservations about talking to Elaine she was glad that she had finally opened up. She felt a sense of lightness. 'So that was London,' she said.

'And how were things between you and Alex in Hong Kong?'

'Hong Kong? That was when the fun really started.'

Part II

23

Barnet, North London

'You look well, not like when that picture was taken. Do you feel better?' Elaine asked, her eyes moving from the picture on the desk to Celeste.

She nodded. 'I eat well, I run. I even go for a swim when I get the chance.'

'How do you feel about being here?'

'This place?' Celeste looked around her and shrugged.

'Is talking to me helping?'

'I suppose.'

'Clichéd I know, but a problem shared is a problem halved.' Elaine smiled.

'You sound like my mother. Please don't treat me like her.'

'How does your mother treat you?'

'Like I'm a foxglove – delicate and fragile but dangerous at the same time. I catch her looking at me sometimes, staring. Like she's waiting for me to do something. Sometimes I think I should do something just to give her a scare.'

'Like what?'

'I don't know, but we all know what I'm capable of.'

'Do you think your mother is trying to hurt you?'

Celeste shook her head. 'I'm not stupid. She's helping. I wouldn't be here otherwise. I only came here because of her. I owed her that.'

'Parents can be like that. They know their children better than we think.'

Did her mother know what was going through her mind? Did she know what she needed to do to make the pain truly disappear? Is that why she was keen on suggesting this place?

'So, Hong Kong?'

Celeste chewed her thumbnail.

'Water?'

She nodded. Elaine stood up and walked over to the water cooler. She poured water into a cup and handed it to Celeste before she sat back down.

'Take your time. We have time.'

'Do we?' Celeste raised an eyebrow.

Elaine looked at the door.

'Some of my best memories with Alex are from Hong Kong. But it was there that my life changed. There are some recollections I wish I could erase from my mind.'

'They're painful?'

'Raw, infected wounds that won't heal. Sometimes I want nothing more than to pierce…' She trailed off, tears brimming, her fists clenched.

'What kind of memories?'

Celeste shook her head.

'Okay, tell me about some of the good times. Did you move to Hong Kong straight away?'

'In the beginning I lived between London and Hong

Kong. We had the money to allow me to do that. Well, Alex had that kind of money. I got on a plane as if it were a bus. Fourteen hours in the air business class is not so bad.'

'But you eventually settled there?'

'Until about two years ago, Hong Kong was my home.'

24

2nd April 2009
Causeway Bay, Hong Kong

The air was thick and humid. The taxi stopped as close to *Cross* as the roadworks permitted, and Celeste had to walk past herbal medicine shops and fast food chains advertising prawn balls with xo sauce and all-you-can-eat dim sum before she reached the cool air conditioning of the store.

'I can't believe you still take a cab,' Jinny said, as Celeste walked into her office complaining about the disruption to the roads.

'Taxis here are cheap.'

'Walk around, take the MTR. Experience the real Hong Kong. How much of Hong Kong have you actually seen?'

'I would if I had the time in the morning. Plus, Alex has been away.'

'That's not an excuse.' Jinny pulled a pencil out from a container on her desk.

'I've been here and there. I've even walked through Stanley Market and bought a stone dragon I didn't need.'

'Put it outside your front door. It's good luck.'

'I watched them burning incense at the Man Mo temple. Had my fortune told at another, visited the fish market and

I've taken the tram up to the Peak.'

'Why the fish market? I thought Alex didn't eat the food you cooked.'

Celeste made a face. 'He may have had enough of my attempts at cooking, but I still like to try.' She thought of the last time she surprised Alex with a candle lit meal in their rental. At least he had attempted the food before calling for a delivery.

'Get out of Central. Go to the Jade market. Eat some fung jau in Wan Chai. Hop on the ferry and go to Macau. Gamble some of that hard earned cash.'

'Chicken feet? I tried them once – never again.'

'You know the word for chicken feet? I'm impressed, gweilo. But listen, life doesn't stop when your husband goes away. He's always away. Come out with the girls and me sometime. In fact, come out with us tonight. We're celebrating Mo Li's birthday.'

'It's Mo Li's birthday?'

'She's only gone on about it for the past month. Get your head out of your sketches for once and listen in to your team. We're going to Lan Kwai Fong to party all night.'

'Toby will be here in an hour. He wants to see my latest designs. Have the pattern cutters been to pick up the blue files?'

Jinny shook her head. 'Does he? Or does he want to see you?'

'Oh no! Where is the design for the sleeveless blazer?'

'It's there, where you left it, on top of the filing cabinet.'

'Where?' Celeste asked, frantically rummaging through stacks of paperwork.

'Relax boss. Toby's a pussycat.' Jinny walked over to the

cabinet, retrieved the designs and passed them to Celeste. 'I don't think you can do anything wrong in his eyes.' Jinny winked as she headed for the door.

'He doesn't fancy me Jinny, so get that out of your mind. He has a meeting with Harris and wants to show him what our team's working on. We have to prove ourselves to keep our jobs.'

Jinny rolled her eyes. 'You're never going to get fired. Tea?' she asked as she left the office.

Toby Cain was the last person Celeste wanted to think about, despite his obvious good looks. He was tall, with dark eyes and broad shoulders. The kind of guy she would look twice at in a room full of people. And there were times when she felt a weakness around him, but she was married. She had made that clear to Toby the last time he had put his hand on the small of her back and complimented her on her perfume.

She thought of Alex; she missed him. Stupid, bloody Graham. Alex was close to burning out, continually flying between London, Shanghai and Hong Kong – all because Graham lacked any business acumen. 'Why can't your dad hire someone else?' she had asked two weeks ago, before he had left for the airport.

'It's a big job, one that has to be retained within the family right now. It takes time to employ the right people.'

'They can get a consultant in the interim,' she had said, knowing full well where the conversation was going. Warwick was not a pushover when it came to his business, even though he seemed to be letting Graham get away with doing bugger all.

'You want to eat, don't you?'

Like they couldn't afford to eat. The way they had been

spending money of late they could have bought a chain of restaurants if they wanted to. But Alex was right, they were used to this kind of spending power now, and he had to earn his money. Plus, every time he went away he bought her back the most beautiful gifts: silk pyjamas from Shanghai and a *Chopard* necklace from London. It went perfectly with the new white linen dress she had designed for the cruise collection. She touched the diamond around her neck. If there was one thing she couldn't fault Alex on, it was his thoughtfulness. Jinny walked back into Celeste's office and handed her a cup of green tea.

'Toby Cain may appear like he doesn't care but he has a job to do. He tells Harris everything.'

'Have you met Mr Elusive yet?'

Celeste shook her head. Not meeting Mr Harris had bothered her at first, but Maryanne had reassured her that he was a busy man and that Toby Cain had been appointed specifically to run *Cross*. 'Unless there's a problem, Celeste, you won't hear from Harris, and trust me, it's probably better that way,' she had said when they had first set up the store. Celeste had taken her at her word, and even Alex agreed.

'Harris is no relation to Bill is he?' she had asked Alex one day, when they were eating microwave popcorn and drinking red wine in front of an old movie.

'Didn't you say your Harris was South African?'

'He sounds it, so I suppose he has lived there at some point.'

'Well Bill doesn't have any family there.' Alex had laughed at her suggestion. 'I'll look into his background,' he offered. Three days later Alex gave Harris the all clear. 'Seems above board. He's probably just busy, and *Cross* isn't a priority for him. Don't worry about it.' Celeste took Alex at his word, as she had increasingly started to do, and she let it go.

'Come out, just this one night. We'll look after you,' Jinny said, and Celeste shook the memory away.

'I don't know how you do it. Party all night and work the next day, I'd be shattered. I look at some of Alex's friends' wives and they can't keep up. Most of them have jacked in their jobs to nurse their never-ending hangovers. I don't want to be like that,' Celeste said, and she meant it. But thinking of the other wives made her miss her friends. She had made up with Alicia over coffee and cake at *Fortnum and Mason* before she had left for Hong Kong. And she had considered picking up the phone to Bonnie as well, but somehow she never got around to it. She reasoned that they had drifted apart, but she still missed her. Who else knew she loved reading *Wallpaper* magazine, and had even sent her copies when she was out travelling? She spoke to Alicia most days, but it wasn't the same having a friend thousands of miles away. And when was the last time she went on a girls' night? She didn't want to admit it but she was lonely, especially when Alex wasn't around.

'Hong Kong's a party town. Here you work hard, play harder. And girl, you've been working so hard. This is not London. You have to do things here the Hong Kong way.'

Celeste looked down at the sketch of the structured evening jacket with three quarter length sleeves next to the sketch of the sleeveless blazer Jinny had given her. Either one would look beautiful with the black *Armani* dress Alex had just bought her. She could wear that dress tonight – without a jacket of course. She bit her lip thinking of what Alex had said to Bill when he mooted the idea of her going out with colleagues. 'It's bad form,' he had said. 'She's a Renshaw now – she's got to elevate herself from all of that.' What would he say when he found out? Lan Kwai Fong with its plethora of bars, bright lights and girls in short skirts was like Piccadilly on speed. He would hate it if she went there without him. But this was a girls' night with Jinny, someone she actually liked. They were all designers after all. What did it matter if she managed them? She couldn't always listen to Alex. So far, life in Hong Kong wasn't what she had imagined. She certainly wasn't experiencing the glamorous lifestyle Alex had promised her. She had made attempts to contact the other ex-pat wives, Jackie and Melanie and they had met on occasion, but they were so dull. All they could talk about was how much champagne they drank and the diamonds they had acquired. She instinctively let go of her Chopard necklace. She was about to accept Jinny's invite but when she glanced at her phone there was a message from Alex.

'I can pick you up at eight?' Jinny said.

She looked up with a smile. 'Sorry, I can't make tonight. Alex is back.'

25

2nd April 2009
Lan Kwai Fong, Hong Kong

Celeste stepped into the grid of roads and alleyways that made up Hong Kong's most famous nightspot. She held on to Alex, a little tighter, as a drunken man in a white vest and silver trousers brushed passed her. 'Are you sure you are up for this after such a long flight?'

'Sure,' Alex said, checking his phone. 'It was a good suggestion. I promised you the high life and I haven't kept my word.'

She leaned towards him and kissed his neck. The smell of his cologne, the sandalwood and the spice, made her forget any misgivings that she had about Hong Kong. 'Forgiven,' she said. 'You should have told me you were on your way back. I thought it was odd that I couldn't get hold of you this morning.'

'I wanted to surprise you.'

'Nice surprise. How was London?'

'Not the same without you, Heavenly,' he said, putting his phone away. She smiled. She loved it when Alex called her that. Their private joke from when they first met in Thailand. It always reminded her of that time when things between them were unadulterated.

'Wait for me,' a girl in a skin-tight, hot-pink dress shouted from one of the many bars that spilled out onto the street. 'Sexy,' she said, as she passed Alex and Celeste and caught up with her friends.

'Was she saying that to me or you?' Celeste asked. Alex smiled and led her by the hand towards the entrance to a bar. A huge man with a thick, short neck stood in front of a queue of about twenty people standing behind a rope. She sighed. It had been years since she last had to do this. In London they were always VIPs.

'Boss,' the bouncer said, as he greeted Alex.

Alex nodded and the doorman quickly pulled across the rope and let them through. They were shown into a lift by another doorman, which took them straight to the top floor. Stepping out onto the terrace of the bar, Celeste took a deep breath. It was cooler here and sophisticated too, away from the chaotic streets below. 'Something tells me you used to hang out in this bar quite a bit.'

'Ronnie, the door guy, does quite a few of the bars. I've only been here once or twice.'

She smiled. If Alex was on first name terms with the doorman she was sure he had met him at least a dozen times. Alex signalled for a waitress and ordered two Mai Tais. Another waitress spoke to three young Chinese men sitting at one of the low tables. They quickly got up and left and the attendant started clearing the table. Yes, Alex had definitely frequented this bar before.

'Please,' the waitress said, nodding at Celeste and Alex and pointing towards the table.

Alex unbuttoned the top of his white shirt and sat down.

'That wasn't necessary,' Celeste said, as she looked over at the young men. The men were leaning against the railings with their bottles of beer looking down at the street below.

The waitress smiled politely. 'It's fine,' Alex said. He took out his phone and tapped something into it.

'Why did she just do that?'

'We're going to be drinking a lot more tonight than those lads who have probably been nursing one beer each since they got here.'

'I see.'

'It's business, honey, pure and simple.'

She shrugged, supposing Alex was right. It wasn't her problem. She avoided looking in the direction of the young men and downed half of her drink as soon as the waitress returned with it.

'Remember in Koh Phi Phi, we got absolutely smashed on these, one night,' Alex said, giving the waitress a two hundred and fifty dollar tip.

'I see why we got the table.'

'Why do you think you never have to wait for anything when you're with me? Like I say, there is no such thing as a free lunch,' Alex said returning his attention to his phone.

She had to admit, there was a certain finesse to Alex's way of living. These days she thought of her life as *Before Alex* and *After Alex*. Before Alex, she stood outside in the pouring rain trying to get into a club. After Alex, she realised tips large enough to feed a family of four got you everywhere. He was right, of course. When she was out with him the service they received was first class, and who was she to complain. They were seated, the waitress was better off, and the three young lads, well, perhaps they were used to it.

She had tried tipping big the first time she ate out in Hong

Kong without Alex. It hadn't quite worked. She wanted to leave more than a twenty per cent tip, but she couldn't justify it. The service had been shoddy and it just didn't feel right.

Alex leaned forward and kissed her. 'So, I have a surprise for you.'

Celeste put her drink down. 'We're already married. You're not pregnant are you?'

Alex laughed. 'Better than that.' He produced a key from his shirt pocket.

'It isn't what I think it is?'

He nodded.

'Don't joke with me. I haven't seen anything decent yet. All the apartments here are like shoe boxes.'

'Not this place.'

She narrowed her eyes.

'It's going to be our new home.'

Celeste took the key from Alex. She hesitated. She was happy, of course she was happy. She had been on at him to get something sorted for a months. But she hadn't expected him to do it alone. It was going to be their home and she wanted to be involved with choosing it. It wasn't as if she got to make many decisions. Their London home had been decided for them. Kealana had even decorated it. Hong Kong, she had thought, would be up to her. 'What about us looking at places together?'

'I was speaking to Warwick and he let slip that the tenants had moved out of this place. Call it a company perk.'

'I thought you said there was no such thing as coincidences?'

He kissed her on the lips.

'Don't try and blindside me.'

'Fine, I knew about this place and put a word in. Wanted it

to be a surprise for you. You'll love it when you see it.'

She wanted to be angry but it was hard when he put it that way. Guilt replaced her irritation. Alex was trying to do something kind for her, and she was acting like a princess. She forced a smile. He pulled her towards him, downed the remnants of his drink and kissed her again. He ran his hand along her back. 'This property has been lying around from when my parents lived here and it's perfect for us.'

'So is this apartment going to be ours, or your dad's, just for us to use?'

'Ours. Warwick can be reassigned to an apartment in the *Four Seasons* when he's here.'

'So then what are we doing here?'

'You wanted a night out.'

'Not over this.'

'I thought you were desperate to go out and see Hong Kong in all its Lang Kwai Fong glory?' Alex said, with a hint of sarcasm.

Celeste looked around. 'Let's go.'

'And then those lads will have moved for nothing,' Alex said, pointing to the three men who were holding on to their empty bottles of beer.

'Tip them,' she said with a smile.

'Celeste!' A familiar voice broke through the low thud of the music.

'Jinny,' she said, standing up.

'Ah, so you made it to our infamous Lan Kwai Fong. The queue here was terrible. Never again.'

'Alex, you must meet Jinny. She is one of my best designers,' Celeste said, feeling a little guilty. She hadn't seen them in the queue and she hoped they hadn't seen her skip it.

He stood up and greeted Jinny with a kiss on each cheek.

'And Mo Li,' Jinny said, pointing to her left. 'Hmm, she was here a minute ago. Never mind.' She looked at Alex. 'You must take Celeste on the night ferry to Macau after this. Do some gambling, Hong Kong style, and eat breakfast at the docks on your return! Don't worry about the seagulls.'

'Sounds like fun,' Alex said flatly.

'There she is.' Jinny said, as she looked behind her. 'Mo Li, Mo Li, why you run off like that? She doesn't bite.'

Celeste felt her cheeks colour.

Mo Li looked at Celeste and then at Alex. She smiled politely and then walked off in the direction of the bar before they could wish her a happy birthday. Jinny rolled her eyes and shook her head. 'You know how shy she is. She's even worse around men.'

'You carry on,' Celeste said. She hugged Jinny and turned around to see Alex on his phone.

Jinny looked over at Alex. 'Next time you're coming out with me, girls only,' she whispered.

Celeste nodded and looked back at Alex, knowing it was unlikely that a girls' night with Jinny and Mo Li would ever happen.

26

2nd April 2009
Mayfair, London

'You did it. You were the one to break poor William.'

Rachel took both glasses of champagne from the waiter and passed one to Sophia. She straightened her back. 'It took me a while to get him to agree, but yes I've been away with William. And I wouldn't put the words "poor" and "William" in the same sentence.'

'Certainly not poor. I don't think he realises how the other half lives. It's like that man is in his own little world filled with white lines, sexy women and limitless pots of cash.' Sophia took a sip of her drink. 'I have to hand it to you. I never thought it would ever happen. Tell me, Rach, what have you got that countless women before you don't?'

Rachel swallowed some more champagne. If Sophia meant what she had just said as a form of flattery, it certainly didn't sound like it. She was quite sure she could hear the scorn in the woman's voice. 'Must be persistence,' she said confidently.

Sophia opened her mouth to say something, hesitated, put her champagne glass down and looked Rachel up and down. 'No, that's not it,' she said with a matter of fact tone. 'Do you know how many people have tried to get on a flight with that man?'

Rachel shook her head, careful to supress her smile of achievement.

'Look around you.'

It was early in the day and the club wasn't busy. Rachel looked through the glass doors into the garden. A few women like she and Sophia were sharing a bottle of fizz and enjoying the first sunshine of spring.

'You must have something about you.'

'Her, over there?' Rachel asked pointing to a blonde woman in skin-tight jeans.

'Probably,' Sophia said.

'Alicia?' Rachel asked. She had spoken to Alicia in depth about William, and she had never said anything, but then they were not that close. She hadn't seen her or Bonnie in ages, but with their wealth she wouldn't be surprised if one of them had had a fling with William in the past.

'God no, not Alicia.' Sophia smirked. 'Now Bonnie certainly has the looks Willy would go for. I haven't seen her in a while. Could be because she's moved out of London. Wouldn't surprise me if she had a thing with him.'

Rachel bristled. It made her skin crawl when she thought of William with another woman, especially a good-looking one like Bonnie. But she realised Sophia didn't really know who William had dated. She was just speculating.

Sophia took a sip of her champagne. 'He isn't making you do ghastly things in bed, is he?'

Rachel leaned away from Sophia. 'God, no! What an awful thing to say.'

'Oh lighten up luvvie. It wouldn't be the first time someone like that had an unusual fetish. Willy was certainly above board when I knew him, but there was a colourful time in the history of *The Emerald Rooms* when all sorts used to go on.'

'Like what?' Rachel said, draining her glass and pouring another. There was something about hanging around with Sophia that made her want to drink like a fish. She thought about going to the bathroom and doing a line but she was trying to cut back during the day, especially as it was so freely available whenever she was with William. How did the super rich stay focused when their kind of money allowed them to buy cocaine as if it were a packet of sherbet? No wonder *The Emerald Rooms* on a Friday night was so full of excess. If you ever saw one of the private parties in the suites after an event, you would see a plethora of half drunk bottles of champagne, white residue by the *Jacuzzi* and most probably someone's panties.

'This club had a reputation for swingers. But *The Emerald Rooms* is in the middle of a residential area so the local neighbours complained. What spoilsports. Must have been "*The Emerald Room* widows", as we used to call them. This place is notorious for luring young men away from their dull wives.'

Rachel pursed her lips. She tried stopping herself from asking, but she just couldn't. 'So were both you and William members back then?'

Sophia sipped her champagne. 'I love bubbles in the afternoon, don't you? Where is Willy?'

'Away, again.'

'Well, he can't help that. He has to earn his living and so has to put in the hours,' Sophia said, with a coy smile. 'Let me guess, away for months at a time and only ever in London for a couple of nights.'

'These days, yes. Is there anything I need to know?'

Rachel had been dating William for over a year now, but she still felt like there was so much she didn't know about him. He had told her about his boarding school upbringing and his brother, the apple of his father's eye, but he was cagey when it came to talking about exes. He was also pretty evasive when it came to business trips abroad. He only seemed to tell her his itinerary a couple of days before he had to fly somewhere.

On several occasions she had asked him about the numerous trips he had to make but he always had a valid answer. There were factories to visit, business meetings to attend and potential land purchases to be made. Sophia was right, William had his finger in several pies. But like he always said to her, you have to work hard to get what you want in life. She couldn't fault him there.

Her friend Bella had said she was lucky because his job meant they never spent too much time together. 'You'll never get bored of each other.' But then Bella had commitment issues. Rachel certainly didn't feel lucky. She felt as if her relationship was just a stopgap in William's life. But what could she do? She had fallen in love.

Sophia laughed. 'Nothing you need to worry about.'

'Worry?'

'Most of the men at this club are the same. I'm surprised he doesn't have a private jet. Give it time.'

It wasn't the answer Rachel was hoping for, but she had come to expect this of Sophia. Plus, she had to be wary of her. There was never any truth in what came out of her mouth. She didn't know why she had even bothered to ask. William had already warned her that Sophia was a woman scorned.

'So, what was Paris like? Did he spoil you rotten?'

'He bought me this,' Rachel gushed and pointed to the black

and gold bag slung on the back of her chair.

Sophia flashed her teeth in a bid to smile. 'A trip away and a *Louis Vuitton*. Must be serious, Rach. You'll be moving in soon.' Sophia held her gaze as if she were waiting for an answer.

'He's asked me to move in.' Rachel watched the bubbles in her glass as they rose to the top.

Sophia's eye's widened. 'The country place?'

'His apartment, around the corner from here.'

'So, just the apartment?'

'We've talked about it, but it's not right for William,'

'Ah, so you know.'

'I know what he's like, yes.' Rachel knew William was not going to be tied down just yet. Yes, he had said he loved her and had asked her to move into his apartment to save him travelling into Zone two – or 'the rear end of London' as he put it. But William wasn't ready for the full commitment of moving into his country abode. The trip to Paris had been her first small step to getting a ring on her left hand. Now it was only a matter of time.

'The location is better suited to my work too.'

'Oh yes, that.' Sophia leaned back in her chair. 'So this is what you have that other women haven't? Staying power.'

'I told you I was persistent.'

'I'm glad. All I had was a fling with Willy. God, he was a good lover, but not that good.'

Rachel poured herself another glass. It gave her goosebumps every time Sophia mentioned her thing with William. Jealousy was unbecoming, and according to William his relationship with Sophia lasted the duration of a taxi ride from Mayfair to Regent's Park. No wonder she had it in for her. Spiteful wench.

She could see a flicker of hesitation in Sophia's eyes. 'Is there something about William that I should know?'

'William,' she said, absentmindedly. 'You tell me.' Sophia looked around the room before returning her gaze to Rachel. A smile formed on her lips. 'Oh dear, you don't know.'

Rachel opened her mouth, not sure what she was about to say, but she didn't get the chance in any case. Two regulars at *The Emerald Rooms*, Ali and Patrick, walked in and crooned around Sophia completely taking away her chance. Instead, Rachel finished her glass of champagne whilst she reflected on just how malicious her so-called friend was.

27

2nd April 2009
Mid-Levels, Central and Western District, Hong Kong

As soon as Celeste walked into their new apartment she knew that Hong Kong was no longer just a change of scene, it was her home.

Alex laughed as she ran towards the panoramic glass wall in the lounge and put her hands up, flat against the window. From the thirty-ninth floor the view overlooking Victoria Harbour, Hong Kong side and Kowloon was breath-taking. The Hong Kong and Shanghai building with its diagonal white lights stood out – an iconic building that was close to Celeste's heart. It seemed apt that she could now look out at it every day.

She turned back to Alex, scanning the lounge. Kealana had left her mark – white lilies on the entrance table. Her enthusiasm waned a little, but then she noticed the stairs close to the entrance leading both upstairs and downstairs. In her initial excitement she hadn't noticed them, but now she was curious to see where they led. The apartment was larger that any other she had seen on her quest to find them a perfect home, and it was in the Mid-Levels – the Beverly Hills of Hong Kong, or so Jinny had once said. 'It's fantastic,' she said, resisting the urge to run around the flat and find their bedroom.

'Told you, you'd love it,' he said, tapping on his phone. 'I did good.'

Celeste walked back to him, put her hand around the back of his neck and kissed him. 'You did more than good.'

Alex slipped his phone back into his pocket, took off his suit jacket and dropped it on one of the chocolate leather sofas. 'Champagne?'

'You've stocked the fridge?' She followed Alex to a room at the rear of the lounge. 'Ah, the kitchen'

'Upstairs is our bedroom and en-suite and the door to the terrace. Downstairs is a room I'm going to use as my office and another room we can use as a guest room. There's also a gym down there. Give me a drink and I'll give you the grand tour.'

Celeste smiled. She was waiting for this. Alex liked to be in control, show her things on his terms. He hadn't appreciated it when she had torn around their London mews looking in every cupboard and drawer, squealing excitedly and not giving him a chance to talk. He never said anything, but she could tell. She kicked off her shoes, found the bottle of *Krug* in the fridge and passed it to Alex. He opened the bottle, poured and handed her a glass.

She eyed Kealana's signature flowers out in the entrance and pouted. She didn't want to say anything to spoil the moment, but she just couldn't let it slide.

'You've furnished the place.'

'Kealana did it. She's good at this. Well, she should bloody be by now. Been with us long enough. Knows what we like.'

'What you Renshaws like, you mean.'

'You're a Renshaw now,' Alex said, raising a single eyebrow.

'Did you want to go traipsing around in this heat looking for the right kind of furniture?'

She fiddled with Alex's collar. 'I guess not,' she said, biting her tongue. She would have loved rummaging through antique shops to find the perfect lamp, or stumbling across the perfect *shoji* screen. It was like Alex kept forgetting one small fact – that she was a designer, a clothes designer, but a designer nevertheless. Anyway, it was done now. 'Jinny was telling me about this place in Ap Lei Chau which has twenty-eight floors of furniture.'

'Where do you think we got most of this stuff from?'

'You went there?' Celeste asked incredulously.

'Kealana did.'

Celeste's shoulders dropped. 'Of course she did. I'm surprised your dad never married her.'

Alex laughed. 'She certainly knows the man's tastes.'

Celeste swallowed the lump forming in her throat with a large sip of champagne. She had been getting ahead of herself. This may have been presented to her as her home, but it was nothing more than a *Renshaw* asset.

Alex put his arm around her and pulled her close. 'She's done it tastefully, don't you think? It reflects the essence of Hong Kong.'

'There's quite a bit of red and black going on.' Celeste looked up at an oppressive, red glass chandelier that hung in the lounge above the dining table. 'But I like the koi carp picture in the living room. Not like Kealana at all.'

'If you don't like it, change it. It's your home. So, if you want to rip it all out and start again, you can. I only wanted to make it easier for you. Let's go upstairs. I want to show you what's up there,' Alex said, taking her hand.

She lifted her glass of champagne to her lips. So what if the place had already been furnished? Like Alex had said, it was one less job for her to do. He was being thoughtful, and she was acting like a spoilt brat. She turned to Alex and kissed him, tasting the *Krug* on his lips. 'I couldn't ask for a nicer home.' Alex lifted the bottle of champagne with his free hand. They were about to turn towards the kitchen entrance when Celeste heard an unfamiliar voice, making her jump.

'Sir,' the voice said. 'Let me take that for you.'

Celeste swivelled on her heel, nearly head-butting Alex in the process.

'Ah, Lada.'

Celeste looked at the small, plump woman with short hair and small eyes who stood before her, her hands outstretched.

Alex passed Lada the bottle of champagne.

'Pop it in a cooler, would you, Lada.'

Lada nodded. 'And glasses?'

'We'll bring them up. Lada, this is my wife.' Alex turned to Celeste. 'Lada lives here. Look, that's her room,' he said as he walked out of the kitchen.

Lada blushed and bowed her head. 'Sir, I was taking nap. No hear you come in.'

'Never mind that.'

Lada lifted her head and returned Celeste's startled gaze with a smile before she went into the kitchen.

She felt awkward. They had a cleaner in London, but a live in maid? This was alien to her. She peered into the small room. She hadn't even noticed the door just outside the kitchen.

'Don't stare, it's rude. We've had help before.' Alex put his arm around Celeste's waist and gave it a squeeze.

'It's tiny!' Celeste whispered. 'I bet the smallest bathroom in this apartment is bigger than her room. It's a bloody broom cupboard.' She followed her husband upstairs towards the terrace.

'It is a lot bigger than most of the rooms the staff get in Hong Kong.'

'Never.'

'Do you remember the first Sunday we got here, and there were a bunch of Filipinos sitting outside the MTR stop near IFC?'

'And?' She asked. At the time she had wondered why so many people had gathered in the walkway that linked the metro to the main road. Hundreds of women had been sitting on old bits of cardboard, playing cards and eating from tiffin boxes. She had assumed it was some sort of protest. But she had noticed that it was a weekly affair and she had meant to ask Jinny about it.

She stood behind Alex whilst he wrestled with the door handle. Eventually he opened the terrace door and she followed him out into the humidity.

'Those women live in rooms so small you can touch the sides with both hands - elbows in some cases. Sunday is their day off and they need space, so they go and sit outside. Terrible problem for the government. Hardly tourist friendly. They should improve employment laws here.'

Celeste put her hand to her mouth. How naive she had been. A protest! Ha! 'But we must offer her a bigger room. We're not expecting guests anytime soon.'

'Lada's worked for us for over ten years. Don't you think we've offered her something bigger?' He shook his head 'Don't make out like we are the bad ones here.'

She frowned. 'What do you…' she started, but Alex shot her

a look as Lada arrived at the top of the stairs and placed the champagne bucket on the table with a bowl of nuts.

When she had disappeared down the stairs, Alex hugged Celeste. 'You care hon and that's what I love about you,' he said, before he kissed her so deeply she almost forgot what they were arguing about.

'I suppose Kealana doesn't stay in a room like that when she's in Hong Kong.'

'She stays in the staff apartment my father has in Wan Chai.'

Kealana had an easy life, thought Celeste. Jetting around the world on someone else's coin, but then she held her tongue. It couldn't be easy looking after all the requirements of the Renshaws. She probably had to ignore the needs of her own family just to make sure that the Renshaws had white lilies in the entrances to their homes.

'So what do you think about the terrace?'

She looked out into the shimmering night-lights of Hong Kong. 'Beautiful,' she said, turning to take in the full view. A bubbling noise caught her attention, making her turn towards the far left corner of the terrace. 'Oh my god, Alex,' she said, spotting the spa pool. She put a hand on his chest. 'This is so *Playboy*.' She walked over to the hot tub and sat on the edge then she dipped her hand in the warm water.

Lada appeared again with towels, which she placed on one of the wooden recliners before she disappeared again. Celeste looked at the towels. It would be odd having someone in their private space all the time. Would they ever get any alone time?

'What are you thinking?'

She took another sip of her champagne. 'Nothing.' Alex seemed so comfortable in the presence of Lada. She supposed he had been used to having staff constantly around him since he was a child. She remembered him telling her that if it wasn't for boarding school, he wouldn't have known how to make a bed. She smiled now, remembering when she first met him in Thailand. She had thought that he was travelling on a shoe-string like her. But how wrong she had been. Life with Alex was certainly different to anything she had ever known. Some days in London she had felt like an impostor, living the life of luxury. But Hong Kong was going to be a different league altogether. It would certainly take getting used to, but she really couldn't complain. Having someone to cook and clean for you was an indulgence. This way she could spend more time with Alex. And she could perfect the new capsule collection for *Cross* she had been working on. Wasn't this what she had always dreamed of, all those years ago, growing up in East Row?

'I want you to like it here. Screw that. I want you to love it here. It's our home. Change whatever the hell you want.'

'I can't say Kealana has decorated it the way I would have, but it's fine. I don't need to change anything. Not just yet.'

Alex walked over to her. He bent his head towards her and lifted her chin with the tips of his fingers. 'I'll have someone bring our stuff from the rental tomorrow.'

'Urgh, I need to pack. I hate packing.'

'So you won't have to. Leave it to me.'

'You're going to pack for me?'

'Someone will. It'll all be here for you by the time you get back from work tomorrow.'

Celeste smiled. This, she could get used to.

28

7th August 2010
Mid-Levels, Central and Western District, Hong Kong

Celeste waved frantically through the glass doors.

'Mrs Renshaw, where is your key card?' Charlie, the doorman at the apartment building, asked as he let her in.

'I've left it at work. Could I borrow another one for a couple of days?'

Charlie made a face. 'My computer has just crashed. I need to restart it.'

In a high security residential building where some of Hong Kong's richest lived there was paperwork even to borrow a spare key card, and Charlie had the slowest computer she had ever encountered.

She rubbed her temples. Today had been trying. She had lost one of her designers and a supplier had let them down at the last minute. She and Jinny had spent three hours in the afternoon sun, traipsing round the trims market in Tsim Sha Po looking for the perfect clasp for a new line in ladies' purses. 'I have a splitting headache and need to get to bed. What if I promise to return it on Monday evening?'

'I'm on leave next week. I'm going home.'

'To see your wife? How lovely.' In the year and a half she had lived in Hong Kong she had grown fond of Charlie and knew just how much he longed to go home to visit his wife. She also knew he was a bit of a pedant when it came to security. She assumed he'd had his fingers burnt before by his manager who had a reputation for being a bit of an ogre. 'I'll keep the card safe and I won't tell a soul until you are back,' she said, making a motion of locking her mouth with an invisible key.

Charlie hesitated. He went into the back room and returned with a plastic white card. He handed it to her. 'This is a spare, but be sure to return it when I get back. It's not registered. I'll get into trouble.'

'I promise Charlie. I won't forget. It's white unlike the black residents card. I'll know to return it.' Celeste tucked the card into her wallet and walked towards the lift.

'Oh, I almost forgot, Mrs Renshaw, a package for you.' Charlie went into the back room and returned with a brown package, which he handed to her before he called the lift.

As the lift ascended the thirty-nine floors, Celeste made a tear in the parcel and pulled out a note on lilac paper. She instantly recognised Alicia's signature lavender scented paper, and a smile touched her lips.

She read her friend's news and then she read it again. The shop was doing well, and Alicia had a lovely wedding day. She had married her boyfriend, Tom, in an intimate ceremony in Tuscany with only their immediate families present. She winced as she read this. At one time she would never have thought that she would miss Alicia's wedding, but the oceans between them seemed to have kept them apart. She was meant to fly out for the week to celebrate with Alicia but at the last minute Alex had been violently ill for no apparent reason, and she couldn't leave him. It was only later that they found out it was a stomach ulcer. By the time he was better, Alicia was on her honeymoon.

It was odd thinking that her one-time best friend, who after a night out drinking declared that she would never marry anyone unless Celeste and Bonnie approved, was now married to a man she hardly knew. When they were in university, life had seemed so simple. They had promised each other that they wouldn't miss each other's weddings for the world. But life had got in the way and they had all moved on, not bothering to take each other along.

Now, she blinked back the tears knowing that she wouldn't be seeing Alicia anytime soon thanks to bloody Mr Harris. Twice now Alicia had booked flights to Hong Kong only to cancel them because of Celeste and her unpredictable and demanding boss. Both times he had ordered her to attend design conferences in China on the same days that Alicia had planned her visits, and both times he was unwavering. She had never met the man but he was stubborn, and, she assumed, a fat pig. She had loved the South African accent before hearing Harris speak. Now it made her shudder. She had no intention of wanting to meet him face to face, especially as those conferences had been an epic waste of time. She had complained bitterly to Alex, but he was unsympathetic. All he could say was, 'If you don't like it, quit.' That was no good to her – she needed to keep her job, for her independence, if nothing else.

Reading Alicia's words made her realise just how much she missed her friend. She missed sitting in her front room eating ice cream straight from the tub, talking about men and watching box sets of *Sex and the City*. She scanned the letter, looking for news of Bonnie, but there was nothing. A part of her was desperate to know what her old friend was doing, but too much time had passed now, and her pride would never allow her to make contact first.

Stepping out of the lift, she let herself into their apartment and realised her dad had been right. 'Time goes by faster with each year that passes,' he always said to her. It was true. And since moving to the Mid-Levels her work and social life had gone up a couple of notches. The days were filled with long hours at *Cross*, tending to the needs from the ever absent but demanding Harris, and the evenings were filled with cocktails and champagne in order to keep up with the glitterati among their new circle of friends.

As the *Renshaw* empire established itself in Hong Kong, it became Celeste's duty to attend the lavish cocktail parties and business dinners with Hong Kong's wealthiest. The expats flashed their diamonds and drank champagne endlessly. None of them cared to work, but Celeste kept at it.

She looked at the four-carat diamond ring on her finger – the engagement ring that Alex had only recently upgraded from its original two carats. She couldn't deny that she did enjoy the sneaky glances it received from the other wives when they thought she wasn't looking. The diamond was beautiful, she had to admit it – it represented everything she ever wanted growing up in East Row. But it also made her feel uneasy sometimes. She often had to turn the stone towards her palm when there were no cabs and she was forced to use the MTR. And she always lied and said it was a fake when young shop assistants asked her if it was real. She didn't want people to know that she had such wealth. It felt wrong when there seemed to be such a divide between the rich and the poor in Hong Kong. The Filipino ladies on their cardboard mats were just one example. Like Charlie and Lada they were just saving up to send money home, but one day they would have enough to go back for good.

Coming back to Alicia's letter, she couldn't help but wonder when she had last done something for herself. Over the last eight months she had been busy getting the design team at *Cross Hong Kong* off the ground and making sure she spent time with Alex whenever she could. She had to be flexible, because Alex certainly wasn't. Bloody *Renshaw* always came first. Alex had been flying non-stop over the last six months, 'chasing money.' Most recently a new project in Shanghai was being talked about incessantly. She had asked Alex several times what it was about, but so far she had only gleaned that a new branch of *Renshaw* was opening over there, and with government red tape it was even more complicated than they had first envisioned. The standard trip of a month was turning into three.

Celeste sometimes felt like she was losing him, and that always made her feel restless and nervous. She had broached the subject of Graham taking on some of the work, but that hadn't gone down well. She had even threatened to speak to Warwick herself, but Alex would have none of it. 'Graham'll screw it up,' he had screamed so loudly she feared that the neighbours would complain – like they had the last time they had a fight – over what, she couldn't quite remember. 'You don't want to stop living this life because of my incompetent brother, do you?' He had asked her this same question so many times now, she had lost count. It was at times like these that she would look at the rock on her finger and know that she would sacrifice it just to spend more time with Alex. To be able to lay her head on his lap and watch an old movie like they used to, or go for a simple Chinese meal at a local restaurant without the interruption of mobile phones and emails that always required an immediate response. Only last week had she said this to Alex , but he had ignored her. Ignored her! He would never have done that a couple of years ago. Now she felt like she had no choice but to let him carry on running himself into the ground.

'Our marriage is strong, it will survive,' she kept telling herself each time Alex went out to some late night business dinner or boarded a plane. It couldn't fail. Life without Alex was unfathomable. Those brilliant blue eyes and his cheeky grin that made her smile no matter what her mood. He still kissed her in the mornings, bought her gifts every time he went away and occasionally sent lunch to her office. She was on his mind as much as he was on hers. He was busy, that was all.

She greeted Lada outside the kitchen who was putting empty bottles of champagne into a recycling bag – remnants from their impromptu party last night, which reminded Celeste of her splitting headache. She wasn't sure how much of it was a hangover and how much of it was working for Harris. And Bill was a bad influence. He had pretty much moved to Hong Kong and was staying in another apartment building in the Mid-Levels. With his wife Angela and the kids back in England, and business keeping him in Hong Kong for weeks on end, he was pushing their already hedonistic lifestyle over the edge. It was never too early to start drinking in Bill's eyes.

Walking upstairs to their bedroom, she pulled a silk top out from the brown parcel Alicia had sent. She held it against her body. It suited her. She put the top on a pile of clothes on the armchair that she had recently bought. She would give them to Lada later for ironing and hanging in her closet. She still felt guilty about leaving all her ironing for Lada, but not as guilty as she would have felt six months ago. And as Alex kept reminding her, she was keeping Lada in a job.

Celeste poured herself a glass of the water Lada had put on her bedside table and took two paracetamol from the drawer. She swallowed the tablets, finishing the contents of the glass. Her phone beeped. She looked at the screen. Bill was trying to convince her to join him and Alex at the club in Repulse Bay so Alex would agree to go. It was hard to say no to Bill. He always had such a convincing argument, and when Bill was around Alex never needed much convincing. She stood up and opened her wardrobe to decide what to wear for the party. Picking out a black dress she glanced around her bedroom decorated in whites and blues. Her bedroom wasn't to her taste. But Kealana had spent so much time on it, or so Alex had said when she mentioned changing the décor, that she felt she ought to leave it. After all they wouldn't want to hurt Kealana's feelings.

Kealana was a thorn in Celeste's side – someone she needed to discuss with Alicia. To everyone else, this woman was a saint. Whether it was London or Hong Kong, Kealana was always hanging around, bringing fresh flowers to their home and no doubt reporting back to her beloved Warwick whatever she noticed. Since they had moved to Hong Kong, it seemed that Kealana had moved there too.

'Delivering the flowers yourself? I thought you would get one of the office hands to do that?' Celeste had one day asked.

Kealana hesitated. 'Oh, I like to keep on top of things. Make sure everyone is doing their job.' She narrowed her eyes and nodded towards Lada's door. A shiver ran down Celeste's spine. There was something about the woman that put her on edge, especially after she had caught her snooping around when she had returned home early from work one day. Kealana had been looking in the trash for an old bill, she said, which was not exactly a crime, but suspicious nevertheless.

After that, Celeste was sure that she was being spied on. But who had asked her to? Warwick? He didn't strike her as the type of man who could be bothered with spying on his daughter-in-law. Surely it was beneath him. Although she was sure he didn't get to where he was without being underhand. And what would Kealana report back? It wasn't like she was siphoning money from *Renshaws* or having an affair. It didn't make sense. Perhaps Warwick, like Alex, was a control freak. And she knew after being with Alex for so long that knowledge equalled power. How many times had Alex told her what exactly was going on with Graham – information he had learned, not from Graham, but from other *Renshaw* staff. He always seemed delighted that he knew what his brother was doing, even though it was rarely scandalous or anything untoward. Perhaps Warwick too had to know what was going on with his son and his daughter-in-law at all times. Or perhaps, and this she knew was most likely, she was just being paranoid.

29

Barnet, North London

'Alicia's letter made me realise that I needed to talk to a good friend. I should have stood up to Harris. I've never been a person with plenty of friends – just a few good ones. In Hong Kong I had no one.'

'What about the expats?'

'Jackie and Melanie? People who would talk about me the minute my back was turned. That was Hong Kong for you. In London I would have stayed away from such socialites. But in Hong Kong we were friends, in a superficial sort of way. We talked about watches and clothes, new spas and shopping, that sort of thing – never anything meaningful. Everything changed in Hong Kong. I changed in Hong Kong. Money does that to you. Growing up in East Row I dreamed of having money, but in Hong Kong I had more money than I knew what to do with. I bought my shoes from *Peddar Red* and dresses from *Lane Crawford*, when I wasn't wearing my own designs. I never wore the same outfit twice, and when Alex was around we were out almost every night. Either sipping martinis in Lang Kwai Fong or picking at sushi in some expensive restaurant like *Nobu* or *Zuma*. Looking back, I can see it for what it was, but at the time we didn't seem to bore of it. We thought that eating thin slivers of raw fish at extortionate prices was bloody marvellous.'

'Do you miss that now?'

Did she miss that life? Her mother hadn't yet asked her this – probably afraid of her answer. Scared it would point to an obsession with her past, her old life. Her mother had used that word – obsessed. She wasn't obsessed or so she had said. But he was still the first thing she thought of when she woke every morning and the last person she thought of when her eyelids closed at night. She had it all planned. She closed her eyes. Yes, she knew what she would do if she could see him one last time, just one last time.

Elaine, with her curly hair and floaty skirt, was the first person to ask her if she missed her old life. Would she go back to that life? Could she go back to that life? It was a shallow existence – where friends wore *Cartier* and *Chanel* and met at the club in Repulse Bay to eat shrimp and drink white wine, where she wore strings of pearls and flawless diamonds to black tie events, and went to yacht parties where champagne was chilled to perfection, and *Michelin* starred chefs cooked something rare and exquisite. She was living a life straight out of those lifestyle magazines. Women looked at her with envy. And they were brazen, these women – often disregarding her and eyeing Alex, looking past her as if she didn't exist. They only had eyes for her husband. They didn't seem to care that he was married or that his wife was standing next to him. So it felt pretty good when Alex would put his arm around her, like his most precious possession, and kiss her madly on the lips for all to see. It felt even better when she noticed their eyes glancing over to her ears or neckline to see the glittering jewels Alex had bought her: a five-carat aquamarine, a ruby brooch, a rock of emerald. She could see the envy then. But as the years passed by, that feeling of triumph began to fade. These women who wanted to snare a millionaire didn't realise what was happening behind the glamour. The escorts who accompanied some of the men in their group were even worse, wanting a glamorous lifestyle, no matter the cost. 'Those money-grabbers wouldn't know the difference between *Laurent Perrier* and *Cava*,' Alex had said, ridiculing their unnatural breasts and button noses. The moral standards that she had set so high for Bonnie had started to slip. Slip? They were positively in the gutter. Bonnie – another friend she had lost. The memory of when Bonnie first met Alex suddenly came to her mind. The way his jaw had dropped when he saw her. Her bee stung lips, her glossy dark hair. Her beauty was certainly natural. She missed Bonnie. She missed Alex.

'So?' Elaine interrupted her thoughts. 'Do you miss that life?'

'Hmm,' Celeste mumbled, coming back to the present. 'Occasionally, I miss that life – the parties and the luxury. But I suppose it was all a lie. So I guess I could never go back, unless I wanted the lies again. Plus, what Alex did…'

'What did Alex do?'

Celeste looked at the clock and pressed her lips together.

'Can you picture that sort of life without Alex in it?'

Elaine, she was so naïve. Alex was the embodiment of that life – the fast cars and the flash meals out. Alex had been her rock in a changing climate and he was thoughtful – he dropped her to meet friends and he always messaged her to check she had got home safe after work, even when he was hundreds of miles away. He was always checking to see if she was okay. She missed that. She bloody missed that. Celeste touched her bumblebee pendant again, and shrugged. 'I don't know that life without Alex. He showed me how to live it.'

'But you were enjoying Hong Kong, no?'

'I was having a great time, but things had started to turn sour. The alcohol fuelled late nights – you can only do that for so long. Alex was away more than ever and that was hard to get used to. My thought process had warped. I wanted to discuss it with someone. I wanted to talk to a true friend.'

'Alicia?'

Celeste nodded. 'Her letter made me realise that.'

'So you went to see her. You reached out to her.'

'Eventually, I booked a ticket. But before I got on that plane something happened that changed things.'

'What happened?'

'Like I said before, Bill was pretty much living in Hong Kong. He had rented an apartment and was almost a permanent fixture in the Mid-Levels party scene. His wife came and went but was mostly in England.'

'And this changed things?'

'Bill and Alex's motto had always been work hard, play hard. I couldn't see the work Bill was doing but he was certainly playing hard.'

'What do you mean?'

'Bill bought a boat.'

'A boat?' Elaine asked. 'And this was a bad thing?'

'It was. You could say it was poison in the water.'

30

14th September 2011
Mid-Levels, Central and Western District, Hong Kong

Celeste put her hand over her eyes as the bright sunlight hit her face. She could hear movement but her head was throbbing and she felt nauseated. She heard a clunk on her bedside table and opened her eyes to see Alex replacing an empty glass on his own bed-side table. Old habits, she thought as she allowed her lids to close again.

'Drink it. You'll feel better.'

She could sense him next to her.

Opening one eye, she took in Alex's half naked body and his hand holding out a tumbler full of fizzing water. She waved it away so he placed the glass on her bedside table again. Alex kissed her as he moved past her and she savoured his lips before he pulled away. It was rare to have a lazy morning together. No Bill, no Lada. Moments like this reminded her of their time in Thailand. Back in Krabi, Alex had been skinnier, now his back was broad and his shoulders defined. When had he started working out? She reached out and put her hand on his bicep. 'Remember Thailand?' she asked before she stretched out in-between their *Frette* bed-sheets.

He took her foot in his hand and ran his finger down the

sole of her foot.

'Stop it,' she shouted, suppressing a laugh. 'I feel sick.' She groaned and put her hand over her eyes.

Alex stood up. He walked over to his wardrobe and pulled out a white polo. 'We're leaving in fifteen minutes,' he said, pulling on a T-shirt and leaving the room.

Celeste looked over at the alarm clock and realised it was noon. Not enough sleep for a weekend. She propped herself up and swallowed the contents of the glass by her bed. Last night had been fun. Jackie was on good form regaling stories of the countless jobs she had before meeting Geoff and moving to Hong Kong. After stepping out of a club at some deathly hour, she remembered they had gone to a local eatery and sat next to a row of marinating ducks whilst they ate beef ho fun and drank jasmine tea. Food had been a good idea. She focused on the door of the bathroom. 'Just a couple of steps,' she said, trying to coax herself into movement.

*

'This car is so loud,' Celeste said exactly one hour later, as she adjusted her dark glasses. The car emerged from the underground car park into broad daylight.

'Do you like it?' Alex said, turning to look at her.

'Love it.' Celeste gave her husband a well-practised smile. In reality she didn't care. It was a car. A loud, expensive car that Alex had only bought because Jackie's husband had a *Ferrari* something-or-the-other delivered last week. The *Maserati* was just what Alex needed to make himself feel better. You couldn't get over twenty miles per hour in most parts of Hong Kong, with its narrow streets and traffic jams. Having a super car was a joke. But if it put a smile on Alex's face, who was she to question it. It was his money in any case. Like Alex kept reminding her, the money she earned couldn't buy a first class ticket to Mainland China.

'Like the colour? Went for the Nero black leather interior to go with the silver.'

'It's great,' she said, careful not to mention that she scratched the door with her watch just moments ago. He would find out soon enough. 'Good choice,' she added in the hope of sounding more enthusiastic.

'You're not in the least bit interested, are you?'

'I am.' She looked at her new watch with a diamond-encrusted bezel that Alex had given her last night after arriving from his latest Shanghai trip. Then she leaned back in the passenger seat. Memories from Thailand came back to her again. Back then she wore a *Casio* and if she could remember correctly, Alex didn't even have a watch. Now, as his gold *Rolex* reflected the sun, she couldn't help but smile. She looked out as they drove past the harbour away from the city. It was nice to get out, to see some open spaces after being hemmed in by skyscrapers in the Mid-Levels.

'Repulse Bay,' Celeste said, as the car turned the corner and the sea glimmered in the sunshine. 'The club?'

'Aberdeen,' Alex said. 'The boat has arrived.'

31

15th September 2011
Aberdeen, Southern District, Hong Kong

'Bill can't be up at this time. Last night he drank a bottle of *Blue Label*. And Angela, wasn't she flying back today? Something about the children?'

Alex looked at his watch. 'Her flight took off an hour ago.'

'She made it?'

'Bill doesn't let his wife miss flights. Far too expensive.'

'You make Bill sound like a dictator.'

Alex smiled.

'He wont be able to share this big moment with her.' There had been talk about this boat for some time. Bill, a master of impressions, had had them all in stiches last night speaking like Popeye and referring to Angela as Olive Oyl as he anticipated the arrival of his beloved boat. He never mentioned its arrival today.

'It's not his first boat. And she'll be back. Bill loves a celebration. That's why he invited us. It cleared customs sooner than he expected,' Alex said, as if reading her mind. 'She wasn't that keen in any event.' Alex made a face. Celeste nodded. Alex didn't like Angela. He never said as much but she got that impression. Angela pretty much kept herself to herself. She probably resented the time Bill spent with Alex, especially now that Bill had pretty much followed Alex to Hong Kong. She imagined Bill blamed a lot of his late nights on Alex too, which was pointless because everyone knew Bill was always the instigator of a night out.

Alex parked at the clubhouse and they walked the short way to the marina. In the distance there were a couple of sampan boats taking tourists to *Jumbo*, the iconic floating restaurant. The largest yacht in the harbour was at the end of the decking of the marina. 'That has got to be it,' Alex said. 'Larger than the last, certainly ostentatious. I love it.'

'Carbon credits must be doing well,' Celeste said. She noticed Alex grimace. 'You wouldn't be jealous, would you?' she asked as they stood outside the ninety-foot boat. Remember when we first met, you said you'd own a boat like this one day. Seems like Bill has beaten you to it.' She watched Alex for a reaction but he just grinned. Her comment was payback for all the recent comments he made about her insignificant job at *Cross*, but her words didn't have the effect she was hoping for.

A man in a white and grey T-Shirt walked down the plank to where Celeste and Alex were standing. 'I'm Roger,' he said with a nod of the head. 'Bill's on board. Please take your shoes off and come up. There is a sea-grass box just over there for your shoes. I'll bring it on board when we're due to set sail.'

'I'm so short without my heels,' Celeste complained with a mock pout.

'Haven't you ever been on a boat before, honey? You can't wear heels on a boat – it's just not practical.'

She narrowed her eyes. 'And how many times have you been on a boat?' She put her hand on Alex to steady herself whilst she unclasped a red *Jimmy Choo*. 'Don't answer that.' She adjusted her red and blue tunic that she had designed for *Cross*'s last Cruise collection. Roger handed them both towelling slippers with Bill's initials embroidered on the front.

'Bloody hell,' Alex said. 'A bit much, don't you think?'

Celeste smiled. 'It's his boat. I think the initials look great.' The slippers were actually a welcome relief with her hangover. 'I was wearing flats when we first met,' she said, looking up at Alex from her new height.

'Why so sentimental today?' Alex asked, as he advanced along the walkway to the boat. 'Next you'll be saying you want a baby.'

Celeste hesitated. 'God no,' she said, a little too quickly. She dared not tell him that she had stopped to coo at a baby one of the merchandisers brought into the office last week. Alex was right though. She had been reminiscing of late and she couldn't pinpoint why the past – their past – kept playing in her mind. Was it because she wanted things to go back to the way they were? Thailand had been fun – a time when they were both on the same adventure. Now, it often felt like she and Alex were on different paths that crossed every so often after one too many Sambucas. It had been months since they had spent any time together. Bill, Jasper or Geoff were always around and there was always some party or event to go to. When was the last time they went for a meal, just the two of them?

'How's the head, Celeste?' Bill asked. He pulled open glazed doors at the rear of the boat and stepped outside. He kissed her on both cheeks. 'Bloody muggy today, isn't it. I've been sitting inside watching the cricket.'

'The head is manageable,' she said. Bill looked surprisingly fit, even if his nose was a little red.

'Much larger than the last one, though we didn't see much of that boat,' Alex said.

'You were here…or perhaps not. Perhaps you didn't see too much of it, Renshaw. This one's my real baby,' Bill said with a wink. 'Come, sit down,' he instructed, as a lady in grey shorts and a white T-Shirt served them flutes of chilled champagne.

'Bill, your initials are everywhere.' Alex said.

Celeste rolled her eyes.

Alex mumbled something but Celeste didn't catch what he said. Instead she took a sip of the pale liquid from her glass. Coupled with the rocking motion of the boat it didn't sit well. She sat on the white seats of the lower deck and looked out over the harbour. 'So what's this one called?'

'*Premier Cru*,' Bill said.

'But you named the last one after your daughter. What about your son?'

Bill smiled. 'You wanted me to name a boat Tristan?'

'You'll give him a complex,' Alex said.

'Well, we sold *Seraphim* so it's no longer in the family. He'll get over it. He needs to learn that life is not always fair.'

'You sold it? I thought you were keeping it as part of the deal.'

'What deal?' Celeste asked.

Bill waved his hand. 'Never mind all that. After this I couldn't go back to a smaller boat, could I? Once this goes, my boating days are over.'

'That's not like you Bill.'

'What?'

'You've just got this one. Why are you talking about when it goes? In Bill's world everything has a silver lining.'

'True. Never a grey cloud in my life.'

Alex shrugged. 'I'm not sure I like *Premier Cru*. It sounds...'

'I just liked the name.'

'And it has nothing to do with you, being the first born of your clan, inheriting your father's vineyard in Bordeaux.'

'I forget how well you know me, Renshaw. The vineyard isn't profitable.'

'Not the point,' Alex said.

'Well I suppose that had something to do with it. *Premier Cru* – It means first growth. So being first born I thought it quite apt. What would you call your boat?'

'Heavenly,' Alex said, winking at Celeste.

She smiled. Bill did too, which wiped the smile off her face. Had Alex shared their private joke with him? He probably had. But it was nice of him to think of 'Heavenly' as a name for a boat. He was thinking of when they first met in Thailand too. Perhaps they hadn't grown as far apart as she had thought.

'That's a bit wet if you ask me,' Bill said, draining his glass. A member of crew came out on deck with a mobile phone on a little silver tray. Bill took the device and slipped it in his pocket. 'Tell me, Renshaw, are you bull or bear?'

Alex laughed. 'Definitely bull, mate.'

'Not this again.' Celeste swallowed the contents of her glass. She felt a little perkier. 'Let me guess, the market is up?' One would always ask the other if they were bull or bear – something to do with the financial markets that went straight over her head.

'Yes, this again,' Bill said with a wink.

'I've invested well and I think I'll be reaping the rewards,' Alex said. 'Bill clearly hasn't done the same.'

'On the contrary...' Bill started, but he was interrupted as

Celeste's eyes fixed upon a tall black woman walking towards them from the front of the boat. She wasn't crew – Celeste could tell that from the way she walked, or rather glided, towards them, but the electric green *Cavalli* kaftan was a bit of a giveaway. Her flawless skin and immaculate cropped hair made Celeste touch the back of her own head. Was her hair styled as it should be? Had her lipstick smudged? She shifted in her seat and sat upright glancing around her to check if there was a mirror nearby she could steal a glance in.

'This is Anya,' Bill said, putting his arm around the woman and kissing her on the lips. Anya called to a crewmember to bring out the canapés.

Celeste held her tongue. Last night Bill had drank his body weight in alcohol and had told anyone who would listen that Angela was the love of his life. He was fawning over her like a lovesick teenager. Of course she had always known that Bill was a flirt, but this... it looked more than just flirting. And Anya ordering around the crew with Angela barely out of the country spoke volumes. She looked over at Alex who raised his eyebrows. There was no use Alex pretending this was news to him. He and Bill were attached at the hip. He would have known about her. Why would he keep this secret from her? Was it because he felt guilty for being so hard on Bonnie all those years ago? Her stomach turned as a member of crew she hadn't even notice approach her to top up her glass.

'You're staring,' Alex whispered in her ear.

'How long have you known?' she muttered back.

Alex smiled at the member of crew filling his glass. 'I've seen her on and off. Thought they were business colleagues.'

'Alex, don't.' Celeste said quietly, thinking of Angela. Her loyalties were with Bill, but she still felt for her. How would she feel if it was Alex playing away from home? She would want to know.

Alex hesitated. 'Only found out recently. I don't approve of this kind of thing. You know that.'

'But you haven't said anything to Bill, like you did to Bonnie.'

'I never said anything to Bonnie.'

Celeste opened her mouth to protest and then closed it again. Alex was right. He'd never spoken to Bonnie about her affair. He had just made it clear to Celeste how he felt and she had been the one to vocalise his thoughts, which had been the beginning of the end of their friendship.

'You can't, seriously, be worried about this,' Alex said, motioning to Anya with a slight movement of his head. 'Everyone we know in the Mid-Levels is sleeping around. Even that couple who live in the apartment below us.'

'This is different. We know Angela.'

Alex gave Celeste a steely look. Then he stood up and walked over to Bill and Anya.

32

1st October 2011
Mid-Levels, Central and Western District, Hong Kong

'Sure you don't want to come?' Alex asked. He laid out his tux on the bed.

'I've a ton of things to do before the design meeting on Monday.'

'Your loss, it's going to be one helluva party.'

Even Maryanne had asked her what she was going to wear for Bill's birthday bash. Celeste picked up her sketch of the maroon, high-waisted, cropped trousers she had been working on and scrunched her face. 'They want me to use CAD for my design work. I hate that. I much prefer sketching.'

'Still computer illiterate after all these years?'

Celeste shrugged.

'You can't go to the office now. Jinny isn't even there to help.'

She looked at her design. Alex was right. There was nothing more she could do. Tonight she would probably drink the last bottle of *La Grande Dame* 2007 that they had been saving and feel sorry for herself, whilst watching a *Bridget Jones* movie.

'This isn't about work.' Alex said intuitively. 'This is about Bill's mistress.' Alex sat at the edge of the bed and put his socks on.

'They've been out at every social event in the last two weeks.'

'So?'

'So, it's one rule for your friends and another for mine?' She couldn't stand looking at Bill and Anya together without regretting what had passed between her and Bonnie.

'Bill's my friend. I can't just cut him out like that.'

'But I cut Bonnie out.'

'That was your decision.'

Celeste wanted to protest, but he was right. 'But we know Angela.'

'Angela is no angel herself. Bill and Angela have problems that not even Bill will talk to me about. Nothing is black and white, hon, and sometimes it's best to stay out of other people's business. Everyone we know in Hong Kong is having affairs. Are you going to stop coming out altogether? Let it go.'

'Have you ever cheated on me?' Celeste tilted her head to one side and stared at her husband.

'I'm not even going to dignify that question with an answer.'

'What was the name of the businessman who gave you that escort service card?'

Alex stood up and put his hands in his pockets. 'You still remember that?'

Celeste nodded.

'I never even called the number.'

'You've been to strip clubs though.'

'And I've told you every time. It's the way they do business here. If I wanted to hide it, I wouldn't tell you, would I?'

Celeste put her design down and folded her arms across her chest. She remembered the first time Alex had told her about the strip club. It had made her feel so inadequate. She thought Alex wanted more than she could offer. Even thinking about it now sent a shiver down her spine.

'Think I want to go to those hovels with women who are too ugly for daylight? You know how business works here.' Alex walked over to his cupboard, took a white shirt off the hanger and put it on.

'Fine,' she said. He had won, again. Her eyes flickered to the black dress hanging in her half open cupboard. The dress would be a perfect compliment to the new diamond necklace Alex had given her – four one-carat solitaires hanging on a platinum chain.

'If you don't want to come.'

How many parties would she miss if she chose to hold Bill's philandering against him? So, she had made a mistake with Bonnie. She couldn't lose another friend over something that didn't concern her, could she?

'If I go alone, think of all those women that'll be throwing themselves at me.' Alex flashed her a cheeky grin.

She couldn't help but smile even though she knew it was probably true. She jumped off the bed. 'I'll be ready in half an hour. Can you get my new necklace from the safe?'

Alex smiled. 'Sure.'

33

Barnet, North London

'There was no "being late" in Hong Kong. You arrived at parties when you wanted to. It was an unspoken rule of the rich over there. The richer you were, the later you arrived.'

'How did it make you feel when you decided to go to the party?' Elaine asked.

'On the way to the party Alex said to me that Bill was the same person I'd always known. He was right. He made me realise that my fight with Bonnie was in the past; that I couldn't take it out on everyone else. I planned on booking a flight to London the next day and I planned to make up with her when I got there. So, I felt pretty good'

'So what changed? You said the boat was poisonous before. That it changed everything.'

'Alex changed. He was away a lot before. Now it was like he didn't exist. He was always on that wretched boat. If he didn't answer his phone I called Bill. It was that simple. They were inseparable. If they were not on the *Premier Cru*, they were looking on the *Benetti* homepage. "Boat porn" I used to call it. And I was so foolish, I didn't say anything. I had all the opportunity in the world and I didn't say a word. I was scared that if I did I would push Alex further away. I didn't want to be a nagging wife and end up cuckolded like Angela.'

'You wanted to be the cool wife. The one that said "I trust you, do what you want".'

Celeste nodded. 'At the same time I was also glad that they were looking at fast cars and yachts. I thought it would keep Alex's eyes from wandering to other women. There were always stunning women on Bill's boat. He attracted them like bees to honey.'

'So you never told Angela about Bill's women?'

Celeste shook her head. I knew Angela, but I wouldn't call her a friend. She was always pleasant to me but she kept her distance. She was so preoccupied with her children and she had a close-knit group of old school friends in London so we only met up occasionally. Plus, I believed what Alex had said about her.'

'Do you want to expand on that?'

'Alex drip fed me information about Angela,' she said, fiddling with the hem of her cardigan. 'Over dinner, not long after I met Anya, he told me that Angela had a violent streak. At the time I believed it. I didn't have reason not to. Angela had a temper when things didn't go her way. I once saw her throw a glass figurine on the floor, smashed it to smithereens, all because she couldn't get a massage booked at the time she wanted. I think she forgot she had company. She took one look at me standing next to her, gawping at what she had done, and apologized profusely. Said she thought it was plastic. Like Bill and Angela would have had any plastic ornaments. It was shocking to lose your temper over something so trivial, but it just made realise I didn't know Angela at all. So when Alex said she had been known to physically attack Bill I believed him.'

'Did you ever ask Bill or Angela about it?'

'I didn't want to get involved. I mean Alex said Bill would die if he found out that I knew.'

Elaine made a note in her journal.

'Now, I look back and I can see why she threw that ornament. She probably knew what Bill was up to. It was probably a special day for them and he was out screwing a nobody in a short skirt. Her inability to get a massage booked was just another disappointment on a terrible day.'

'The straw that broke the camel's back. Is that what you think?'

Celeste looked out of the window. It was almost light outside. 'Bill's birthday party was everything I imagined. We were dancing with the glitterati of Hong Kong like teenagers. But I kept my promise to myself. After the party, after my big design meeting, I called Kealana and asked her to book me a return trip to London. I wanted to catch up with Alicia, make up with Bonnie, see Maryanne and spend time with my family.

'And did you?'

Celeste shook her head.

34

19th November 2011
Mayfair, London

Celeste looked at the old white and blue vase that she had found in a little shop in Primrose Hill. She touched it with the tips of her fingers and as she walked around her old home she adjusted the various ornaments she had once collected. Items that Kealana had no involvement with. Everything had been cleaned before her arrival and fresh white lilies had been placed in the said vase – on Kealana's instructions, no doubt. There was milk, bread and her favourite chocolate spread in the fridge. The wine rack had been re-stocked and the towels and linen had been freshly laundered. Despite her suspicions of Kealana, who had also moved some of the furniture around, she couldn't discredit her running of the *Renshaw* properties.

She turned up the heating and pulled her dressing gown around her as she opened her wardrobe. She examined the red *Valentino* dress Alex had left in her wardrobe with a note telling her that he missed her, and smiled at his thoughtfulness. But rather than a note she wanted him there. Lately, she had been trying to make an effort, cancelling important meetings just so that she could spend more time with him. She had even offered to go with him to Shanghai but everything she did, everything she said, seemed to spark an argument between them.

'I thought you had to work on the next collection?' he asked when she had offered to accompany him.

'I do. But you're more important than that. I can ask Jinny to lead on this.'

'And blame me when it all goes wrong. I don't think so,' he had said. 'You did that once before, remember?'

'That was different. It was a capsule collection that Harris specifically asked me to work on and…'

'Never mind. Why is this house so filthy? And my shirts, look,' he said, taking one out of his drawer. 'It's creased. Lada's not taking any care anymore. She knows how to fold them. She's been doing it for years. She just needs reminding. Maybe…' Alex started and then stopped.

'Maybe, what?'

'Don't worry.'

'No, say it.'

'Maybe you need to keep an eye on what the staff do. We can't have Kealana here the whole time checking their work. Remember, you don't like her.'

'So you'd rather I stay here and watch Lada clean than spend time with you?'

Alex had sighed. She noticed his shoulders drop. 'Honey, sorry. I didn't…Come to Shanghai –' he started but she cut him off, slamming the bathroom door and running herself a bath to drown out his apologies.

Now she ran her hand over the silky fabric of the *Valentino* dress. It was better than nothing, even if Alex had asked Kealana to pick it out.

As she examined the cut and the neckline of the garment she wondered if Alex too had felt the distance between them of late and was trying to bridge the gap. Was the dress his way of saying he was sorry that he was never around anymore? 'This is my job,' was his usual response when she complained about all the travelling he was doing. Already he had been to Shanghai twice in the month and it was only the nineteenth.

She couldn't keep track of where Alex was most of the time. When she had first complained he had installed an application on to her phone and his own, which pinpointed their whereabouts on a map, but even this bit of technology couldn't seem to keep up with him. She had used it a couple of times, just to know where he was. It always felt better when she could see the little blue flag on the map, pinpointing Alex's whereabouts. But lately it seemed to have stopped working. Perhaps it needed updating or something. The last time Alex was in Shanghai it put him in Scotland and she knew he was in Shanghai. It was always Shanghai. Making in-roads through the mountain of red-tape that surrounded the *Renshaw* office set-up.

Celeste let the thought go. It felt odd being back in London. London had given her so much – her degree, an amazing career and two friends who she had once thought the world of. But before she had left for Hong Kong it had all turned sour. *Cross* London was financially close to ruin and the friendship between her and Bonnie had been lost. Moving to Hong Kong at the time seemed to have preoccupied her. Her focus had been her new husband and *Cross* Hong Kong.

The move seemed to have paid off, for *Cross* at least. The recent red cape she had designed had been a sell out in Hong Kong, but had barely sold in London. *Cross* London was still failing, or so Alex had said. She had felt foolish when he had broken the news to her. He often did that – told her what was happening to *Cross* before she found out from Toby Cain or

Harris. She hated when he did that, hated that he had friends in high places with insider knowledge on just about everything.

She was looking forward to catching up with Maryanne. When was the last time they had spoken? She couldn't remember and she felt a slight pang of guilt. She should have made more of an effort with her old boss, but the wild nights and busy days in Hong Kong seemed to have distracted her more than she realised.

And Bonnie – how could she have let a petty argument get between them? She should have forgiven her for her harsh words and called her. And of course there was Alicia, the person whose letter had sparked this trip. Alicia had always been there for her. But just before she left Hong Kong Alex had told her something, something that changed the way she regarded her close friend. Now she wasn't sure if she wanted to speak to Alicia, let alone see her. What Alex said had hurt. It wasn't so much what Alicia had done, but her failure to confide in her that stung. Did their friendship mean nothing to her?

She sat on the bed, staring at the red dress. It was a first for Celeste to be alone in London. She looked at her phone. She would call her mother for a chat or watch a movie. But just as she was about to dial her mother's number, the screen of the phone flashed up with a name she hadn't seen for a while.

Celeste answered apprehensively. An hour later she got dressed and left the house.

*

'Darling,' Celeste said, kissing Angela on each cheek. She noticed Angela's long brown fur and estimated it at around eight thousand pounds – far too much money to pay for a coat that made her look like a Shar Pei.

Angela turned to stub out her cigarette. 'Bill mentioned that you were in London, possibly at a loose end.'

So Alex had spoken to Bill – of course he had. That explained it. It wasn't as if she and Angela were friends. They were the wives of two friends, pushed together by familiarity only. It was rich, Bill asking his wife to keep her company, especially after what Alex had just told her. Did he want her to tell Angela? Was that it? Well, she wouldn't be doing his dirty work.

'The children are with their nanny, and I just needed to get out and have a drink.'

'Shall we go in?' Celeste said, as a sharp gust of icy wind caught her. 'I've forgotten just how cold it can be here in winter. But I have to admit, it's a welcome relief from the constant mugginess of Hong Kong.'

'You've been holed up in that place for far too long.' Angela opened the heavy black door to *The Emerald Rooms* and walked into the reception area of the club. 'Bill's told me to come out there, but I just can't do it. I'd miss my friends and family too much. It's a good job he doesn't mind flying up and down so much. Alex must be the same. I suppose they get used to it. Angela flashed her membership card to the front of house who greeted them.

'They never refer to you by your name here. Some odd tradition,' Angela said. 'It's always sir or madam. Makes me feel old. You a member?'

Celeste shook her head.

'I'll sign you in as my guest,' she said, writing her name and then Celeste's on the register. 'Been here before?'

'I think so. When I got back from travelling. I came with

a friend, but she doesn't live here anymore. We kind of lost touch. Her name's Bonnie. Bonnie Notman. She used come here with a girl called Alicia and two others – Rachel and Sophia, I think.'

Angela looked blank. 'Can't say I know them. But with the kids I don't come here that often. It's nice though to have membership – somewhere where everybody knows your name.'

'Like an upmarket *Cheers*?'

'You could say that. Get Alex to sign you up. He just needs to add your name to his membership. If they close the list then you're screwed. Alex practically lives here when he's in town.'

'Does he?' Alex had never mentioned *The Emerald Rooms* before. He always said that it was full of wannabes.

Angela hesitated. 'Well Bill's here all the time when he's in London so I assume they are together. What do those two get up to?' She walked upstairs, towards the Drawing Room bar. Celeste followed thinking about what Angela had just said.

It was obvious that Bill was using her husband and *The Emerald Rooms* as an excuse for his indiscretions. She watched Angela's blond hair swaying as she walked, wondering the real reason as to why Angela had called her? Was it because Bill had asked her to, or was Angela suspicious of her husband? Was she going to interrogate her after a few glasses of wine?

Angela would have had to be completely blind not to know what Bill was up to. The whole of Hong Kong was talking about his affairs, and after what Alex had just told her she'd be surprised if the gossip hadn't spread to London. It wasn't as if Bill's infidelity was limited to Hong Kong. Celeste accepted a glass of champagne from Angela and took a sip. She couldn't disclose any of Bill's affairs. Not without hurting everyone around her.

She followed Angela to a sofa next to a large Georgian window and looked out. It was dark, yellow lamps lit the street. She watched commuters make their way towards the tube station, after a long day's work, reminding her of her own days spent working in London, before Alex – going home to her bedsit in Finchley after a long tube ride that she would have spent standing in heels, heels which pinched her toes and gave her blisters. Even then, she had thought that this time of the day, when the sun had gone down and the street lamps were lit, was when London was at its best. Celeste looked down on the street scene from the warmth of *The Emerald Rooms* and for the first time since her arrival in London felt glad to be back. Hong Kong was busy and always full of life. She loved the noise of the busy market places; the glazed ducks hanging in windows and hawkers selling curious meats, shouting for your attention, and the stark contrast as soon as she stepped into an air-conditioned building, away from the grime of the streets – the clean lines and the courteous manner. But London was different – the British reserve, the icy wind in winter that took your breath away, crisp autumn leaves and conkers. She missed all that.

She looked back to Angela now talking to a woman in a ruffled white shirt, which looked very Anne Fontaine. She smiled at the stranger and turned back to the window. Now she was out of the house she realised she wasn't feeling sociable at all. But as they had just arrived she could hardly make an excuse to leave. Being at home with a take away and Alicia for company would have been a much better plan. In fact it had been a plan they had made weeks ago. But there was no way that that was going to happen anytime soon. What Alex had told her before she left their home in Hong Kong had rocked her to the core. She closed her eyes, remembering their conversation.

'You're meeting Alicia?' Alex had said, putting his arms around Celeste.

'As soon as I get off that plane.'

'I'll miss you.'

She pouted. 'Why don't you come? Come for a couple of days.' Her voice rose in anticipation. It had been a long while since they had been away together.

'Shanghai.'

'Of course.'

'Listen, before you go, there's something I've been meaning to tell you.'

Celeste froze. 'What?'

Alex was silent.

Her hands began to tremble as her darkest fears began to invade her thoughts. Was he going to explain the distance he had been putting between them of late? Had Bill's infidelity rubbed off on him? She tried to rationalise her thoughts. Alex didn't have time to cheat on her with the Shanghai project ruining all their plans. And he despised cheating. He would never put her through what Warwick had put his mother through.

'You look worried.'

Celeste released herself from his grasp and adjusted her scarf. 'What are you trying to say?' she asked, avoiding his gaze.

'Sit next to me a minute.' Alex sat on the bed.

'The taxi will be...' *We've grown apart*. That's how he would start.

'The cab can wait. I just want you to hear this before you go, so you're prepared.'

Prepared? For what? She looked at him, silently praying that he wouldn't make her nightmare a reality, anything but that.

'It's about Alicia.'

Alex and Alicia? She shook her head. He would never, she would never. 'What about her?'

'Bill and Alicia have been seeing each other on and off since our wedding.'

Celeste laughed. 'That's it? Okay.' She took a moment whilst the news registered, relief that it had nothing to do with Alex flooding her mind.

'You know?'

She shook her head. 'Of course not. You mean Bill is not only screwing half of Hong Kong, but my best friend as well?'

'Sorry.' He took Celeste's hand in his. 'I thought you should know before you see her.'

'Since our wedding? You've known all this time and you're telling me now.'

'I only recently found out.'

The buzzer sounded. Celeste stood up.

'I know how the whole Bonnie episode got out of control. I wanted you to hear this from me.' He stood up and picked up her bags. He followed her downstairs and out of their front door where he called the lift.

The news was shocking, but she was glad it was only about Alicia and not about them. It made her realise that something was amiss with their relationship, something severe that she needed to resolve. Previously, she'd never had the courage to think they had a serious problem, worried she was expecting too much from a husband who was trying to make their lives perfect, working so that she could have diamonds and business class flights. She wondered if she should cancel her trip and spend time with Alex instead, try and work out what was going on with him, why he was working later and later each night, creeping into bed just before sunrise. He was taking on the lion's share of the work at *Renshaw*; why wasn't he getting another consultant on board like he did when they opened the Hong Kong branch? Her thoughts were fleeting. What good would come of her cancelling her trip? Alex was flying out to Shanghai, plus she needed a break from *Cross* and also needed to renew her visa. Toby Cain had told her to take a break now before she had to start working on the summer collection. He had also confided in her that profits were down. Even though her designs were selling out, company overheads were high. They were thinking of making cuts; he even mentioned closure of the store, which didn't make sense, and this worried her. But there wasn't anything she could do. Speaking to Maryanne would help and she was in London. The trip would be worth it. She kissed Alex goodbye and stepped into the lift when the doors opened.

'Love you, Heavenly' Alex said, passing her bags to her.

Celeste smiled. Alex always knew how to make her feel better. She put her hand on her neck, looked at her soulmate and blew him a kiss as the doors to the lift closed.

35

19th November 2011
Mayfair, London

'Bad day?' Angela asked.

Celeste opened her eyes. 'I found out my best friend is having an affair with a married man. And she's married too.'

'I hate men who cheat,' Angela said nonchalantly.

If Angela knew that Bill was cheating on her she wasn't giving anything away. But this wasn't about Angela. She had considered what Alex had told her about Bill and Alicia for fourteen hours – from the time her flight took off to the time she landed. What was going on in Alicia's mind to have slept with a married man? Had she cheated on her husband, Tom? Alex hadn't implied that the affair had ended. But what galled her was that Alicia didn't trust her enough to confide in her.

Alicia had confided about her brief fling with another woman back in university, and she had confessed her battle with bulimia. Celeste had been the one to make sure that she had got the right help at the time. And she too had told Alicia things even Alex didn't know. Alicia was the only one that knew of her shame walking into school with clothes too small for her and shoes with the soles falling off because her parents couldn't afford to replace them. Alicia even knew about the brief encounter she had with a man who liked to cross-dress on the occasional weekend. Now, Celeste wondered if, after their spat in London, things had not gone back to how they were, like she had foolishly thought.

Alicia was a talker. Celeste could confidently say that. She wore her heart on her sleeve and her secrets didn't stay buried for long. She was the opposite of Celeste and Bonnie who could bottle up emotions for months. So whom had Alicia confided in? One of her new friends, Rachel or Sophia? Although she rarely spoke to them these days, or so she said. Or perhaps it was Bonnie? Only recently Alicia said that Bonnie had ditched Matt and that she had taken up with another married man. Had they talked about their adultery and sniggered behind her back? Bill was her friend and Alicia sleeping with him felt like a double betrayal.

Celeste took another sip of her drink. She was tempted to tell Angela, if only to hurt Alicia. But she was better than that. And Alex had validated Bill's actions by telling her about Angela's violent streak. Although looking at Angela now, with her kind smile and soft brown eyes it was difficult to imagine her being violent towards another person, smashing a glass figurine sure, but a person... Celeste sighed, she didn't know what to think anymore.

'I hate men who cheat too,' she said, raising her glass to Angela's. 'And I suppose it's not my problem. I shouldn't get involved.'

'That's the safest bet. If I were you I'd stay out of it.'

There was an awkward silence between the two that Angela soon filled. 'So how's work? I hear that you are going from strength to strength – I almost bought that fabulous backless dress you designed the last time I was in the store, but they had sold out in my size. I should have gone straight to the source and called you.'

'You should have.'

'The London store isn't well stocked. And is it true what I hear – that *Cross* Hong Kong isn't doing well?'

Was there anything that Alex didn't tell Bill? The news had come as a shock to Celeste when Toby had given her the news. 'We have a recovery plan in place. But times are tough. The finance director is looking at making some changes. I'm going to see Maryanne tomorrow.'

'I've heard rumours that they want to close the store. Is that true?'

Celeste swallowed the contents of her glass. She hadn't breathed a word about that to Alex for fear of one of his "told you so" remarks.

Angela must have seen her surprise because she was quick to explain herself. 'Bill mentioned it. Business, eh! Hong Kong isn't a big place. Oh, I am sorry. I hope I haven't upset you.' Angela reached out for Celeste's hand. 'Don't worry I am sure things will be okay. This recession has taken its toll.'

Celeste's mind was racing ahead. If Bill knew, so did Alex, but he hadn't mentioned it. Was it because he was too busy with *Renshaw*? Or just indifferent to her career? She looked up and as she did so Angela smiled. There was no malice there.

'I'm looking forward to catching up with Maryanne,' she said, moving the conversation along. 'I seem to have lost touch with her since the move to Hong Kong. The occasional email isn't quite the same. And you? Are you working again as you had planned?'

Angela laughed. 'I wanted to, but with Bill being away so much I just don't have the time. As Bill says, it's best that I deal with the running of the house and the children. It's a full time job in itself.'

'Sounds like something Alex would say.' Celeste silently hoped she would never be as naive as Angela. Her husband was having multiple affairs, and Angela was dependent on him – so much so, she failed to see what was happening around her. Although Celeste could see how having children didn't help matters. Alex was against the idea of having children and she had been too, but as her biological clock had started to tick she often found herself thinking about starting a family.

For now and the foreseeable future *Cross* would be what defined her. She couldn't let them close the store. She imagined Alex would take some joy if *Cross* closed its doors. Not only would it prove him right, but he would have a good argument that she no longer had to work. He never came right out and said it, but she knew her working at *Cross* made him feel like he couldn't provide. It was ridiculous. Everyone knew just how rich the Renshaws were. It was so typical of Alex. She wasn't just one of his office hands, he couldn't control her like he did them. Then she smiled, thinking about him. Despite his flaws, she already missed him terribly.

'And the children, how are they?'

Angela started to tell her about Tristan and Seraphim's latest school play. Celeste's eyes wandered over to the other side of the room. Standing near a marble statue of a wild boar stood a woman with vibrant red hair. It was similar to Alicia's. She wished she were chatting to Alicia instead. There would be no pretences and superfluities. It was easier talking to someone who knew everything about you including your faults, instead of speaking to a socialite like Angela – someone who only knew you on a superficial level and valued their friendship with you less than their *Prada* handbag. The woman with the red hair walked out of Celeste's line of vision. She couldn't help but wonder if Bill had brought Alicia to *The Emerald Rooms*.

She should have asked her when they spoke this morning, when they had that bitter row. She could have made Alicia squirm, but she hadn't. She had been too angry for that.

*

'You're here!' Alicia had said into the receiver. 'I'd've picked you up from the airport. You were going to call.'

'I just wanted to get home and sleep,' Celeste lied. She couldn't face seeing her friend after what Alex had told her.

'Come over. Tom's dying to see you. Aren't you Tom?'

Celeste could hear Alicia's husband mutter something in the background.

'Tom is absolutely the most perfect husband,' Alicia whispered into the phone. 'I suppose after all those frogs I finally found my prince.'

'You certainly changed your luck.' How much longer was Alicia going to keep this up? 'Heard from Bonnie?'

'She is besotted with her new man. This time it's love. He plans to leave his wife soon. But don't they all say that?'

Alicia had walked into Celeste's trap. 'You would know about that, wouldn't you?'

Silence.

'Tom doesn't know about Bill, does he? You've not been married long. You should still be in the honeymoon phase, not screwing Bill.'

'You know.' The joy from Alicia's voice disappeared.

Celeste could hear Alicia moving around. Into another room, probably, so Tom couldn't hear her.

'Who told you?'

'Who told me? The whole of Hong Kong is talking about it.' She wasn't going to let Alicia off lightly. 'I've been your best friend for years. Why didn't you tell me?'

'It was on and off. I stopped after things with Tom got serious. We only met once after I married.'

Celeste was silent.

'Tom and I were just married and I don't know... it's not an excuse, but I was worried that I was going to be with the same person for the rest of my life. And it was like the fear of commitment caught up with me after the wedding. I freaked out and I went shopping to calm my nerves. I stopped in *Harrods*, at the *Dress Circle*, for something to eat and Bill walks in. The connection re-kindled. It was so silly of me. I know that.'

'Silly is buying a top two sizes too big, not something as big as this.' Celeste hated Alicia's naivety sometimes; her need to make light of everything; the way she used the word silly all the time. It was childish. She thought back to her wedding. She remembered Bill talking to Alicia, placing his hand on the small of her back. How he leaned in to speak to her. She could see why her friend had been attracted to him. She herself had felt that attraction, albeit briefly, before Alex had claimed what was rightfully his. Bill could be persistent – she knew that. But there was a difference between her and Alicia. Alicia had acted on her feelings. Celeste had been grown up enough to walk away.

'Let's meet up and talk about this face to face.'

'You let me pour my heart out to you about Alex whenever I have doubts and you never told me a thing.'

'I would have told you, but it got complicated with Tom.'

'You know all my insecurities.'

'Let's just meet.'

'I need to think about it. '

'I haven't seen you for years. I need you right now. You did this to Bonnie and now you're doing it to me.'

'I did this to Bonnie? I regret what happened with Bonnie. Maybe we shouldn't have been so quick to judge her. We were young. Clearly, everyone is screwing around. But this is different. Bonnie told us what she did. She trusted us. You don't trust me.'

'So you're going to spend a week in London and not see me?'

'Yes,' Celeste said, although she already doubted her snap decision. People made mistakes. Alicia was right, she should have learnt from the mess she made of her relationship with Bonnie. But before she had the chance to take the words back she had already slammed the phone down.

36

19th November 2011
Mayfair, London

'Madam,' the head of house said. His eyes narrowed as they looked at the computer screen in front of him.

Had her membership lapsed? Of course it wouldn't have. William was sure to have paid the subscription for the year. He never forgot things like that. Plus, she was known at the club as William's other half – a title she relished. The staff loved his big tips. They wouldn't let a lapse in membership get in the way.

'Welcome,' he said eventually. 'I haven't seen you here in a while. Can I take your coat?'

Rachel shook her head.

'Oh,' Sophia said, lifting her eyes from the guest book.

'What?'

'Someone I know has signed in here. Someone I haven't seen for some time.' Sophia shared a wicked smile with the head of house. One that said she knew something Rachel didn't.

Rachel wondered why, after all these years, she was still hanging around with this old has-been who was clutching on to her youth, like a sailor to a wreck. Then she remembered. Recently, all her friends had deserted her, or had she deserted them? Her friend Suzie had hinted that William was not treating her right, because she had overheard a conversation between them on a day when William was being awkward about taking her away with him to his country estate. Not that Suzie could talk. At least William didn't ask her to split the bill like her partner did. Jo was mad because they missed her baby's christening because William had to suddenly fly off somewhere on short notice, and Bella, well Bella didn't say anything. But Rachel could tell she was jealous because she was still single.

Through all her friends' criticism though, Rachel knew the real reason as to why her friends didn't want to know her anymore. Quite simply they were jealous – jealous of William's wealth and her elevation in society. How many times could they say they were gifted *Gucci* handbags and taken to dinner at London's finest?

'In fact,' Sophia said, hesitating, 'why don't we get some cocktails and I can tell you all about her. I think you'll find her very interesting.'

'Two cosmos,' Sophia said to the passing barman. 'We'll take them upstairs.' They climbed the mahogany staircase to the bar, took off their coats and found a cosy sofa in the corner of the room.

'I'm not sure if I should have a drink.'

Sophia's eyes widened. 'Our Willy hasn't got you pregnant has he?'

'No!' Rachel laughed nervously, putting the scare to the back of her mind. 'It's just I have a bit of a hangover.'

'Being in *The Emerald Rooms* without alcohol is like being in hell without having sinned. I don't suppose poor Willy has had the chance to get you pregnant has he? How many days has he been in London this year? I mean we never see him anymore. He's up and down like a yo-yo. Wouldn't surprise me if he has citizenship somewhere else!'

'He comes down for a couple of nights here and there.' Rachel said, but truthfully he she had not seen much of him at all.

'You've done well to put up with his baggage for so long.'

'This has got to be the worst seat in the bar. Let's move over there,' Rachel said, trying to change the subject. She stood up and pointed to the armchairs by the large window. Sophia always had to say something to make her feel insecure about her relationship. So what if William had been away a lot. At least she had a relationship. Men in London were hard to come by. William was a far better option than what Sophia had – sitting in *The Emerald Rooms* every night drinking her body weight in alcohol and doing a couple of lines. With William there was a chance to settle down once he had earned enough money to stop flying here, there and everywhere.

'No,' Sophia hissed. 'Trust me. You don't want to be sitting there.'

'Why not?'

'Here look our cosmos have arrived. Get this down you and I'll explain.'

Rachel sat down and took a sip of her drink. No doubt this was one of Sophia's usual games. Inevitably this would be about William. All Sophia ever did was talk about William. 'When are you moving in to his country house?' she would ask or 'has he taken you away again? Have you seen his house? The one in the country?' Sophia thought she knew all there was to know about him, but she was wrong. And the way she said 'our Willy,' made Rachel want to slap her across her haggard face. As far as she could tell Sophia was full of shit. Just an attention seeker wanting to create drama wherever she went. Sophia had almost guaranteed her that William would never take her away with him and that he would never show her the inside of his country house. Well ha! She had done both on more than one occasion. And she had moved into his flat in London. But she had to admit he wasn't around much anymore, and things between them had not been so certain of late. The bloody pregnancy scare hadn't helped, and after their awkward meeting with Bonnie things definitely seemed to have cooled.

*

She had been late. Eleven days late to be exact and she had missed a couple of pills so it wasn't completely impossible to be pregnant. In fact, a quick search on Google told her it was highly likely. She wasn't worried about it. A baby on the way excited her, but she should have taken a test before she blurted out her suspicions to William. He had been distant with her for some time now, cancelling dates at the last minute without a decent excuse. She could feel him losing interest and at he back of her mind she wondered if a baby in their lives would draw him back in. How wrong she was.

'I think I'm pregnant,' she blurted out in between courses at William's favourite fish restaurant.

Instead of the joyful look she expected, William's face turned ashen. 'What?'

'I said…'

'I know what you said. You also said you were on the pill.'

'Nothing is fail-safe.'

'Well you can't keep it.'

'What?'

'It's not up for discussion.'

Rachel held her tears back. 'Why?'

William took the napkin off his lap, scrunched it into a ball and threw it on the table just as the waiter came over with two plates. William put his hand out to stop the waiter. 'We're done here, Victor. Put it on my tab, we're leaving.' Then he stood up and started walking out of the restaurant.

Rachel could feel the eyes of the other diners on her, but she didn't dare turn around. It was the first time she had seen this side of William. She managed a polite smile for the waiter after which she stood up and followed her lover out. He hailed a taxi and was gone. The next day her period arrived.

The way William had reacted to her faux pregnancy was just so out of character, she knew there had to be something at the root of it. Had he previously lost a child with another woman? Or did he just not want to have children? Some men were like that. A text telling him that she wasn't pregnant after all had smoothed things over. Just. But their relationship didn't feel the same and then they had bumped into Bonnie the last time they were out, and that had certainly set alarm bells ringing.

It had been a casual encounter outside the juice bar on Marylebone High Street and Rachel was pleased to see a friend whom she had not seen in ages, but when she introduced her to William a strange look had passed between them. Was it a look of familiarity; had there been a history between them like there had been with Sophia, or was it something else? Whatever it was it had set her on edge. She couldn't compete with Bonnie's lustrous brown hair and ethereal good looks. She had been so rattled by the meeting that she had tried to ask

William about her, but he would not entertain any discussions on the matter, claiming he had only heard of her in passing. She was almost certain that she did not believe him.

Was this acceptable behaviour? Did William love her like he claimed or was he in love with someone else, someone as stunning as Bonnie? The usual signs were there – the new clothes, the heavy aftershave, the late night calls. She could drive herself insane with these questions or she could forget about them. Worrying was pointless. So she decided on the latter.

*

'Go on then,' Rachel said to Sophia draining her first cosmopolitan. 'Every time you're about to tell me something you stop. Just tell me why we can't go and sit over there.'

'You see those two women. The blond and the one with the short black hair,' Sophia pointed to the sofas by the large Georgian window.

'Those two so wrapped up in themselves they're unaware of anyone else's presence?'

Sophia smiled. 'Well that one over there,' she said, pointing, 'that one is William's wife.'

37

20th November 2011
Mayfair, London

'Come in.'

Celeste heard the familiar voice and smiled. She opened the door and saw Maryanne sitting on her gold throne, her signature fuchsia carpet underfoot.

'It's been a while darlin',' Maryanne said, rising to her feet.

'Oh, don't get up.'

Maryanne waved Celeste's comment away. 'Look at me, as fit as ever.'

'That you are.' They embraced but Maryanne didn't look fit; she looked tired. Her eyes were sunken and her skin sagged.

When they each had a cup of tea and the pleasantries were over Maryanne asked the inevitable. 'What's this I hear about *Cross* Hong Kong?'

'I was hoping you'd tell me.'

'Bah! Harris tells me nothing these days. I should expect that though. I'm only here in name. When I sold the majority share I made it a condition that I could come into the office daily, but they have no obligation to ask for my opinion or even take it when I offer it – which I often do.'

Celeste looked at her one-time boss. This was as good a time as any to ask her what she wanted to know. 'Why did you do it, Maryanne? Why did you sell the majority share in *Cross*?'

'I had my reasons, darlin.'

'Tell me.'

Maryanne hesitated. 'A man like Harris can keep the name of *Cross* alive for years. An old woman like me can't.'

'You created *Cross*.'

'And it cannot die with me, kid. When you've a child you'll know. You have to set them free eventually. It's the same with *Cross*.'

Celeste pressed her lips together. Maryanne was putting on a brave face, but it wasn't just *Cross* Hong Kong that was suffering. It sounded like Harris was soon going to get rid of *Cross* altogether – the rich kid had gotten bored of his latest toy, and Maryanne wasn't stupid. She knew what was happening.

'I've heard that Harris is considering closing down *Cross* Hong Kong? They want to make cuts to my design team.'

Maryanne nodded. 'I hear it's not going as well as planned.'

'I thought you'd know more. They don't share their finances with a mere designer like me.'

'I'm surprised.'

'Why?'

'Oh nothing, kid. But you've got more respect in this company than I have. I guess we'll have to wait and see what happens. If I hear anything you'll be the first to know. I owe you that.'

'Owe me? You've done enough for me.'

Maryanne waved the comment away with her hand. 'And darlin' how are you finding life in Hong Kong?'

'One big party.' Celeste thought about the night before she left the city. One of Alex's acquaintances had invited them to a new fusion restaurant. They were supposed to leave by midnight but had stayed until three, drinking bellinis and eating cerviche. She had thought that London would have been a break from the sleeping at dawn lifestyle, but last night had turned into quite an event in itself.

One minute she was having a conversation with Angela and the next a woman was accosting her, accusing her of being married to a chap called William. After a bottle of champagne it had taken Celeste a good few minutes to figure out that William and Bill were one and the same. Of course it was the same name. By a stroke of luck, the drunken woman had mistaken Celeste for Angela and chose a convenient time when Angela was in the bathroom to have her outburst. How many women had Bill been sleeping with? She had told Alex when he had called her last night, and they had laughed together. Clearly Bill was a pro at this cheating game, using his full name like that. Celeste couldn't help but smile at the memory. Alicia was welcome to him.

The blond haired creature had attacked Celeste, shouting abuse at her, and Celeste hoped that Angela would return from the bathroom to hear what the girl had to say. At least that way she would know what her husband was up to – in the unlikely event that she didn't know already. But before Angela could return, *The Emerald Rooms*' front of house was charging up the mahogany stairs, two at a time, commanding two waiters to escort the woman off the premises. Angela returned to her seat seconds later and none the wiser. Celeste could see why Bill chose *The Emerald Rooms* as his club of choice.

'The Hong Kong lifestyle can be a little hectic,' Maryanne said. 'When I first met you, you were so young and naïve. Now look at you – Diamonds and *Dior*. Your friends must be envious.'

'Apparently we're the glitterati of the Mid-Levels, or so they say. I have to keep pinching myself to check it's real.' Celeste raised a smile. She enjoyed the champagne lifestyle, but now she was back in London the sheen had come off the superficial luxe. 'Maryanne, can I ask you something?'

'Anything.'

'Tell me the real reason as to why you sold *Cross* to Harris?'

'I just told you.'

'Don't you trust me?'

'Celeste, at some point in your life you'll look back and wish you'd made some different choices. I often think like that when it comes to *Cross*. Sometimes I think it was better to go under than to sell to that man.' Maryanne looked away from Celeste. She hesitated. 'But we have to stick by the decisions we make. It was my time to step down.'

'But I… You never even offered me any shares in *Cross*. I could have afforded it,' she said, although it probably wasn't true. Alex and she were not even married back then and Alex had always thought *Cross* was a dying brand.

'Let's just say I needed the money more than I needed *Cross*.' Maryanne put her hand in the air to stop the conversation. 'Let's not talk about it any more.'

Celeste opened her mouth and then closed it. She could tell by Maryanne's rheumy eyes that whatever it was that made her sell out, it must have been a hard decision.

'Before you go, kid,' Maryanne said, opening her desk drawer. I want you to have this.' She took out a fuchsia pouch and handed it to Celeste. Celeste noticed just how frail Maryanne's hands were. Dark veins shone though her almost translucent skin. She placed her hand on Maryanne's and squeezed it before she took the package. Peering inside the pink pouch she took out a long gold necklace with the bumblebee pendant. 'It's beautiful.'

'The bee reminds us to be hard working. It's a small insect but it has great strength. Whenever you feel weak, darlin', and you don't know which path your life is taking, wear this pendant. It'll guide you.'

'Thank you. I'll remember that.' Maryanne had always been so good to her and so perceptive. Could Maryanne see that her time designing for *Cross* was coming to an end?

Maryanne leaned across the table and lifted Celeste's chin with her hand. 'And remember if a bumblebee ever feels under attack it has a nice sting in its tail. You're strong Celeste. Remember that. If anyone tries to put you down, you just remember my words.'

Celeste couldn't help but smile.

38

Barnet, North London

'Is that the pendant you're wearing now?' Elaine asked.

Celeste clasped the bee in her hand. 'I've not taken it off since…'

Elaine waited but Celeste didn't continue. She smoothed her skirt and looked at her notes. 'I'd like to go back to my original question. Why did you do it?'

Celeste let go of the pendant. 'You wouldn't understand. I don't want you to get…' Celeste trailed off as her throat caught. She looked at the clock. 'I want to finish my story first. If that's okay with you? I can't see why it wouldn't be.'

Elaine nodded. 'Whatever you're comfortable with.'

'That was the last time I saw Maryanne. I was too blind to see through her smile that she was dying. The woman who had given me my chance in life was fading and I didn't know. I was too preoccupied with Alicia and Bill, or William or whatever he was calling himself. Maryanne died a month after my visit. I never even attended the funeral. Of course, it coincided with some Renshaw family emergency and Alex couldn't spare me. What a fool I was to place my utmost trust in that man. I found out later, much later, why she sold *Cross*. I had been so naïve, or as Alicia would have gently put it, I had been silly. Very silly indeed.'

'So why did Maryanne sell? How did you find out?'

'Before she died she wrote me a letter. A letter Alex kept hidden from me, but strangely he never destroyed it. That surprises me. He should have known better than to keep something like that.'

'Maybe Alex didn't know what the letter said.'

'Oh he knew. It had been opened. It told me everything I needed to know.' Celeste met Elaine's gaze. She had said enough for now. The contents of the letter could wait. 'Being in London at that time was no good for me.' She looked into the distance. The sun rising, dawn breaking. 'I never wore that bumblebee until…it wasn't bling enough for me back then. If it had been encrusted with diamonds, then maybe I would have.'

Elaine smiled.

Celeste noticed that her smile was crooked. Just slightly, but now after all these hours sitting in front her, looking at her face, her kinked smile became obvious. She wondered if Elaine knew she had a wonky smile. Did she obsess over it, like Celeste obsessed over her minor flaws? *Obsess*, the word made her think of Alex. No Mother, I am not obsessed.

'Well at least you didn't throw the bumblebee out. And you have it now. There's a reason for that.'

'I hid it in a drawer and went for it on that terrible day. I pulled off a fine, white-gold chain I was wearing. It felt good at the time to get rid of the necklace Alex had given me. Like I was removing a noose around my neck. Maryanne said it would give me strength. It did in the end.'

'Did you see Alicia on that trip?'

Celeste shook her head. 'I think I was self-destructing back then. Pushing away those closest to me.'

'You were hurting because she betrayed you. Not only that. She was sleeping with Bill. Someone you held close to your heart, despite his philandering.'

'Graham and Sarah came over one day, which was nice. Warwick had told them I was alone in London. Alex would never have wanted his brother to visit me on my own in case I said something I shouldn't about *Renshaw*. It was stupid of him, but then back then I didn't realise just how much he had to hide. It wasn't often that I saw Graham and Sarah without Alex. We shared a bottle of Rioja and talked about the good old days. The fabulous Sunday lunches Warwick used to host. Graham was concerned about Alex. He never said it but I could tell from his questions – was Alex enjoying what he was doing? Was he away much? Did he seem stressed? How was I coping with Alex? He made him sound like he had an attention deficit disorder! Alex hated me talking about him, especially to his brother, so each time he broached the subject I moved the conversation along.'

'And did you meet your parents when you were in London in 2011?'

'That was the one good thing about my trip.'

'Did you see them at home in London or in Bristol?'

'London.'

'Tell me about the time you spent with them.'

'Nothing to tell. They stayed for a couple of nights. We ate out, watched movies. I bought them new clothes from designers they had never heard of. It was nice showing my mum images of my new designs. She was always so proud of my creative side. Whenever there was a *Cross* advert in a magazine she would cut it out and ask me if it was one of mine. She has a scrapbook of my designs, some really old designs too – like the ones I did in university. It was nice spending time with mum. Dad was his usual self, but they were worried about me. Even back then – perhaps they could see the storm coming. And as usual they told me I had lost weight and that I needed to eat more. Dad fussed that the food in Hong Kong was too foreign, which he thought was the reason why I had gone down a dress size. That sort of thing.'

'And did you meet Bonnie and make up with her like you said you would?'

'You know 2011 was the same year that I saw Bonnie in Hong Kong. Well, I thought I did. I was sure I caught a glimpse of her in the *IFC Mall* in the *Mont Blanc* store. I was a fair distance away and by the time I got to the shop she had gone. I looked around in all the nearby shops, but she wasn't there. Alex said I was imagining things.' Celeste took a breath. 'But to answer your question, I called her, yes.'

'And?'

'She was cold, aloof. I guessed too much time had passed between us. The damage to our friendship had been done. In university Alicia, Bonnie and I were inseparable, like sisters. When we did have time apart, we always managed to pick up where we left off. I expected some awkwardness, but I received hostility. She was surprised to hear from me. We made small talk, but she had this wall up. I assumed she didn't want me to attack her again, but…' Celeste's shoulders dropped. Tears began to stain her cheeks.

Elaine handed her a tissue.

Part III

39

Barnet, North London

'Feel better?'

Celeste nodded. She looked at the clock again. Time was running out.

'In 2011, how did you feel about Alex?'

'I still loved Alex despite his increasingly long absences. But the distance had grown between us, I couldn't deny that. Alex was away much of the time and when he was in Hong Kong Bill was around. He spent more time on that boat with Bill than with me. It wasn't just Alex going away that upset me. Evenings would be spent entertaining associates or he would be working late. I picked fights with him about it. It didn't help matters.'

'How did Alex respond when you questioned his late nights?'

'He always told me where he was beforehand so I couldn't complain. Always had his brother, dad or some other businessman as an excuse. Of course, I would never check, but he was so confident I didn't have any cause to mistrust him.'

'Did you ever bring it up with him?'

Celeste nodded.

'And how did he make you feel?'

'This big,' Celeste said, holding her thumb and index finger less than an inch apart. 'But sometimes he made me feel like I was a million dollars. He'd put his arms around me and tell me how much he loved me, bought me gifts, paid for spa treatments. He sent Kealana round to check on me when he was out of town. I didn't like her then, but it was sweet of him. Plus, he had reason to be working late and he made me see that. In the middle of the recession Alex was earning more than anyone I knew. I could have had caviar for breakfast and it wouldn't have made a jot of difference. I loved my life – the parties, the free flowing champagne. I knew that Alex had to put in the hours if we wanted to sustain that lifestyle. I'm not blameless in all of this. And living in the Mid-Levels, it was all about keeping up with appearances as well. I felt a terrible burden of expectation from our expat friends.'

'Go on.'

'Friends would say that our marriage was a fairy-tale. And I felt that was what we had to give them. We were so bloody convincing, I believed it myself.'

'The Pygmalion effect.'

Celeste raised her eyebrows.

'What you just described is a common phenomenon. That's what it's called, when you live up to someone else's expectations.'

'Hmm.'

'You just mentioned that sometimes Alex made you feel small. Tell me about that?'

'Insignificant is the correct term. I don't know. He'd laugh at me if I brought up the idea that he could be cheating. Told me he wasn't going to have this conversation again. Said I was just picking fights with him because my job was a waste of time.'

Elaine frowned.

'He didn't value my job at *Cross*. It didn't make any money. Not the kind of money Alex made, so he didn't respect that. He kept it hidden for a long time, but soon the snide comments about my work, my designs, would slip out of his mouth. He always knew more than I told him. I should have known then what he'd done.'

'And what had he done?'

Celeste shrugged.

'But you said that he would have been happier if you didn't work.'

'His control over me would have been total then.'

'Would you say that in 2011 Alex was not the man you married?'

'We had both changed. My head was in the sand. When I did find out what Alex had done, was doing…Well, we all know what happened then.'

'Tell me, Celeste.'

Celeste looked up at the ceiling. 'After that trip to London, when I returned to Hong Kong it was the beginning of the end for me. I should have seen it coming, but I didn't. Looking back on that time is painful for me.' She held the gold bumblebee tightly in her fist.

Elaine turned the page of her notebook and wrote something on a blank page. She looked at the clock. 'What happened?'

'I missed Alex. Even when he was around I was still lonely. I worked hard, but I also began drinking to fill the emptiness. I cried a lot.'

'How did Alex react?'

'He tried to appease me with words. He told me the kind of

pressure he was under to pull off this new venture in Shanghai. I felt guilty. He assured me that he would try and make time for our marriage. He was temperamental though. Sometimes he ran me a bath or cooked me dinner. Sometimes he bought my happiness with jewellery, or he would send Lada to the international store to get me marmite or something else from England that I missed. Perhaps he thought it was some sort of delayed homesickness. But more often than not he would just stay out late and come home drunk without an excuse. Sometimes he wouldn't even come home – instead he would stay with Bill. Bill would call and tell me that my husband had passed out on his sofa. That way at least I didn't have to sit up all night, worrying.

'I started to drink more and more. Then one day I thought to myself, I just can't do this anymore. I was about to confront him. I realised I was better off without him than being trapped in what had become a miserable marriage. But then something happened which made me think that things were going to change.'

'What happened?' Elaine asked. She looked up her pen poised.

'Alex took me back to Thailand.'

40

26th February 2012
Krabi, Thailand

Celeste sipped on her second Mai Tai as she lazed on the pool lounger. Alex walked up to her with the top two buttons of his shirt undone, his sunglasses on. She had rehearsed what she was going to say to him. Accuse him of not prioritising their relationship, let alone her. Surely, for their first holiday together in years *Renshaw* could have waited, but no, on the day of their flight out, Alex had called her to say that something had come up. He couldn't leave the office. Could she take the flight out and he would meet her a couple of days later? She had reluctantly agreed, but her anger had been bubbling ever since. But now, as he sat on the edge of her recliner, with that same cheeky grin that had first attracted her all those years ago, her heart melted. She play punched him on his arm and he leaned over to kiss her.

'Heaven isn't it?'

'We haven't done this since…'

'I know,' Alex said, holding his hands up. 'My fault. Let me make it up to you.'

She stood up and let her sarong slip to the floor. Then she plunged into the swimming pool. Surfacing, she said, 'If you mean it, put that off.' She pointed to the mobile phone in his hand.

Alex nodded and put the device back in his pocket.

She swam up to the edge of the pool. 'Did it go okay?'

'What?'

'Shanghai. The big emergency.'

Alex smiled. 'Oh that, yeah, completed yesterday. Left the rest to Warwick and whatever Graham can manage.'

'So you're winning?'

'I'm always winning, hon. But when we get back, work is going to be intense. This is one last fling!'

Celeste frowned. This wasn't going to be a last fling. This was the beginning. They were going to put the last few years behind them and be a proper couple once again. Weekends away, dinners just the two of them and perhaps even a trip to the cinema if that wasn't too much to ask. They would talk, tell each other how they really felt and just spend time together. Once Shanghai was sorted things would return to normal and that was imminent, Alex had said so himself. Thailand was the perfect place for them to get their marriage back on track. After all, Thailand was where they had met, and coming out here had been Alex's idea. She watched him as he disappeared past the palm trees to their whitewashed villa.

41

26th February 2012
Clapham, South West London

Rachel lay in bed watching a spider making its way to the window. She pulled the duvet over her head wondering how long she could stay under the covers without thinking of what had happened. It was impossible. She had no choice. Three months had passed and still the memory of that God-awful day was etched in her mind. How happy Sophia must have been to break the news to her and then leave her to her own demise.

What had she been thinking? How had she not seen that William was married? She had been to his country house in Staffordshire, yes. But her visits had been fleeting only accompanying him when he had to pick something or the other up. She had told Sophia that she had been in his house, and she had been, but it had been just the entrance. Neat and tidy – no trace of a wife or family. And of course, whilst she was staying in his London apartment he had another much larger property a few streets away, a property his wife knew about. The apartment she stayed in was just for her. She didn't want to think about how many other women he had brought back to that flat. What a sick bastard, she thought, even though she still loved him.

She had heard of girls who spent a lifetime as a mistress. They usually got a holiday in the sun once a year, and the occasional weekend here and there. Never Christmas. Definitely late night booty calls and jewellery. Jewellery was always part of the deal. She looked back on her time with William – the designer handbags, expensive meals and yes, late night calls. How had she not seen it before? Now she knew what Sophia meant when she showed admiration for Rachel for putting up with his baggage. Well, she wasn't going to be a mistress all her life. She shook her head. No she wasn't.

It was Sophia's fault. The stupid bitch had known about William's wife all along but hadn't said anything. She thought it was curious, the first time she was introduced to William, when Sophia had double-checked his name. It must have been a secret code between them. Of course Sophia had known about his wife. She knew every sordid little secret of *The Emerald Rooms*' members. No wonder they were all so nice to her. It must have been bloody good entertainment for her over the years. Would William have ever told her? Maybe he wouldn't have, keeping her dangling for years until she was well and truly trapped in his web.

Fragments of that whole sorry episode came to her. Sophia had plied her with drink after casually pointing out William's wife.

'That's your lover's wife. She calls him Bill.' Sophia said, as casually as picking her dinner from a menu. Rachel hadn't quite caught it the first time. By the time it had sunk in, Sophia had ordered a vodka martini and a shot of something thick and syrupy and encouraged Rachel to down them both, promising her it would take the edge off. 'It's either that or coke darling, and I'm all out.'

As her vision blurred, Sophia promptly left *The Emerald Rooms* for the evening. Of course she didn't want to stay for the fall out and tarnish herself with the same brush. She would rather hear what had happened the following afternoon from the bar men and the usual gossips – their lives so empty they had to laugh at other people's misery.

Rachel remembered approaching the woman, telling her that she was in love with William and that they were going to be married. What had she been thinking? Before she knew what was happening, two staff were showing her the door. They had known! That part had stung the most. The waiters, the security, every employee and probably every member of *The Emerald Rooms* knew that William was married and no one had had the decency to tell her.

What must they have thought of her, following William around, telling everyone she was his girlfriend? How smug she had been. She must have been the butt of all their jokes. And to think she had believed that he was her true love. She had told him he was the one! And he had let her believe it. What kind of man would do that?

She had tried calling him frantically as she stumbled to his apartment that night. No answer. His wife had got to him first. What would she have said? That she had been accosted in the club by a drunk claiming to be his lover. Would William admit his adultery? Would he tell her he was going to leave her? She could only imagine. But it was more than likely that he would deny all knowledge and the bar staff would back him. Why wouldn't they? The stupidly large tips he paid out now made sense.

After a week with still no contact from William, Rachel had

started to worry. Had something happened? She had asked the doorman at his apartment block, but when that didn't prove fruitful she knew she would have to go back to *The Emerald Rooms* as Sophia had predicted. She was refused entry and walked home cloaked in humiliation. A humiliation, which was only deepened when she returned later to their apartment to find that the locks had been changed and her possessions boxed up and waiting for her outside the front door.

Rachel's hands had felt numb as they reached for the hand-scribbled note stuck to one of the boxes, tears pricking the back of her eyes. 'Sorry' was all it said. No explanation, no excuse. Nothing. It wasn't even signed by William. But she knew his hand, the same way she knew that he liked a brandy nightcap before bed, plenty of water in the morning – usually to combat his hangover – and his eggs sunny side up. She thought she knew everything about him. Everything, except that he had a wife, and now she knew he had no heart either.

42

2nd March – 14th May 2012
Mid-Levels, Central and Western District, Hong Kong

'Why didn't you tell Lada to get some food in? It's late and I'm bloody hungry,' Alex said, as they opened the front door to their apartment. It was as if he had transformed somewhere over the South China Sea. She had tried with him, she really had, but with every kind gesture, Alex made it his mission to put her down. He had done nothing but snap at her from the time they landed at Chek Lap Kok and she had spent the entire journey home looking out of the taxi window as rain washed Hong Kong's dusty streets, sending hawkers running for cover and blurring the city lights.

'It's her day off,' Celeste muttered trying not to lose her patience.

'Day off? The day we land. You don't know how to run a house.' Alex took his phone out of his pocket. 'You could have asked Charlie. What's the point of having staff if you don't use them?'

She took a step back and dropped her case at the door. She had a headache. She wanted to leave Alex to call Kealana and retreat to the bedroom, but she had promised that she was going to make more of an effort. They both had to try if they wanted their marriage to work. Alex wasn't making it easy though. What had happened to the man who, only a couple of days ago, had held her hand as they climbed up to the temple in the Tiger Caves and had massaged her aching legs later that evening?

'We can manage. I'll make something.'

'You can't bloody cook!'

Celeste took a deep breath. 'Delivery?'

Alex opened his mouth to say something, but the phone in his hand rang. He answered it and walked down to his office. Celeste breathed a sigh of relief and retrieved the folder of takeaway menus that Alex had, typically, filed alphabetically. She wondered if she too was now just one of his possessions that had a fixed place in his life. She studied the menus. Alex would want roast duck and rice, and vegetables of some sort. She would have normally just ordered for him without hesitation, but these days he was difficult to read, and the last thing she wanted was to get the order wrong. He would just snap at her again.

She left the folder on the table in the lounge and made her way up to their bedroom with a glass of water. She wanted to be angry with him. Was it the pressures of work that had put him in a foul mood or was she just making excuses for his awful behaviour? Warwick had called as they were waiting for their luggage. She hadn't heard what had been said and Alex had walked away from her when he saw that she was trying to listen in. He told her that it had something to do with Shanghai. He had cursed himself for taking the time off, and she knew by the way he looked at her with his steely blue eyes that he blamed her. She wanted to point out that Thailand had been his idea, but she bit her tongue. Instead, she let him complain, like a broken record, about Graham and his inefficiencies.

*

The next morning she woke to find that Alex had already left. She had slept so soundly she wasn't even sure if he had slept next to her that night, let alone eaten. She dragged herself to *Cross* at Causeway Bay and threw herself into her work.

'Get me Mr Harris,' she said to Jinny as she walked in through the office. For months now there had been rumours that *Cross* Hong Kong was going to be closing its doors, and that her team was going to be one of the first to be cut. Her staff were worried and Toby was being as vague as ever. If she didn't get to the bottom of this soon she could lose some of her best designers. She drummed her fingers on her desk. Jinny and Mo Li were the best she had. She was lucky she had hung on to them for so long.

'I have Toby Cain,' Jinny said. Celeste rolled her eyes, but took the call and put her questions to Toby.

He avoided answering them in that snake-like manner, which he no doubt must have picked up from Harris over the years. She put the phone down and scrunched her face. She had to tell her staff something. So she gathered them and told a half-truth. *Cross* was doing better, and if they continued to make steady progress then they would continue trading. She needed a hundred and ten per cent from everyone and they would review the future of *Cross* Hong Kong after the next collection. It seemed to work. Jinny and Mo Li left her office somewhat happier, but she knew they would still be looking for similar positions coming up with other designers and she couldn't blame them.

Celeste was going to lead by example. She rekindled her old relationships with merchandisers in Italy and managed to get some rare pieces for their autumn collection. She ensured weekly design meetings were attended by all staff – no excuses. And though she had been working long hours she had kept her promise to make things work with Alex. But it had been difficult. He wasn't around much, his promise to leave Shanghai alone once the branch was set up turned out to be an empty one. Most of his time was spent either there or in London. And lately she felt anxious, a feeling that she couldn't shake. At night she worried if Alex was safe, irrationally thinking about car accidents and emergency rooms; she worried whether her designs were good enough for *Cross* and she worried about her health that seemed to be deteriorating. She hadn't been feeling well for some time now and seemed to pick up a cold every other week. She needed Alex with her. She wanted to tell him that the travelling had to stop if they were going to make it work, but she could never find the right moment or find the courage to initiate the conversation. It wasn't until Lada had announced that she had saved enough money to go back home to the Philippines, and Kealana had moved in, whist she tried to find them a replacement maid, that she was pushed to say something.

'You're not eating much?' Kealana said to Celeste one day when she was helping tidy away after lunch.

Celeste smiled without responding. The woman got on her nerves, commenting on every little thing she did or didn't do.

'Everything okay?' Kealana asked with that butter-wouldn't-melt look.

'It's fine.' It was a lie. She felt nauseous. She hadn't felt right since Kealana had moved in. The very presence of the woman was making her feel ill. She had never liked her and now she was growing suspicious of her.

She hated the way Kealana watched her every move, constantly asking her if she was all right and refusing to take time off when Alex wasn't around. She had even started cooking for her. 'You can't eat takeaway all the time. I will cook,' she had said and ever since then there was a meal waiting for her no matter what time Celeste returned home from work. The food had been good, tasty and nutritious, but there was something about Kealana's manner that put her on edge. Kealana disliked her, she knew that, and only yesterday she had seen a movie where a man was slowly poisoning his wife's food with selenium, which had made her think. Her nauseous feeling had only arrived when Kealana had, and the woman insisted on cooking for her. Having no girlfriends that she could trust, she confided in Alex the next time she spoke to him.

Of course he had laughed at her. She had expected that. 'Why would Kealana want you dead?'

'I don't know. She loves you Renshaws. Maybe she doesn't think I'm good enough for Mr Alex.'

'You're being a hysterical.'

'Maybe if you were here more often things would be better between us and she wouldn't see the need to bump me off. She probably thinks I'm ruining your life.'

'Is that what this is about? You know why I work. You want to give up your diamonds?' he said, looking at her engagement ring.

'I don't –' she tried. She wanted to say that she didn't care about diamonds. She would give it up in a heartbeat to have their relationship back to how it had been in the beginning, but Alex interrupted her.

‘Do you know how ridiculous this sounds? Look, if you’re worried, go and see Dr Asthall. It’s a small private clinic, so it won’t go any further than that. We would need discretion for something like this. You can’t go around accusing people.’

Alex had made her feel foolish, but her anxiety ensured that she made an appointment almost straight away. She saw Kealana in the doorway as she put the phone down. Her heart leapt. How long had the woman been standing there?

Two hours later Kealana brought Celeste a cup of lemon and ginger tea. ‘You’re not eating and you feel nauseous. I don’t want to speak out of turn, but could you be pregnant?’

Celeste gave the woman a cold stare as her stomach turned. She couldn’t be, she was on the pill.

That evening as the eight o’clock symphony of lights at the harbour started, Celeste returned with a home pregnancy test. She peed on the test stick. In the two minutes it took for the result to show she wondered what it would be like to be a mother. She had agreed with Alex that children were not for them, but now she felt alive with the hope of a tiny being inside her. The persistent nausea suddenly didn’t seem to matter anymore. She bit her lower lip as she thought about Alex’s reaction to the news. Surely he would come round after the initial shock. He would tell Warwick that he was going to stop travelling so much, like Graham had done. A smile formed on her lips. Their relationship would return to what it had been when they first met. They could be a real family. Yes, a baby would make everything right.

Celeste looked at the test result.

She checked it twice.

It was negative.

43

Barnet, North London

'You thought Kealana was trying to poison you?'

Celeste narrowed her eyes. 'I was paranoid, and I had reason to be. Okay, it was a stupid suggestion at the time. But maybe if I'd been more wary back then I could have saved…' She touched her wrists, her eyes glazed over.

'Saved?'

She could have done a lot of things back then but she didn't. She didn't want to live through any more could have, would have, should haves. Now everyone was offering their advice. 'Go for long walks,' her mother said when she complained of being unable to calm her mind. 'Meditate,' Elaine had said previously. She was tired of listening. She knew what she had to do to put her mind at rest – to stop the nightmares and the pain.

It's not healthy to think that way. Of course it wasn't, she knew that. But sometimes you couldn't stop those thoughts. He had clearly thought that way, and no one had stopped him.

'Did you think Alex had something to do with the way you were feeling? Or did you only suspect Kealana?'

Celeste looked up at Elaine and then she returned her gaze

to her hands, clasped together in her lap. 'I didn't think he wanted to cause me harm. We'd grown apart, but that was all. He reminded me of that when we were in Thailand.'

'You were close during that trip?'

She nodded.

'Kealana on the other hand, with her beady eyes always on me, I was sure that she was trying to cause me harm. She had been with the Renshaws since Alex was a kid. Alex was like a son to her. But ultimately it was a mistake going to the doctor. Well it was and it wasn't.'

'Did he find that you were being poisoned?'

Celeste looked at the clock. They were running out of time. And now she had started she needed to finish telling Elaine her story. She shook her head. 'I don't even think he tested me for that. He seemed to know straightway what was wrong. My husband was right, I was being reckless and he knew Dr Asthall so well he probably explained what I was thinking before I even saw him. But Dr Asthall did find something.'

'What did the he find?'

'Turns out those home pregnancy tests are not always accurate. He told me I was pregnant.'

44

17th May 2012
Mid-Levels, Central and Western District, Hong Kong

Celeste closed the door behind her and went straight to her bedroom, ignoring Kealana. She had tried calling Alex, but his phone kept going to voicemail. What the hell! He was attached to that phone, yet he never seemed to answer when she called. She could hear his usual responses resounding in her ears. 'I was in a meeting,' he would say, or 'I left my phone in another office.' Blah, blah, blah.

'I'm going now,' she heard Kealana say. 'Will you be okay?'

She rolled her eyes. 'Fine,' she shouted. 'Of course I'll bloody be okay you miserable wench,' she said under her breath.

'So, I'll be back after one week to check on things. The new maid, Ruby, arrives tomorrow. I wish I could be here but Warwick needs me at the office.'

Thank God. Celeste hoped he needed her in the London office. She walked through her bedroom door and peered down the stairs towards the front door of the apartment, making sure the woman was really leaving. 'Thanks for all your help,' she said, forcing the words from her mouth. 'You go and take care of Mr Renshaw.'

As the door clicked shut behind her she let out a sigh,

walked down to the kitchen, opened the fridge and peered in. Kealana had left two containers of food, but even though her mad notion of being poisoned had been put to bed by Dr Asthall she didn't fancy Kealana's cooking. You could never be too sure. Apart from the two containers, there was a half finished bottle of *Veuve Clicquot* and a whole Camembert. Celeste held the cheese it up to her nose, sniffed it and then put it in the bin. When was the last time she and Alex had eaten together at home, something home cooked? It was always instant noodles or takeout. She looked at the champagne and touched her belly.

Closing the fridge she rooted around in the cupboards and found a packet of crisps, which she took to the lounge to eat on the sofa. Her size eight figure would soon disappear and that made her smile – no more fad diets, no more denying herself chocolate, she should even stop dying her hair black. She had heard that it was unhealthy if you were pregnant. Anyway, she was tired of the jet-black cropped hair that Alex loved, but was never there to see anymore. Instead she would go back to her natural brown hair and perhaps let it grow.

It hadn't taken her long to get used to the idea of having a baby – something she could nurture and love unconditionally. But every time she thought about Alex's reaction her fingers started to tingle. 'Too expensive,' Alex would say to friends when they asked the baby question. He would put his arm round her waist and say, 'I can just about afford Celeste.' He loved that line, but now it was all going to change.

She retrieved her phone from her pocket and pulled up a picture of Alex. She wanted to feel his hands on her belly, but given he was in Shanghai, it was highly unlikely. Instead she called up the application he had installed on her phone so she could track where he was in the world. She urged it to work this time. But it showed Alex in Hong Kong just a few blocks away. 'Stupid app,' she said, making a face and putting her phone away. It was no good even trying. She bit her lip. The longer she waited to tell Alex, the more nervous she felt. She tried to shake away the feeling. He was her husband, after all, despite the rocky patch they were going through. He may be apprehensive at first about the news, but he would come around. Wouldn't he?

*

Celeste woke with a start. She had fallen asleep on the sofa, the television was still on and the lights were bright. She checked her watch. It was three in the morning. She heard a key in the front door.

'Alex,' she said, as he stumbled through to the lounge.

'What?' Alex's blue eyes looked straight at her, as if he had caught her doing something she shouldn't have been. She felt like the guilty one although she had no reason to feel that way. 'I said not to wait up.' He put his keys on the console table and walked into the kitchen.

She followed him into the kitchen. He looked in a foul mood.

'You look tired. Why don't you go to bed?' he said.

'What time did your flight get in?' she caught a whiff of his alcohol laced breath and strong sandalwood cologne. 'Where've you been?'

'Nightcap.' He poured himself a glass of water. 'Went out for a few after my flight.'

'Bill?' She kept her tone steady, but it took some effort. She couldn't tell him her news when he was like this.

He shook his head. 'You have no idea how stressful my work is, do you? You like the money I earn, you just don't want to hear about my day.'

'I ask you all the time about your work. You never want to talk about it. I asked you a couple of weeks ago but you said it was boring and confidential. Said I wouldn't understand. I ask – you never let me in.'

'You're lucky you have a job.'

'What?'

Alex waved away her question with his hand. 'Forget it. You wouldn't understand.'

'Stop saying that. Try me.'

'Nah.'

'I never know what you are thinking. Tell me what do you do in Shanghai. Tell me what is so wrong with me that you go out with Bill as soon as you land. Remember when we first moved here, you couldn't wait to get off your flight and come home to me. We used to sit up chatting about our work, what we had missed in each other's lives whilst we were apart. We talked about our hopes and our dreams. You wanted a big house in the country with Great Danes and an *Aga*. I wanted my own design studio. What's happening to us? I've no idea what you want anymore.'

'Our hopes and dreams!' Alex let out a low laugh. Then he looked into the distance and his eyes glazed over. 'Is working at *Cross* a dream? Because it's over, or it will be soon.'

Celeste clenched her fist and thumped it on the counter. She turned and walked out of the kitchen. He was angling for a fight, but she wasn't going to bite.

45

18th May 2012
Mid-Levels, Central and Western District Hong Kong

'I'm sorry,' Alex said, waking up and turning towards Celeste. 'It was a bad day yesterday and I took my anger out on you. I went out with Bill because I needed to let off steam about some business associate we've both had bad dealings with.'

Celeste was silent.

'If it's any consolation, I feel like death.' He nuzzled her back.

She wanted to hate him, but she couldn't. Instead she pulled the sheets back and turned around to face him. She looked into his eyes, the same loving eyes that she had married, and pouted. 'You were horrible last night.'

'I shouldn't have taken it out on you.' He put his hand on her thigh. Let's call in sick and spend the day together. Dim sum lunch?'

She sat up in bed and kissed his bare shoulder. 'I'd love to but I can't let the team down. We have a meeting with the merchandisers that I don't want to leave to Jinny.

Alex sat up and poured the water from the carafe on his bedside table, into a tumbler and drank it. She watched him. Now was as good a time as any to tell him. She got up from the bed, padded over to her wardrobe and picked out a navy shirt-dress before returning back to the bed. 'I'm pregnant,' she said. Her eyes locked on his and she could see the shock in the brilliant blue.

'You're on the pill.' He looked at her bedside table and back at her. '*Where* are your pills?'

'I stopped keeping them in full view when we moved to Hong Kong and have had staff in the house. They've been in my bedside drawer since we moved here.' Celeste tried to keep her voice from shaking. 'I wouldn't go behind your back.'

'But you're pregnant? You're sure?'

'It happens,' she said, walking into the bathroom. Sadness displaced her anger. She had expected shock, not accusation. He was angry with her, she could feel the anger radiating off him. She took a deep breath to stop herself from bursting into tears and looked out through the bathroom window at the silhouettes of people in the apartments around her. They were all going about their daily routine, getting ready for the day's work. Their apartment was higher than most of the buildings surrounding them. It felt like she was always looking down on people – like a god watching mortal souls. Usually she felt lucky to be in this palatial apartment compared to her neighbours' tiny rooms, but today she was jealous. She wanted their normality where you worked hard for what you wanted in life. Life had other difficulties in store for you when your basic necessities in life were met.

Alex appeared behind her as she stripped her pyjamas from her body and turned the shower on. 'What do you mean, it happens?' he stared at her only slightly protruding naked belly. 'When did it happen?'

'Thailand. I'm nearly fifteen weeks.'

'And you didn't know? How could you not know?'

She ignored him and turned to face the back wall of the shower, letting the warm water wash her. Contraception was not 100% guaranteed, but she didn't want to admit to Alex that she had also become complacent with taking the pill everyday. She had forgotten countless pills over the years after drunken nights out but she had never had a pregnancy scare before, so she had stopped worrying about it.

How had she missed that she was pregnant though? She had to give him that. Her erratic pill taking had meant that her cycle was irregular. There had been no need to worry, not previously. But she should have been aware that her body was changing. Did that give Alex the right to be so cold? She had been naïve thinking a baby would solve their problems. It was only going to make things worse. She stood under the warm flow of the shower and let the water wash away her tears. When she turned to face Alex, he was no longer there.

46

Barnet, North London

'How did you feel when you realised Alex didn't want the baby?'

Angry. She had felt angry and sad. Sad because her one soulmate seemed a million miles away from her. Celeste played with her fingernails. How did she feel? That was all anyone ever wanted to know. It was a loaded question because she knew what they were trying to say was: are you at risk? Are you going to do something you're going to regret? She had enough regrets already. Another couple wouldn't hurt.

She supposed Elaine was different. Well, Elaine was different. In a way she had chosen Elaine and not the other way around. 'I could do with a smoke,' she said. 'I've never really smoked. Tried it once at university, but I never took to it. Afterwards though. After the… I don't know I wanted to smoke then. Its strange isn't it when your body craves something its never had before. I wonder what that means.'

'Perhaps it's a comforting smell. Did your parents smoke when you were little?'

'Yeah,' she said, somewhat impressed by Elaine. 'I think they did.'

'What happened after you told Alex about the baby?'

'That evening, after work, I came home tired and hungry. Alex was already in the lounge. I wondered if he had even made it out to work that day, but he had left the house before I did so he'd made it somewhere. The news of the baby must have shocked him. I remember that evening so clearly. He was wearing a blue shirt unbuttoned at the neck and dark grey suit trousers. He had a glass of whiskey in his hand. I wondered if he had been drinking all day.'

'What did you do?'

Celeste touched her lips. 'I went over to him and put my arms around him. He was as stiff as a bit of cardboard. Anyway, I hugged him. I wanted things to be right between us. More than that, I wanted him to want the baby, our baby. He didn't hug me back, instead he said, "Celeste, there's no room for a baby in our lives." I took a step back and looked at him. I looked at those unflinching, blue eyes when he told me. He meant it. Then he told me to abort it. He didn't say get rid of the baby, he said "abort it".'

Elaine shook her head.

'I wasn't sure what to do. Alex was the only person I had in Hong Kong. I didn't want to share my news with the expats just yet – they were not very baby friendly and would have probably agreed with him. Jackie had put both her children in boarding school and Melanie used a surrogate, not because she couldn't have children but because she didn't want to ruin her figure. After the birth of her baby she deposited it with a nanny. I couldn't call Alicia.'

'Why?'

'We still hadn't made up after I found out about her affair with Bill. It was stupid. I was holding a grudge unnecessarily.

Without Alex's support I was lost. I couldn't call my mother either. She's so sensitive. She would have hated Alex for even suggesting something like that and I didn't want to add that to the mix. I had no one I could trust, so I made the decision with Alex. I let him make the decision for me…for us. Although I knew then that we would never be kindred spirits again.

'The day we went to the clinic, there was a typhoon approaching. There was a yellow warning. I wanted to stay in, huddle up and cancel the appointment with the doctor, but Alex was adamant that we go. He didn't want to waste time. "You always said you didn't want children," he said to me in the taxi on the way to the clinic, like I had planned the whole thing. I just looked out of the steamed up taxi window. I wanted us to crash. He held my hand the entire ride there. He hadn't done that since Thailand. He never held it again after that day.'

'What happened at the clinic?'

'They asked us why we didn't want the baby. They weren't interested in the answers. It was just a check sheet they had to complete.' Celeste held the gold bumblebee in the palm of her hand. 'I was so weak back then. I think back to my youth and wonder how I went from someone who once got her belly button pierced after a night out to who I was that day at the clinic and I can't reconcile the two. At work I still appeared like some Amazonian woman who could make things happen, but inside I was crumbling, and with Alex I was always the weaker one. Always in his shadow. I thought if Alex didn't want this baby, and I had always said that I didn't want a baby, then it was only fair to go through with the abortion, even though I had changed my mind.'

'Do you think you were still trying to please Alex?'

Celeste nodded. 'And he was so bloody hard to please.'

'What happened?'

'Dr Asthall was laughing with Alex about something. They knew each other from the club at Repulse Bay. At first I didn't want to see someone Alex socialised with peering into my vagina, but Alex said he was the best. He was an obstetrician but expats went to him for all sorts of things because the clinic was private and the doctor was British.'

'He was the one you went to when you thought Kealana was trying to poison you?'

'Alex developed a mild stomach ulcer shortly after we arrived in Hong Kong. It was the reason I didn't attend Alicia's wedding, because Alex was in so much pain. Asthall treated him. He gave him something for it.' Celeste let out a sigh. 'Before we sat down, Alex shook my shoulder and said, 'I hope you haven't been drinking.' He said that not looking at me, but at Dr Asthall. It was crazy. He wanted me to have an abortion and he was worried that I had been drinking. At the time I wondered why he would say something like that. For the record, I never touched a drop of alcohol after finding out about the baby and Alex knew that. I should have known then what he was doing.'

Elaine pushed a curl of hair behind her ear. 'Some men have the desire to control everything their partner does.'

'I was nervous, I kept reminding myself that Alex knew best, but something inside me would not be still. I thought of my past, from where I had come. Even before Alex, I had got myself to London, made a career for myself and had travelled half way around the world. I think it was those memories that made me do what I did next.'

'And what was that, Celeste?'

'I stood up, said I'd made a terrible mistake and I wanted to keep the child. Alex's jaw dropped.' Celeste smiled. 'Asthall stood up and politely said he would give us some space. Alex tried to stop him from leaving with his usual intimidating look. He used to stare at people right between the eyes until they did what he said. But Dr Asthall left us to it.'

Celeste dropped the bee from her hand and let it swing by her waist. 'We agreed,' Alex said, trying his menacing look on me. A look I was well accustomed to, along with his 'this is not what we want' statements. I averted my eyes, couldn't look at him. I knew I'd submit if I looked at him. So I didn't. I kept my eyes on a silver pen on the doctor's desk. "I want this baby, Alex. Don't take this away from me," I said.'

'How did he react?'

'He put one hand on my knee and then gently touched my chin with the other pulling my face up to his. When I eventually met his gaze I saw a man I didn't recognize, but his words were kind. "Okay," he said. "If that's what you want." I sighed with relief. I thought my nightmare was over.'

'And was it?'

'It had only just begun.'

47

29th – 30th July 2012
Mid-Levels, Central and Western District, Hong Kong

Celeste hadn't felt right in days. She clutched her belly and buried herself further under the duvet.

'It's been two months now. You should go back to the doctor.' Alex moved the damp strands of hair from her face. 'Want a cool towel for your face?'

She shook her head. 'Call Jinny again and say I won't be in. I'll be back at work next week.'

'Jesus, Celeste. Take it easy. You're still running around with *Cross* – Jinny and what's the other one's name?'

'Mo Li.'

'They're doing fine. Jinny is your right hand woman and Mo Li is almost a manager.'

'Did I tell you that?'

'What? How would I know if you hadn't told me?' Alex said, walking towards the back of their room.

'Well you seem to know everything that happens there without me telling you?'

'Are you making this about us again?'

Celeste rubbed her forehead. She couldn't do this now, not when she felt so miserable.

'Oh, I meant to ask. Did Maryanne try contacting you before she died? Send an email or anything?'

Celeste frowned. 'No. Why?'

Alex shrugged. 'Rumour has it that the days for *Cross* Hong Kong are numbered. You should think about handing in your notice.'

'I could take some time off.'

'Severe morning sickness doesn't sound like a walk in the park. Asthall said the symptoms may ease in a month or so, but why have the worry of work as well? Take the time off. Work on the nursery.' Alex adjusted his tie and reached for his cufflinks on the dresser.

'You've spoken to Asthall, again?'

Alex was silent.

'I'll think about it.'

'Should I tell Jackie to pop round?'

'That'd be nice,' she said, although she had been messaging Jackie and Melanie yesterday, and they had made no offer to visit her. They were fair-weather friends. She didn't mind, she knew that from the start. 'New suit?' she asked Alex from the bed as he stood at the bedroom door.

He checked his phone and smiled at the screen before walking back to the bed and kissing Celeste on her forehead. 'Yes.'

'Something funny?' she asked, her interest piqued. He was always with his wretched phone.

'Just Warwick's wicked sense of humour.'

She wanted to ask what it was, interrogate him just a little more than usual, see if she could catch him out, but she didn't have the energy. She had a baby on the way and more pressing things to think about.

*

Celeste didn't have to worry about handing in her notice. The next morning she dragged herself into work and found a large brown envelope waiting for her on her desk. She read the letter as Jinny and Mo Li read theirs. *Cross* Hong Kong was not financially viable. It was closing down. They were redundant as of that morning. Her staff complained – Mo Li in particular was crushed – her eyes red raw from crying had left a lump in Celeste's throat. She had tried to comfort her, but Mo Li didn't want any sympathy and with a cold stare she had walked off. Celeste wished she had been prepared for the news. How dare Harris, or Toby Cain for that matter, not tell her before the rest of her staff? She would have warned her team if she had known. Her mind racing, she called Toby Cain. 'Why wasn't I told about this before the rest of the team?' she demanded. What were their rights, she wanted to know, but her questions were met with the vague answers she had come to expect. She could ask Alex for help, but she new that wouldn't go down well. He never had anything good to say about *Cross*. And why had he asked if Maryanne had tried to contact her before she died? What did Alex care? He never even liked her. Although now she thought about it, it was odd that Maryanne had not made any contact with her in those final months. It was typical of Maryanne, keeping her problems to herself for as long as she could bear.

She touched her baby bump and decided to go home as Jinny and the others made their way to a bar in Wan Chai to drown their sorrows.

*

'I gave that company the best years of my life,' Celeste complained to Alex later that day. 'Maryanne would be turning in her grave right now,' she said, reading her redundancy letter for the fifteenth time.

'Maryanne got out whilst she still could. She got a large payment for a company that was never going anywhere.'

'You don't care about this, do you?' she asked looking up.

'Course I care. But maybe it was for the better. You can spend time at home, making sure everything is in order for the new arrival. How is the new maid, Ruby? Has she settled? Doing what you ask?'

'She's fine,' Celeste said, running her finger over the *Cross* logo at the top of the letter.

'I don't know how to say this. So I'm just going to come out with it.'

'What?' Celeste said, her heart beating a little faster. She felt a kick in her belly and instinctively her hand went to it. 'What's the matter?'

'I need to go away for a couple of days. I hate leaving you in your condition, but I have no choice. It's business.'

'You've only just come back from China.'

'I have to go back there.'

'Graham isn't the only one with a family now. You've a baby on the way,' she said, refraining from reminding Alex that she wasn't well either. She didn't want to play the victim. Can't he go instead of you this one time? Your family put upon you constantly and if you let them carry on like this they'll keep taking advantage. I'm not putting up with this anymore. I'll speak to Warwick myself.'

'I've told you before, leave work to me. Don't ever call Warwick. He has enough going on without getting involved in our affairs.'

Celeste frowned.

'Look, I don't want to upset you. And I don't want you

getting into an argument with my dad, or my brother for that matter. Both of them are stubborn. Let me speak to them.' Alex walked over to the cabinet and poured himself a drink.

'So you won't go?' Celeste said with a half smile.

'This time I have to.' Alex checked his phone. 'It's my job. And it's your job to look after that.' Alex motioned to Celeste's baby bump.

She felt another kick. 'It's not a *that*. It's a baby. I don't think I've heard you use the word "baby" as yet. You do want this child, don't you? It's kicking, do you want to feel it?'

'I'll speak to my father about reducing my responsibilities when I get back. Don't go speaking to them yourself. I don't trust Graham. He can't do a job properly. Also,' Alex looked around the room, 'he's having some problems with Sarah. I didn't want to stress you with this, I don't think she's well.'

'Oh,' Celeste said, feeling a little guilty. 'What's the matter?' She walked up to him, took his hand and placed it on her belly.

'They're doing tests but…' Alex removed his hand. The baby wasn't kicking anymore.

She made a face. 'Graham's usually quite open about these things. I'm surprised he didn't tell me the last time we saw him.'

'Well, this is a little serious, that's why,' Alex said, leaving Celeste feeling wounded. 'So, don't speak to him. He's emotional about it and I can't have him making any more mistakes at work because someone has set him off.'

'I get it.'

'I promise I'll do less from now on,' he assured her before tapping on his phone and holding it to his face as he walked up the stairs towards their bedroom.

She followed him with her eyes until he was out of sight. A minute later he appeared back on the stairs holding the phone in one hand and his drink in the other. 'Oh, and I've asked Kealana to come stay whilst I am away. To keep an eye on you,' he said, before disappearing again.

48

4th August 2012
Mid-Levels, Central and Western District, Hong Kong

Celeste located the email application on her phone and tapped it with her index finger. Amidst the junk emails offering her fifty per cent off beauty products and hair salons, was an email from Alex. She opened it. *Delayed. Another couple of days. Hope you're feeling better. Xx.* She sighed. She was fed up with dubbed Korean soap operas, American chat shows and talking on the phone to her mother who was fussing about her unborn grandchild. She looked out of the window and made a face. Since Alex's departure, her sickness had subsided and today she felt she could manage a trip. Taking a taxi to the Peak was what she fancied. She couldn't sit trapped in their apartment till Alex decided to come home. But when she pulled back the curtains, the black sky outside and the specks of rain that had started to stain the window told her the typhoon they had predicted was on its way. The Peak would have to wait.

She put the television on and her mind began to drift as the weather report started. She had hoped Alex would have softened to the idea of a baby, making him a bit more affectionate in the process, but she had been sorely mistaken.

Since Thailand, when he promised her that he would work less, he had done just the opposite. He flew to Shanghai on a moment's, notice and his calls and texts had now turned into an occasional email. 'It's just you and me, little one,' she said to her unborn child.

She heard a key in the door and looked up.

'Hello,' Kealana said, stepping over the threshold, a brown bag full of groceries in her left arm, her laptop bag hanging off her right arm. 'You're looking well. Mr Alex told me your news.' She gave Celeste a satisfied smile.

'You were right,' Celeste said through clenched teeth.

Kealana waved her hand across her face. 'Sometimes you just know these things. You are happy, yes? Not long to go now.'

Celeste frowned. 'Of course.'

'And Mr Alex?'

'Couldn't be happier.' She picked up a magazine from the coffee table.

Kealana smiled and took the groceries into the kitchen.

Why didn't Alex listen to her when she said she could cope without the meddling Kealana? 'She is not meddling,' he had said, but that was only because she had never interfered in his affairs. 'She has had children herself. All grown up now and doing quite well. It'll be good if she's around to keep an eye on you. Warwick's out of town, he doesn't need her at the office.'

She had protested, but Alex ignored her pleas and eventually she had given in, flattered by his need to have someone to keep an eye on her. 'You're not feeling insecure are you?' she had asked whilst he was packing. Alex had grunted in response and she wondered why she ever bothered trying to talk to him when he was preparing for a trip. She put it down to his mild OCD – he hated the idea that his clothes could get creased in a suitcase. 'Let Ruby do that,' she had said, but he ignored her. He had left soon after that.

As she was fiddling with her phone, it rang. She answered it immediately, desperate to talk to someone.

'Celeste,' she heard through the receiver. 'Glad I got hold of you.'

'Graham?'

'I need to get hold of Alex.' His voice sounded panicked.

'Is everything okay? Is it Sarah?'

'Huh? No.'

'The kids?'

'What? No, no. They're fine. God no. It's about work.'

'Oh.'

'We need to get someone over to Shanghai ASAP. Alex needs to go this time. He may have been lying low recently with everything that's been going on, but this is urgent.'

'What?' Celeste said. Graham was the one who had taken a back seat at *Renshaw* as Alex had repeatedly told her. This was so typical of him, trying to weasel his way back in to the business with a fictitious emergency. She had to be careful – he was just trying to find out information on what her husband was doing. Alex had warned her of this.

'I really need to get hold of him. Do you know where he is?'

She bit her lower lip. He sounded genuine and if he was trying to get information out of her in Alex's absence why would he pretend that Alex wasn't in Shanghai? Graham probably didn't know. Warwick and Alex were always keeping things from him.

'You're mistaken. Alex is in Shanghai,' she said, after some hesitation. 'He didn't tell me the ins and outs of why he had to go, as usual, but he's definitely there.'

There was a silence on the other end of the line.

'Celeste, Alex isn't in Shanghai. You must have heard wrong.'

Celeste gritted her teeth. 'I think you are confused. Check with your father. He knows exactly what's been going on.' That would serve Graham right. His father would put him in his place.

'He doesn't know of Alex's whereabouts. Alex only tells us what he wants us to know. He's been very elusive of late.'

'I-I…err…' she stuttered. If Graham was trying to get information out of her, he wouldn't have spoken to Warwick. She knew Warwick thought very little of his eldest son, Alex had told her as much. But now she was having doubts.

She could hear the urgency in Graham's voice. She thought back to the last time she met him. Alex, Warwick and Graham had been discussing the lack of public trust in the banking industry and the recent insider trading scandal. She had to admit that most of it had gone over her head, but she remembered at the time being surprised when Graham seemed to know more about it and had the winning argument, which Warwick had even toasted. She had been impressed at the time but thought nothing more of it. Was Graham the more intelligent one? After all, she only had Alex's word for it that he wasn't. She had never witnessed Graham's apathy or neglect of his *Renshaw* duties, but Alex was quick to say just how lazy his brother was. Was Alex belittling Graham behind his back solely to make himself feel better?

Kealana brought out a cup of green tea for Celeste and then powered up her laptop on the dining room table. No doubt she was listening to her conversation and would repeat it to Alex as soon as possible. It wouldn't surprise her if she was going to email him this very minute. Alex had warned her not to speak to Graham. But what choice did she have? He had called her.

'Don't worry,' Graham said, as if he had suddenly remembered something. 'I've got my wires crossed. I shouldn't have worried you. Do you know any other numbers I can get hold of him on?'

'He emailed me earlier. Can you email him? His UK phone is on. The number ends in 38 do you have it?'

'Yes,'

'Try that one.'

'Thanks. Goodbye Celeste.'

'Wait, before you go,' Celeste took a breath. She glanced over at Kealana studying something on her laptop. She knew what she was about to ask went against Alex's instructions, but one of the brothers was lying and she needed to know who. 'How's Sarah? How's she feeling? Alex mentioned she's unwell.'

'Unwell?' The line was breaking up. 'Huh? Sarah? She's fine. She's with the kids at *Disney*.'

'Okay, that's good. She's recovered?'

'She's fine. Nothing to recover from. Anyway, I must go.'

Celeste said goodbye and disconnected, pulling her feet off the coffee table as Ruby came down the stairs with a duster. She watched Kealana for a couple of minutes tapping away on her computer then she pulled up the phone application to locate Alex. It was stuck in Scotland. She had meant to speak to Alex about the app not working before he left, but it had slipped her mind. Perhaps if she uninstalled it and re-installed it would work. But that sounded like an effort. Instead, she slipped her phone in her pocket and tried to deconstruct what Graham had said. Alex was not in Shanghai. He had not been doing much for *Renshaw* recently. Sarah was completely fine. Her heart sank. She knew what she had to do. Kealana started talking to Ruby, telling her how to dust the oppressive red chandelier that hung above the dining table. Celeste saw her chance. She got up from the sofa and slowly made her way down to Alex's study.

49

4th August 2012
Mid-Levels, Central and Western District, Hong Kong

Celeste closed the door to Alex's study and looked around the room she so rarely entered. It was a small room but everything had its place. There were two leather chairs, a computer, a desk and a filing cabinet in white lacquer. A clear-framed flat screen television was in the far left corner. She opened the first drawer of the filing cabinet and peered inside, then she looked in the second drawer. A couple of files were inside each drawer. She glanced at the file names but nothing stood out. She took a seat at Alex's desk and she switched on his computer, noticing how her hands trembled as she did so. She had only stepped into Alex's office a handful of times since they had moved in, even though there was no lock on the door, nothing to tell her to keep out.

'I've important stuff in there,' Alex had said to her once when she was looking for an envelope, stapler or something like that. 'You can't just go rummaging. If I lose any papers or if files get corrupted it could cost *Renshaw* millions. We deal with sensitive data. If you need anything just ask me.' She hadn't said anything at the time, but she supposed he was right. She knew part of it was his need to keep everything in order. After that, staying out of his office had become an unspoken rule.

Now she felt guilty for just sitting in his chair. If Alex knew she was in his office he wouldn't like it, she was sure of that. 'What would he do?' She asked herself. She didn't really want to find out. Celeste hoped Kealana wouldn't come looking for her. With any luck she would hear her footsteps as she descended the stairs. The conversation with Graham had startled her, left her with a gnawing feeling that Alex was perhaps keeping something from her.

'I'll laugh about this later,' she whispered to the large silver Buddha on Alex's desk. There were no pictures of her anywhere, but at least he had kept the lucky Buddha she had given him when they first arrived in Hong Kong. She pressed the space bar on the keyboard.

The computer whirred into life, asking for a password. She hadn't thought of that. She tried variations of her name and then tried a couple of names that she thought were special to Alex like Krabi and Renshaw. She even tried Kealana. Nothing worked. She tried substituting i's for number one, and e's for the number three. After seven attempts she was losing patience and was worried that the computer would lock her out, exposing her to Alex.

'You must eat something.'

Celeste spun round to see Kealana at the door. Shit. She hadn't heard her approaching or even opening the door for that matter.

Quickly, she hit control, alt, delete to lock the computer screen. Kealana smiled that knowing smile, making Celeste clench her teeth to stop herself from screaming at the woman. Instead she calmly stood up. 'You can never find something when you're looking for it, can you? I think I will have something to eat.'

'Good.'

'You rest. I'll get Ruby to make it for you.'

'I'll make it myself,' she said, slipping past Kealana and walking upstairs towards the kitchen.

50

4-5th August 2012

Mid-Levels, Central and Western District, Hong Kong

The conversation she had had with Graham played over and over in her mind as she ate a sandwich of ham and pickle. She picked up her phone and dialled Alex's number.

No answer.

She left a message and every ten minutes or so glanced at her phone, willing it to ring. Eventually, at two in the morning she went to bed, but she couldn't sleep. Her eyes stung, but her lids wouldn't close.

At dawn her phone rang. It was Alex.

'You called?' he said, as soon as she answered, his tone nonchalant.

'Did Graham get hold of you?'

'Yes.'

'Where are you Alex?'

Silence.

'I know you're not in Shanghai.'

Alex laughed. 'Where else would I be?'

'I spoke to Graham. He needed you there and you weren't.'

'Graham should've spoken to me first.'

'He couldn't get hold of you.'

'He's playing games, as usual. You know how it is between Graham and me.'

She rubbed her eyes. Alex was right. Graham had done this before, not long after they had returned from travelling. He had implied that Alex wasn't where he said he was when he was late for a family lunch. Alex had told her then that Graham was jealous because Warwick had more confidence in him. And Alex had been right. Their move to Hong Kong had proved just that. She felt her shoulders relax and the tightness in her chest begin to ease.

'I hate not being there, especially now that you are…'

'Pregnant.' She smiled, remembering her priorities.

'I'll see if I can get home soon, hon. Just promise me one thing?'

'What?'

'Ignore any calls from Graham.'

'He's your brother, Alex. I don't have any siblings but I know you can't just cut them out like that. Graham probably has his reasons.'

'Graham's spiteful and he's trying to poison your mind. God knows why! It's not good for your health to worry like this, so ignore him. You get what you see with me. You always have done. I told you about Bill and Alicia didn't I? I don't keep stuff from you.'

'Point taken,' she said, pacified by his concern. 'I miss you.'

'I have to get to a meeting.'

'Don't worry about me.' Celeste disconnected. Seconds later a picture message came through to her phone. It was of Alex standing outside a skyscraper. She tilted her phone and looked at the steel and concrete structure from several angles.

Celeste bit her lip. Could she believe him? The photo could

have been taken in Shanghai. But it also could be Hong Kong or even London. It could have been taken months ago. Nevertheless, she hadn't asked for a photo but Alex had sent her one. Was he trying to hide something or was she worrying unnecessarily? Pregnancy certainly was making her paranoid. First she had thought Kealana was trying to poison her and now this, she had to get a grip.

What would Alex say when Kealana blabbed about her being in his office? She hoped he wouldn't mind. After all, Alex said he had nothing to hide.

*

Celeste took a long bath listening to her iPod to blank out the noise from Ruby unloading the dishwasher. For the first time in days she felt alive. The dull ache in her abdomen had subsided and the sick feeling had completely disappeared. There were times over the last few months when she felt like she didn't want the baby because she felt so ill, but today she felt good, excited for the new arrival. She dressed and walked down to the sitting room. Without work to worry about, she needed something to busy her mind. She decided to sketch. Yesterday, when she had been in Alex's office, she had noticed a blank book and some pencils. She had been in there once, she could go in there again. Alex wouldn't mind her taking items he had probably bought for her. She asked Ruby to make her some porridge and went down to fetch her drawing supplies. But as she stepped into Alex's office, she noticed something was different.

Hearing a noise, she turned. It was Ruby, 'You wan jam or honey in you porridge?'

'Has Kealana been in here this morning? Did she come into this room when I was taking a bath?'

Ruby shrugged. 'Maybe. Bought flowers in lounge. You want me call her?'

The fresh lilies in the hall, of course. Celeste nodded, suddenly realizing what was different about the office. There was a bright orange post-it note on the bland white desk.

'Jam or honey?'

'Jam please.' She walked towards the note. Scribbled on the paper were four letters and two numbers. There was no mistaking the handwriting, the scratchy scrawl she had seen countless times on airline printouts and other paperwork. There was no doubt in her mind that the writing was Kealana's.

She waited for Ruby to leave, pressed the space bar on the computer and then sat motionless as it came into life. Eventually, with shaking hands she punched in the letters into the password box. When she had finished her finger hovered over the enter button. Was Kealana trying to trick her?

She could leave his office now with the pencils and the paper she was after, but she knew this was her chance. If there was any truth in what Graham had said this was the time to look. It wasn't just herself she had to think of now, she had a baby on the way and with Alex's erratic mood swings of late, she couldn't pass up the opportunity. She looked towards the door and saw Ruby hovering with her bowl of porridge.

'Shall I put it down for you, madam? It's hot.'

She nodded.

'You tired. Baby keeping you up?'

Instinctively, she touched the tender skin under her eyes. It felt bruised. Tired. Ruby's question reminded her of Sarah being unwell. And she remembered that Alex had lied about Graham's wife. Why?

She ran her fingers over the orange note. Celeste wouldn't have put it past Kealana to look over Alex's shoulder whilst he was at his computer, just so that she could steal a glance at his password. But, if Kealana hated her why would she help her in this way? Her fingers trembled. Was this a trick?

A feeling of guilt crept up on her, but she had the right to access her husband's computer, didn't she? *If files get corrupted it could cost* Renshaw *millions.*

Celeste buried her thoughts and hit 'Enter'.

51

5th August 2012
Mid-Levels, Central and Western District, Hong Kong

Upstairs, the sound of the vacuum cleaner drowned out Ruby's singing. Celeste looked at the picture of Alex's beloved *Maserati* on his desktop. Immediately, a message icon appeared in the bottom right hand corner of the screen. *Call me when you get back*, the message said.

Her heart began to race. Did she really want to know what was going on with her husband? Once she knew, there would be no going back.

Taking a deep breath she told herself it was nothing.

She clicked on the message.

It was from 0000sporty. She touched her fingers to her mouth and suppressed the nauseated feeling in the pit of her stomach.

She hit reply. Who are you? she typed in the message box, then immediately deleted it before she could press enter. That would sound desperate, plus Alex would find out immediately. She had to restrain herself. She had to be careful.

Minutes passed whilst she considered what to do next. Technology had never been her strong point. Then she noticed a bar to the right of the message. She realized she could scroll up and read the previous messages.

She hesitated.

Would Alex know if she checked his messages? Another minute passed. She made a decision and began to scroll.

'A *V8 Maserati* is a fine specimen. *Nero* leather? My next car is gonna be a red *Enzo*. Imagine 12 cylinders…' 0000sporty wrote.

She laughed nervously. Alex was just showing off. It wasn't another woman. Of course he didn't have time for women in between work and deciding which car he was going to buy next. She had been worrying over nothing and now she felt as if a weight had been lifted from her shoulders. She silently thanked Kealana for leaving her the password. It was the one positive thing the woman had done for her since they had met. Perhaps she wasn't so bad after all. A smile formed on her lips. She was about to log out when she noticed three folders on Alex's minimalist desktop. One labelled *Photos*, another *Finances* and a third called *Miscellaneous*.

The one labelled *Photos* instantly had her attention. Alex wasn't the sentimental type and it had been years since she had looked through any old pictures. She and Alex had taken reams of photos when they were travelling but since then they hadn't bothered. Alex occasionally took pictures on his phone. Would he have any of their premises in Shanghai? She moved the mouse to the relevant folder and clicked on it. Inside were at least fifty different folders neatly labelled and dated. Typical of Alex. None labelled *Shanghai* though. That was curious. He spent so much time there. Had he not taken a single photo of their new offices?

She put the thought to the back of her mind and located their travelling photos, marvelling at how Alex had managed to save them all on to his computer. She had thought they had misplaced most of their memory cards. She imagined some poor work experience kid thinking he was going to learn how to place a trade being lumbered with this task at the *Renshaw* offices.

She flicked through the first couple of shots of Thailand. There was a picture of her in a pink sarong, standing in front of a cliff face on Railay beach, the picture made her feel warm inside. She opened the next folder along. It contained pictures of the Renshaws on family occasions. She was amazed by Alex's mother's bone structure. She had seen countless pictures of her before, but each time she was stuck by this woman's beauty. She could tell that Alex got his good looks from her. Alex and his mother had been close. There were pictures of the two of them skiing, drinking champagne and sitting by the Renshaw's Christmas tree amidst a mountain of presents. Celeste knew that this particular picture had been the last time Alex had seen his mother alive. Where was Graham then?

She felt foolish now for having looked at his computer, and seeing pictures of his frail mother towards the end of her life made her realize how stupid she was being. Alex would never do to her what Warwick had done to his mother. The photos had been a nice reminder that Alex was human too. Just because recently he had grown distant didn't mean he didn't love her anymore. He was just buried under the pile of work Warwick thrust upon him at every possible opportunity.

She selected another folder at random which contained pictures of a gorgeous country house. An estate she had only been to once. She had been charmed by its majestic architecture sitting in acres on land and hoped that when they returned to England they could use it as a family home. It would be a perfect place to bring up a family. The house had been his mother's haven, and after she died, none of them had really used it, just maintained it as a *Renshaw* property. She moved onto another folder containing pictures of construction projects at various stages. She briefly looked at these before moving on. As far as she was aware, *Renshaw* was not in the business of developing property, but what did she know. Didn't all big firms build up their asset base that way?

It was then that the task bar at the bottom of the computer caught her eye. She noticed that Alex's email account was open and had just been minimized at the bottom of the screen. This is almost too easy, she thought. Alex had always kept his email account closely guarded, like his mobile phone. He never said as much but she could tell, by the way he minimized the window when she tried to catch a glance at what he was doing.

'Work stuff,' was all he offered when she had asked him what the secrecy was all about. 'You don't see me looking at your work emails.'

'Feel free,' she had responded, after which she had quickly deleted some of her private emails to Alicia – the emails where she had detailed how Toby Cain had made a pass at her, and those discussing a dreamy sales assistant who had started working at *Cross*. It was girlfriend banter but she wasn't sure if Alex would see it as harmless fun, and she couldn't erase the memory of how Alex had hit that man on the beach in Thailand in a jealous rage.

A shiver ran down her spine.

She heard a noise upstairs and her eyes immediately flicked to the door. She should quit while she was ahead. She had found nothing incriminating so far and she could easily stumble across something innocent and overreact. She wasn't infallible, but she was paranoid, as she had recently found out. Celeste clicked on the inbox. It asked for a password. Again she typed in the same letters and numbers that had been hastily scribbled by Kealana on the orange post-it note.

It worked like magic. She was in her husband's account. It surprised her. For someone like Alex, she expected him to have different passwords for everything he accessed. Maybe she didn't know her husband as well as she thought she did. All the emails had been read but she expected that. Alex was glued to his phone. He checked it every minute. The last email from his father was sent just moments ago. Would he be able to tell if someone else was logged onto his account at the same time?

She looked at the subject bar and sender of the first twenty or so emails, ignoring the spam. There were a couple of folders Alex had created, each labelled with various initials. She had heard some of the initials being bandied about between Bill and Alex. It had to have something to do with trading. She stuck out her bottom lip. Nothing looked suspicious so she clicked on the email from Warwick. 'Call me now. We need to talk about Shanghai' was all it said, reminding her of the urgency in Graham's voice yesterday and the hole in their marriage. She had conveniently forgotten about it just by getting nostalgic over a couple of pictures from Thailand.

Celeste had hoped a pregnancy would bring her and Alex closer together, but it hadn't. They knew so much about each other when they were living in Krabi all those years ago. How well could she say she knew Alex now? And when was the last time he genuinely asked her about her career aspirations?

She couldn't just blame him, though. Before pregnancy she had spent more time in the office than at home. When they were together they had attended a whirlwind of parties fuelled with alcohol and one-upmanship. People they knew referred to them as the Mid-Level's power couple. The couple 'everyone wants to be,' Jinny had once said, but what good was that if their marriage was falling to pieces and both of them had failed to notice. After looking at his account for another couple of minutes she logged out and minimized the screen just like she had found it.

She was about to shut down the computer when her eyes were drawn back to the folder labelled *Miscellaneous* on his desktop. It was odd. Alex was the sort who labelled things as they were. Photos were stored in *Photos*, finances would be stored in *Finances*. Why would Alex need a folder of miscellaneous items? She felt a knot tighten in her stomach as she moved the cursor towards the folder. Her fingers stuck to the mouse as she slightly lifted her index finger to double click. Inside the folder were three more folders labelled *High Stock*, *Low Stock* and *Ultimate Stock*. More trading stuff? She clicked on the folder called *High Stock*. It contained a couple of spread-sheets detailing accounts and property transactions. She was bored now.

Lifting her bowl of now cold porridge, she stuck her spoon in it. Her appetite had returned. She put her hand on the mouse and directed the cursor towards the start button to switch the machine off. But her gaze caught the orange post-it note again. Why had Kealana given her this password? She must have wanted Celeste to know something – something that was on Alex's computer.

It didn't make sense for Kealana to break Alex's trust for

nothing. The only reason she could think of was that there was something on his computer which would drive a wedge between them. She was certain that that's what Kealana had wanted from the start, because she didn't think Celeste was good enough. But if Kealana wanted to break them up, wouldn't it have been easier to poison Alex's mind against her and not the other way around? Alex believed everything Kealana said, whereas Celeste couldn't stand the woman. It just didn't make sense.

She let go of the mouse and put her bowl down. Kealana had watched her every move since day one. Was it because Kealana didn't like her? Or was Kealana looking out for her? And if Kealana was looking out for her then there was something on Alex's computer she wanted her to find. She felt a mild pain in her abdomen and rubbed her belly until it subsided.

With this in mind she had to take a better look. 'It'll be like ripping off a plaster,' Celeste said to the watching silver Buddha before she moved the cursor over the folder labelled *Low Stock*.

52

Barnet, North London

Celeste took the glass of water Elaine offered her with trembling hands. She took a sip. Her mouth was dry and she felt sick to the stomach. This was what Elaine had wanted. The unravelling had started.

'It's a terrible thing to find out your husband's been keeping secrets from you.'

Celeste held on to her bumblebee pendant, rubbing it between her thumb and forefinger. She looked at the clock. There wasn't long now. The gentle tick of the second hand jarred in her ears. 'You need to understand what was in those folders so you understand my state of mind at that point. That picture of me.'

Elaine took the photograph from the desk and passed it to Celeste.

She examined it and ran her fingers over her face. 'I lost everything.'

Elaine nodded. 'Is that what made you pick up the knife? Was it because of what you found in those folders?'

Celeste took a deep breath.

'Is that what made you try and take your own life?'

'Sometimes I think back to that week I was left alone at home, seven months pregnant, without a job. No real friends. Just Ruby and Kealana for company and I wonder if Alex had set it up that way. I was so helpless.' Celeste shook her head. 'Would it have been better to have stayed in the dark? Ignorance is bliss and all that crap.'

'Sometimes we bury our heads in the sand. We don't want to face reality, and there is a reason for that. It's because we feel we can't cope with the truth. We're afraid of reality. It does sound like Alex was isolating you from the real world and trying to induce a sort of learned helplessness on you so that you would be scared to do anything that went against him.'

'I spent a large part of my life living a lie. I can't stop thinking about that.'

'The life you lived in your past makes you the person that you are today. Don't overthink it. Sometimes it is best not overthink things.'

'And what makes you an expert?'

Elaine winced.

Celeste dropped her head. It wasn't right to be angry at Elaine. She was only trying to help. She looked at the clock again. She had to continue. Time was running out.

'What I found out about Alex was horrific. It ruined me. I realised that I didn't know this man who I'd lived with for years. When I met him I was a strong woman, determined to succeed in my career. Yet he managed to somehow manipulate me. When I clicked on that folder, *Low Stock*, it was the beginning of the end for me and for my unborn child, but I didn't see any of that coming.'

53

5th August 2012
Mid-Levels, Central and Western District, Hong Kong

The *Low Stock* folder contained eight further folders, neatly numbered. Alex was so methodical, so controlled, so different from Celeste's ad hoc ways he had once loved. Once when he was looking at some of her latest designs and passing comment, back in the early days of their relationship, he had confessed that part of the attraction was the lack of organization in her life.

'You just want to organize me, don't you?' she had teased and he had mock scowled, playfully telling her he would never. Yet how much she had changed under Alex's influence? Her guarded conversations with Maryanne, her designs neatly ordered by season. At first he had nagged her to keep her clothes tidy as well. He couldn't fathom how, even with a maid, her wardrobe was always in a mess and she enjoyed him commenting on her chaotic ways. But when was the last time he had pleaded with her for order? She couldn't remember.

She clicked on the first folder, expecting to find boring accounts like *High Stock* had contained. But the folder contained just a word document. It had a photograph of a woman with all her details. It looked like a job application.

Her name was Suzan Blythe. She was twenty-five and worked as an administrator at *Global West*. She scanned the rest of the document looking for anything out of place. Nothing. She tried the next three folders. They were all the same. She drummed her fingers on the table as she opened folder five. This contained the details of a Julie Christie, but this folder was different. It didn't just contain a word document. It also contained airline tickets – business class tickets from London to Hong Kong and a credit card statement showing meals out in the upmarket *Wagyu Steakhouse* just around the corner from their apartment. Finally there was a pale yellow pdf receipt from an expensive boutique showing a twelve thousand Hong Kong Dollar spend.

Who were these women and why would Alex have all their details, their CVs? An unnerving thought hit her. Could they be professional escorts or prostitutes? They didn't look like prostitutes. But what did a prostitute look like? Were these women that Alex had slept with? Women he had paid to sleep with? Is that what escort services did these days – sent resumes for their clients to choose?

It could all be innocent, she reasoned, applicants for a job post at *Renshaw*. But the details on the forms didn't say why they wanted a job. It was all very basic – not like job resumes she had seen before. And the women were good looking, but not of a type. One was blond, another brunette, one with glasses, two looked Asian.

The receipt and the airline ticket bothered her. She looked at the receipt again. It was dated a couple of years ago. A year or so after they had moved into their apartment in the Mid-Levels. Alex had started to travel quite a bit by then, returning with expensive gifts. The twelve thousand dollar receipt must have been a gift for her around that time – perhaps a handbag or piece of jewellery. She clicked on folder number six. Inside was a folder called *Bear*. Bull or Bear. She remembered the saying, it had something to do with Bill. She could almost hear Bill call out to Alex, 'Are you Bull or Bear today?' She opened the *Bear* folder and clicked on the jpeg within it.

As she expected there was another picture of a woman, but this time no bio although the face was familiar. She couldn't place her, but there was definitely something about her beach blond hair that made her memorable. Celeste cocked her head to one side and then to the other as she studied the picture. The woman was older than the other girls. Underneath the picture the name Rachel Blake was typed out.

Blake.

She knew that name. Celeste put her in her late twenties. She wore a provocative black dress with a plunging neckline, which made her look sexy, if a little desperate. She tried to place her face but she just couldn't.

Celeste came out of Rachel's file. 'Bull or Bear,' she said out loud. She had asked Bill once what it meant. 'It's to do with the financial markets,' Bill had said. 'Bull is good. Bear is bad,' Alex had said with a grin. She had ignored them. At the time she wasn't interested in financial trends, but now she considered if there was a subtext to the joking around.

She was about to click out of the folder when her breath caught. Of course she had seen Rachel before. She had heard the name Blake as well. Alicia had told her about Rachel Blake, a friend she had been occasionally meeting. She thought back to that cold and miserable day in London when she had fought with Alicia because she had been sleeping with Bill. That was the day she had been to *The Emerald Rooms* with Angela.

Whilst Angela had been powdering her nose, Celeste had been accosted by a drunken and unruly woman – a woman who claimed to be sleeping with William. William was Bill. Voracious, philandering, yet fucking attractive, Bill, using different forms of his name! And Rachel Blake was the unsuspecting victim. It was ironic that Alicia had been friends with Rachel. It was possible that they were sleeping with Bill at the same time. It was positively disgusting.

Celeste put her head in her hands and laughed. This was all about Bill. Alex was keeping records of the women Bill had slept with. It was ridiculous and childish, but at least it exonerated her husband. How foolish she was to think Alex had been screwing around. The Alex she had committed to for life was not a cheater, anything but that. His mother had been her saviour in that respect.

But why would Bill want to keep details of the women he slept with? Was it just a trophy thing? Celeste shook her head. It didn't matter. It wasn't her problem. Poor Angela!

As Celeste's heart rate returned to normal she decided she had done enough prying for one day. It was late morning already. She rubbed her belly. 'Everything is going to be fine,' she reassured her unborn child. 'You are going to be the most loved child, ever.'

She instinctively clicked on the sub-folder labelled *Notes* in the *Bear* file and wondered if Alicia would be featured here or perhaps there would be a *Bull* folder for her. Thinking of Alicia now made her realize just how much she missed her friend. She felt alone looking through these sordid files. She wanted a partner for her crime – If Alicia was in on it they would laugh at how pathetic Bill was, but she could hardly call her now.

54

5th August 2012
Mid-Levels, Central and Western District, Hong Kong

The *Notes* sub-folder within the *Bear* file contained intimate pictures of Rachel, some out and about, some in what looked like an office with a large desk. Celeste had never been inside Bill's office, but it was well decorated. She skimmed passed these pictures. There were streams of saved conversations between RB and WH – Rachel Blake and William Harris. She scanned their first recorded conversation.

RB: Say you love me

WH: You know I do.

RB: Feeling lonely. Why do you always have to travel so much?

WH: I have to earn a living.

RB: :(

WH: :(:(*I miss you.*

This wasn't the Bill Celeste knew. Smiley faces were for teenagers and young lovers, not Bill. How did he find the time to do all this? He had a business to run, a wife to love and two adorable children. There were streams of conversation that looked like it had been automatically saved from an instant messaging service. They talked about where they would meet for lunch or what they were watching on television in their separate homes. No mention of Angela or the kids anywhere. No wonder Rachel was in a state that day. She must have only just found out about Angela. She wanted to feel sorry for her, but Rachel shouldn't have been so naïve. Didn't she question why her boyfriend was away so much? Or had she known that Bill was married? Perhaps she had been given the same sob story Alex had given her about how evil Angela really was.

Scrolling through, Celeste passed the next half hour reading their conversations. They made her laugh, but mostly she cringed. It was like reading the script of a badly written play, yet she couldn't drag herself away. It wasn't as if she had anything better to do. It was fascinating reading the words of two people who were having an affair. She continued to scan the conversations. Bill had taken Rachel to Paris and it looked like they even shared a flat in London. How had he managed to conceal this without Angela knowing? Or was Angela just burying her head in the sand?

Celeste looked at her watch. It was nearly lunchtime. She was about to close the document when a familiar name jumped out at her further down the page she was on.

RB: *How's Cross?*

WH: *That subject is taboo. Let's leave it there.*

RB: ☹

Celeste frowned. Why was Bill talking about her boutique? Well not so much her boutique, but Mr Harris…'

'Fuck!' Celeste said, jumping to her feet, her heart pounding in her chest. 'You have got to be kidding me!' She paced Alex's study, occasionally looking back at the computer screen. 'No way,' she said again. The Harris she had conversed with at Cross was from South Africa. He had the accent. But that was all that it was – an accent, and she more than anybody knew just how good Bill had been at accents. How he could switch from his normal voice to that of Popeye or Frank Spencer without so much as a stutter, and his Somerset farmer's accent had her fooled the first time she had met him. As the discovery slowly sank in she realized just how stupid she had been. How could she not have seen it before? Bill or William Harris, the elusive Mr Harris, had bought Maryanne out and facilitated the whole Hong Kong store.

Bill had never been involved with retail for as long as she had known him. He was in carbon credits and vineyards! There was no way Bill would have gone into retail like this, which was why she had never linked their surnames. 'Harris is a common name,' Alex had said when she mentioned it once before, and she had dropped it. And Harris *was* a common surname.

Yet this conversation was on Alex's computer. He must have known. And if he had known, then surely he was in on it as well. It made sense now why Alex seemed to know exactly what was happening at *Cross*, sometimes even before she did. Even Angela had known confidential information when they had met in London. Why had Alex not said anything to her? Why had Bill bought *Cross* in the first place? It had to have something to do with Alex. Just seconds ago she had ben laughing at Rachel and Angela's naivety. How could she when she hadn't even seen what was under her own nose.

She reached into her pocket and pulled out her phone. She tried Alex's number, but there was no answer. She didn't leave a message. How dare Bill buy *Cross* and not tell her, all this time! The brand had not failed. Her designs had been so successful in Hong Kong, yet they closed the store. Bill had engineered all of it. She was sure of it. He hadn't even the decency to give her any notice of the closure. It was sick. She clenched her phone in her hand. 'Lying bastard!' she screamed.

Alex had to have known about this. She had asked him if he knew who this Harris was and he had lied to her face, without so much as flinching. What else was he keeping from her? She sat back down at the computer and rolled her shoulders back. She had seen a *Finance* folder somewhere on the computer. She needed to look inside it. A niggle in the back of her mind told her that *Cross* had nothing to do with Bill and everything to do with Alex. But Alex loved her. He wouldn't do something like this. Had his need to organize and control her life been that intense? He could have set Bill up with a company to purchase the shares in *Cross*. It wasn't rocket science. Even she could figure that one out. Had Alex really set up the whole thing?

When she started back at *Cross* after her trip around the world *Cross* was on it's knees. She herself had given Alex the information he needed to enable Bill to wrangle a good deal out of Maryanne. She remembered Maryanne saying that Harris knew exactly where to look, despite their creative accounting. Of course he did. She had given them all the information they needed.

When *Cross* had been failing, an investor came in and saved the company, opening a store in Hong Kong in a global recession. It didn't make financial sense. Yet she never questioned it, happy that things were going her way. She never stopped, even for once second, to see how much of a coincidence it was. Wasn't it Alex who said that there were no such things as coincidences? Alex had to be behind it, yet she needed proof. She couldn't believe the kind and generous Alex she married would do this. This wasn't her Alex. Not her Alex at all.

55

5th August 2012
Mid-Levels, Central and Western District, Hong Kong

Celeste clicked out of the folder. She rubbed her tired eyes as a feeling of loss engulfed her. How many late nights had she put in at *Cross* – and why had she even bothered? Had Maryanne known? It wasn't as if she could ask her now. Is that why she hadn't come to their wedding? *Sometimes I think it was better to go under than to sell to that man,* Maryanne had said when Celeste had pressed her about the sale of the shares. Is that why she had given her the necklace? *Whenever you feel weak and you do not know which path your life is taking, wear this pendant. It will guide you. And remember, if a bumblebee ever feels under attack it has a nice sting in its tail.* She had stupidly thought Maryanne was worried about the closure of *Cross* Hong Kong, when all along Maryanne was concerned about Bill. And if Bill was involved, then so was Alex. He had to be. He definitely knew about it. It was on his computer. Why hadn't Maryanne just told her about her deceiving husband outright?

It all started to make sense – the ever-evasive Mr Harris, the last minute design conventions in Mainland China she was made to attend, conveniently when Alicia had planned a trip or when she had wanted to go to London. Had it been Alex – pulling the strings. Had she just been his puppet?

She stood up and made her way to her bedroom. Her limbs were heavy as if she had the flu. She opened the second drawer in the chest opposite the bathroom, searching in between her clothes for the small fuchsia pink pouch that Maryanne had given her. Celeste pulled the delicate gold chain out of its casing. The gold bumblebee swung towards her. This was the chain she had deemed too cheap to wear previously; her diamonds had always taken preference.

Now she needed strength. She let the tears roll down her face as she unclasped her diamond necklace, laid it on the chest and put the gold chain on. She felt better. After an hour of sobbing into her pillow, she sat up on the bed holding on tightly to the golden bee. She looked out over the harbour through the haze and realized then that she had to finish what she had started. She had to look through everything on her husband's computer. She had been in the dark for too long and it was about time she opened her eyes.

*

Back in the cold white study Celeste stared at the folders on Alex's computer. Her mobile phone beeped. She picked it up. It was Alex. He had sent her a picture of himself inside what looked like a shopping mall. She put the phone back on the desk without replying, too tired to care where Alex was right now, too tired to wonder whether or not he was lying.

Opening the folder labelled *Finance* she found at least

a dozen folders inside. She opened the one titled *Property* and scanned the documents. There were dozens of properties owned by different trusts. She located the folder called *Trusts* and looked at its contents. The documents inside revealed that *Heavenly Ltd* owned an apartment in Mayfair that she had never once stepped inside. She cringed at the name. Had Alex really set up a company using his moniker for her? *Heavenly Ltd* solely belonged to Alex. It took Celeste at least an hour to familiarize herself with the different property deeds. Nothing appeared to be owned by both she and Alex. Absolutely nothing. Graham and Sarah seemed to have their family home in Essex in their sole names, but everything else was under the ownership of a company or trust. Did that mean if she left Alex she wouldn't have a home to live in? Alex would never do that to her. She closed the folder and clicked on one called *Bank Accounts*. There were statements from banks she had never heard of and balances in various currencies that made her eyes water. Alex had money, but all this, she had never imagined such amounts. He always said it was too vulgar to talk about money – money he was clearly stashing here, there and everywhere.

Celeste straightened her back, trying to understand what she was looking at. Alex's words of caution came back to her. *If files get corrupted it could cost* Renshaw *millions*. But Alex wasn't scared she would corrupt some files, he was worried she would find out who he really was.

She stopped looking through the folder, skimming over titles such as *Profit and Loss*, *Insurance*, *Utilities* and *Directors*. She paused at the folder titled *Boys' Toys*. After what she had just seen it was clear that Alex could afford a boat like Bill's ten times over. Why hadn't he just bought one?

Finally, Celeste found the folder she was looking for. The folder that would tell her what she wanted to know. She sat staring at the label *Cross* for almost a minute before she plucked up the courage to open it.

56

5th August 2012
Mid-Levels, Central and Western District, Hong Kong

There were hundreds of documents in the *Cross* folder neatly filed. She scanned a saved email exchange between Bill and Maryanne. It didn't tell her much. She closed the document and opened another and then another until she found what she was looking for. She sat back in her chair looking at the document detailing the purchase of *Cross*. *Heavenly Limited*, the company owned by Alex in its entirety, had financed it. So *Cross* had nothing to do with Bill and everything to do with Alex.

Her instincts had been right. She had just hoped on this occasion that she was wrong, that there would be some rational explanation for what she had previously seen, but Alex had orchestrated the whole *Cross* transaction. Celeste clenched her teeth as she read through document after document. Why? Why did he do it?

She searched in the *Cross* folder to find any clue as to how Alex had made this happen, but there was nothing. Not a scrap. And she wanted to know more. The very name of the company Alex had used made her seethe with rage. Had Alex set up the company, *Heavenly Ltd*, to hide behind in case

Celeste had started to dig into find who the elusive Mr Harris was? She had mentioned it so many times to Alex over the years: how she had never met her new boss. In fact, Alex had offered to look into it for her. Of course he had, and she had trusted him. 'Seems above board,' Alex had reported.

Alex had once told her to record all her negotiations with suppliers and other designers, and she had ignored him. He was always paranoid that people would go back on their word. If Alex practiced what he preached, then surely his emails would tell her what she wanted to know. She clicked on the minimized email window at the bottom of the screen and tapped in Alex's password once more to log in. She was getting better at finding information she wanted. Alex had extracted and saved emails between Maryanne and Bill, so it stood to reason there would be more emails that would show his involvement. It wasn't enough that Alex owned *Cross*, she wanted to know exactly why he bought it. *I was trying to help Maryanne out. She was struggling she needed the money. I didn't want to tell you because I didn't want you to think it was charity.* She could hear his excuses as she scanned his email folders.

She picked the folder labelled *W.H.* Now she was certain it stood for William Harris. She remembered the beautiful soft slippers she had been given to wear on Bill's yacht, his initials emblazoned in silver on the white fabric. How had she not realised it then? She double-clicked on the first email in the folder.

Nothing.

She clenched her fists and banged them on the table. She had to find out. If she asked him, he would never tell her the truth. She knew Alex must have had some correspondence with someone about the purchase. He was always tapping something into his phone. Alex backed every spoken business word with a written note because he didn't trust anyone. Of course he didn't, not when he was so deceitful himself.

Celeste decided to use the *search* function in Alex's email account to find emails that mentioned *Cross* and Bill. Twenty minutes later, after opening countless emails, she found herself staring at an email conversation between Alex and Bill. The email had dictated exactly what Bill was required to do.

Bill would act as Alex's representative and deal with Mary-anne when required. Alex was financing the entire project – or the 'dawn raid,' as Bill had referred to it as in his correspondence. A dawn raid, of course. Another sketchy memory came back to her. Alex explaining the trading term for when one company buys a large number of shares in another company at the start of a day's trading in order to take over. How many times had Bill and Alex joked about the dawn raid? 'Share stuff, hon,' Alex had said when she had asked him what they were talking about. 'You wouldn't be interested.' 'I am,' she had protested but he and Bill had laughed it off. She took a deep breath and started reading the email chain.

Won't she know? A rich investor wants to save this dying company and open a branch in Hong Kong. Celeste isn't stupid. She'll twig, Bill had written.

She won't question it. The company's on its way out. My accountant looked over the figures today. Thanks to Celeste, Robbie knew exactly where to look and what questions to ask. I think you'll find we are going to get a good deal. Alex replied.

You're going to lose money on this.

Worth the investment.

You need a stay at home wife like mine, Renshaw. Why don't you just tell Celeste about your plan?

I have to make her believe she's doing this on her own terms.

Because you love her or because you are trying to control her?

Won't answer that, Bill.

Yeah, both you and I know the answer to that. Anyway your choice Renshaw, but don't say I didn't warn you. So now that you've decided you want to burn your cash tell me where do I fall into all of this?

I need to use your identity.

Again? I'm beginning to worry.

Have I ever misused it?

No comment.

Heavenly Ltd is going to buy the company from Maryanne.

Maryanne will know who owns the company if she goes looking.

Maryanne needs this cash more than you know. She'll know not to say anything and I can keep it that way. You'll be the main contact. I'll provide the finance and you'll get a nice bonus out of it.

You say you never misuse my name but I had the Emerald Rooms call me up the other day questioning a rather large spend the other night. What have you been up to? I've told you Rachel's more bear than bull. She'll be moving into your London apartment if you're not careful.

Already asked mate. Shall we make this bonus a yacht?

Now you're talking.

I'll buy a boat under a new company.

I have a boat.

You could do with an upgrade.

I suppose it's time.

You can keep it for the duration of the deal. You can even bloody name it. It'll be delivered to Hong Kong and moored there.

And Celeste won't be any wiser because she will think it's all my doing.

Exactly.

And you're just going to give me a boat?

I'll use it as a joint owner. Once it's over I get the boat back or if you're nice we can carry on sharing it.

Why would you want a second hand boat with a name you haven't even chosen?

Me owning a yacht moored in Hong Kong won't do me any favours with Warwick right now. He is not one for an obvious show of wealth and I don't want Graham to think he can take his kids on it.

Warwick's anti-retail isn't he? How did you manage to get that past him?

He doesn't know about Heavenly Ltd. But back to the boat, he'll come round soon and then I'll have something to sell and upgrade.

Fucking genius. I should never underestimate you, Renshaw. You make an offer hard to refuse. But that's it after this. No more Face Off. *No more Emerald Rooms.*

This is it.

Won't Celeste recognize me?

You'll never need to see her.

And my name?

She knows you as Bill.

Bill Harris and William Harris, really? It's not that hard to figure out. Sure you don't want me to use Clark Kent?

Ha! Sorry to break it to you Bill, but the name William Harris is as common as muck. She won't make the connection and I'll be there to put her right if she does. You never question things right under your nose.

Ok Renshaw, send me the details of what you want me to do.

*

As Celeste read through the email exchange between Alex and Bill again, tears blurred her vision. Now she knew why Alex had been so angry that Bill had put his initials on the yacht slippers and towels – it was because it was his boat. She realised now that Alex wasn't keeping Bill's conquests safe from Angela as she had foolishly thought. He had been using Bill's identity. That's why at *The Emerald Rooms* the drunken blond had targeted her. It was Alex Rachel was having an affair with, not Bill. Rachel knew Alex as William. Celeste looked at the date of the email – it was 2008. Alex had been cheating on her from the beginning.

57

5th August 2012
Mid-Levels, Central and Western District, Hong Kong

'It's not true,' Celeste said out loud. 'It can't be true. This isn't Alex. Not my Alex.' She was smarter than this. He could not have duped her so easily. She was the one who had got that graduate job at *Cross* on her own merit. Alex hadn't been on the scene then. She had worked her way up to being a highly regarded designer. Her clothing had won awards. And then she started relying on him, hanging on his every word. Believing everything he said – without question. When had that started? She had listened, taken his advice, told him about the difficulties *Cross* faced and given him the upper hand, without even knowing it.

Could Graham have organised the whole thing? Did Graham, or even Warwick, have it in for her? She had been certain Kealana had been sent to check up on her when she first moved in with Alex. Had Kealana been ordered by Warwick to set this all up on Alex's computer, especially for her to find? It would be a hoax, an elaborate hoax. But somehow despite the excuses she conjured in her mind, she knew what she had seen had more truth in it than she wanted to believe. The late nights, the frequent trips, the excuses that

Graham was incompetent. They were all diversions and smokescreens created by Alex.

With a trembling hand Celeste checked back in the *Finance* folder, the *Cross* folder and through the emails. She followed the trail of money from one of Alex's private accounts to *Heavenly Limited* and then disappearing right around the time Maryanne broke the news to her that she had sold the controlling share in *Cross* in November 2008. She couldn't deny the transaction. It was all there in black and white.

And the apartment in Mayfair. Alex owned that. She searched online how to check the ownership of a property and realised she could do it on the Land Registry website. Carefully, she set up an account, verified her email and typed in her credit card details to purchase a copy of the record. It confirmed that *Heavenly Limited* owned the apartment. She went back into the *Property* folder and then the folder of photographs. She trawled through the contents until she saw what she had missed the first time – pictures of the apartment being redecorated, Alex sitting behind a mahogany desk. The same desk she had seen Rachel sitting behind. She went back to that picture now. She had thought it was Bill's office. It wasn't. It was taken in Alex's apartment. When she took a closer look, her heart sank. The signature *Cross* letterhead was on his desk. How could he?

She needed to speak to someone, anyone. Just to confirm her suspicions. Everything she read was merging into one. It was too much to take in. She couldn't call any of the ex-pats. Their allegiance was to Alex. Graham and Warwick were certain to cover for him too. Graham already knew he had put his foot in it by calling her to ask about her husband's whereabouts and he was sure to feel Alex's wrath soon. Bonnie didn't want to know her, and Alicia... she had been cruel to Alicia. How could she call her now, after everything she had said?

With no other option she checked the time difference and called *The Emerald Rooms.*

'Hello. Hi,' she said into the receiver. She took a deep breath trying to steady her voice. 'I'm looking for...' she hesitated. Should she ask for Bill or Alex? Did the staff know that Alex was Bill? Bill's email implied that they didn't. But Celeste was sure they would know. Either way, how would she distinguish between the two without revealing who she was? If she told them her name, they would be sure to alert Bill.

'Hello?' came the voice at the end of the line.

Celeste disconnected.

58

6th August 2012
Mid-Levels, Central and Western District, Hong Kong

Celeste stood in the tea bar in the vast lobby of their apartment building holding on to her Styrofoam cup. She was trying not to think about the last two days. She replayed what she had seen over and over in her mind – trying to make sense of it. Trying to think of a logical explanation as to why Alex would do this. But after a sleepless night looking for some explanation it had finally sunk in. She had spent much of the morning looking through Alex's possessions in their bedroom for some clues to his betrayal, but there were none. Alex was smart – she had always known that, but he certainly wasn't the man she thought he was. He had betrayed her. She could no longer deny that. Now she had to find out what else Alex was hiding from her. Were Rachel and those women in the *Low Stock* folder the only ones he had slept with or were there more? She realised that there were eight folders in the *Low Stock* folder, but she had only opened the first six. She needed to finish what she started. She felt a sharp stabbing pain in her abdomen as she walked across the lobby and had to steady herself on the black console table near the elevator. She looked outside the panelled glass windows and could see the street signs swaying in the wind. The streets were deserted.

'You okay?' the porter asked. 'You don't look okay. Don't go outside. Typhoon is still happening. You'll blow over.'

Celeste swallowed. She wasn't okay. Her life was falling apart around her, and there were still folders on Alex's computer that she had to look in. He would be back late tonight.

'I'm not going outside and I'm fine. Please, just call the elevator.'

'Yes, Ma'am.' The porter did as he was told, and Celeste managed a smile, even though her eyes were glazed over.

'You feeling sick with baby?' Charlie asked.

Celeste felt another pain. She had been worried about the dull ache she had been experiencing in her abdomen over the last couple of weeks. She had even been to the doctor for a check up, but he had said it was just a urinary infection. He had given her some tablets and told her to drink plenty of water. It hadn't helped and something didn't feel right. Once the typhoon was over she would make another appointment at the clinic. She took a deep breath, like the doctor had told her, and nodded at the porter. She needed to take it easy. Stress would only make it worse the doctor had said. And she was stressed. Highly stressed.

Back in her apartment she went to Alex's study once again, back to the *Low Stock* folder. There were two further folders she hadn't opened. Methodically she clicked on the first. She saw a picture of Mo Li, one of her designers at *Cross*. In the office she was well dressed and as shy as anything. Here her legs were spread. Did Alex know this was one of her team? Did Mo Li know Alex was her husband? Of course they had both known. They had met in Lang Kwai Fong when she was there. Mo Li had run off at the time and in her ignorance she had put it down to shyness. She never expected this. Without thinking she deleted the picture. They must have laughed at her stupidity together. No wonder when they were made redundant Mo Li had treated her with such disdain. She probably knew that Alex owned *Cross*; that's probably how he got her into bed. Mo Li had thought Celeste knew about the redundancies. Yet she knew nothing – not as a manager, certainly not as a wife.

Folder eight contained a sub folder called *Asian Escorts*. She opened it. The shimmering red logo looked back at her from the screen. It was familiar. She knew where she had seen it before. It was when they had first visited Hong Kong. Right before Alex had proposed. Alex had brushed away her concerns saying that it was common practice when doing business in the East for directors to hand out such cards to single men. He said that people would think of him differently after he was married, they would stop encouraging him to visit strip bars. Had there been any truth in what he had said back then, or was he cheating on her even before they were married?

Celeste felt as if she were having an out of body experience. She could see her pregnant self snooping through her husband's folder of trophy fucks, slowly realizing he loved paying for sex more than he loved her. Humiliation caused her hands to shake as she glanced at pictures of women, younger and more exotic than she was – women with flawless tanned skin and size zero hips.

She closed her eyes and let her tears stain her cheeks. Graham knew. She could see that now. That's why Alex put him down at every opportunity. That's why they stopped socializing with him and Sarah, and the reason for fabricating the illness Sarah was supposed to have. Alex was purposefully putting distance between them. She swiped at the Buddha and it fell to the floor. Then she ran to the bathroom with her hand over her mouth, and returned to his office after she had thrown up. She picked up the Buddha with its permanently happy grin and thought about smashing his computer with it. Better than that, she could corrupt his files – moving items from one folder to another. Alex would hate it and she would get some small satisfaction from it. But before she did that she needed evidence of what she had seen – just in case. She started opening Alex's drawers one by one, then she stood up and looked in the filing cabinet, rummaging through his perfectly lined files for a memory stick.

Nothing. She looked out of the office window. It was dark, and the tail end of the typhoon meant that it was still raining outside. She could go out and try and find a stationers' close by to buy one. She looked at her watch. If she went out now she wouldn't have time to look in the last folder before Alex returned. He said he was going to get back today and due to take the last flight out of Shanghai. So wherever he was he would be on his way back. She weighed up her options. If there had been a *Bear* folder, then there had to be a *Bull* folder. A gut feeling told her that the contents of this folder would be the beginning of the end for her. She started looking for it. Then she went back to the folder titled *Ultimate Stock*.

59

6th August 2012
Mid-Levels, Central and Western District, Hong Kong

Just before she clicked on the file for *Ultimate Stock* she heard the soft click of the office door. Immediately, she turned around. It was Kealana.

'You knew,' she said, her eyes red and puffy, tears staining her cheeks. She would never have dreamt of exposing her raw emotion to this woman before – a woman whom she disliked, but now she no longer cared. She lifted the sleeve of her jumper to her eyes and wiped them.

Kealana entered the room, sat down on a white leather chair and took Celeste's trembling hands in hers. 'I'm so sorry.'

Seeing Kealana, the look of pity on her face, made Celeste wonder if her initial concerns were in fact correct. If Kealana hated her, had she set this up to drive her away? Celeste pulled her hands away.

'They are like this,' Kealana said, so softly Celeste almost didn't hear. 'I've been with the family for years.'

Celeste held her head up. 'Alex hates this behaviour. His mother… He saw what Warwick did to his mother. How much it hurt her.'

'I've organized parties where waitresses have served

cocktails and canapés to the mistresses of the Renshaw men. I sent for their…' Kealana trailed off.

'What? You sent for what?'

'I'm sorry. You're a good woman.'

'Tell me what you sent for?'

Kealana shook her head. 'I sent for their cocaine.'

Celeste sat back. She was expecting Kealana to say prostitutes. Alex would never use cocaine. Not once in her life had she seen him smoke marijuana or take any kind of illegal high. How many late night parties had they attended together? She had always been with him and she had never noticed anything like that. He loved whiskey, and brandy nightcaps. He never needed anything else. Now she knew that Kealana had engineered this whole episode.

But then Celeste remembered, whilst she suffered the next day with a raging hangover, Alex had always been up, bright, breezy and ready to start the day. The day they had been to see Bill's new boat had been a prime example. Cocaine would explain why Alex was so alert all the time, regardless of what time he went to bed or how much he had drank the night before. Still, she would have known if her husband was on hard drugs. She narrowed her eyes at Kealana. 'Why are you lying?'

Kealana stood up and went to the cupboard. She put her hand deep in its recesses and pulled out a small, black, plastic bag. Then she emptied the contents on to the desk. There were three small plastic bags containing white powder. Kealana carefully put them back where she had found them and sat back in her chair.

'Why are you telling me this? Why did you give me the password?'

'I knew the first time I met you that you were innocent. You didn't like me popping in with flowers. I knew that. You thought I was checking up on you. You thought I was trying to, how do I say this? Squeeze you out. But my intentions have always been good. I wanted to protect you. You have no family here and you remind me a great deal of my second daughter.' Kealana tilted her head and looked at Celeste. 'At first I tried to turn a blind eye and forget about what Mr Alex was doing. Should have been easy. I've been doing it for years. But my daughter, she is the same age as you. You both married in the same year and you are both similar the way your hair is cropped short and black. You both like fashion also.' Kealana smiled. 'Like my daughter, your eyes sparkle when you are happy. Day by day I saw the sparkle disappear from your eyes. Same like my daughter. My daughter, I cannot help. I don't even have keys to her house anymore. But you, you I could try to save, especially now you are having a baby. I thought you had the right to know – even if you choose to do nothing. At least you will know the truth.'

Celeste thought back to when she first met Kealana. How the woman had taken over running their home. She had hated her habits of placing flowers on the table, making sure the entrances were always so clean and soulless like a hotel. Now, she wondered if it was all Kealana, or if was it an instruction from Alex and Warwick in case they stopped by at one of their many properties with another woman? She had seen too much for this to be a set up by Kealana. The *Asian Escorts* card, Rachel Blake and Mo Li: at some point she had witnessed a part of each of these lies. Kealana wasn't making it up. She had to believe her. Now a sliver of guilt pricked her conscious. She had always ignored Kealana, even accusing her of trying to poison her. She never even knew that Kealana had a daughter the same age as her, and all the while this woman had been looking out for her.

'Alex took away my job,' Celeste said, remembering afresh that Alex was the true owner of *Cross*. 'I have no way of surviving on my own. I'm carrying his child.' She turned and grabbed hold of Kealana's hand. 'What do I do?' Her eyes scanned Kealana's face for an answer.

'Maybe, for now, you do nothing. It will not be good for your health or that of the baby.'

'You show me all this and then expect me to do nothing?'

'I'm saying think about what you want to do before making a quick decision. Mr Alex's mother always knew what Warwick was up to, but she didn't say anything. It's hard to leave when you are accustomed to this lifestyle. The Renshaws provide well.'

Celeste thought back to her days on East Row. All her life she had wanted to escape from living hand to mouth, but for this? At least everything she had then was true. Now her life was based on lies. 'You said you wanted to save me. Now you tell me not to do anything.'

'I'm telling you to make a plan for yourself to get out. Don't act irrationally.'

'I'm not Alex's mother. I won't let him get away with this.'

'You've no family here. You don't even have many friends. You can't go back into the world on your own. You have to find some strength first. Then leave.'

It was true. She had no friends, not anymore. Her job was a thing of the past and she had a baby growing inside of her that she had to provide for. She wanted to be back in England – back within the security of the four walls in which she had grown up.

Kealana looked around the room and Celeste followed her eyes. Her lifestyle now was a far cry from East Row. Celeste stood up and clasped her hands together. Her mind was clouded with confusion. Then she turned, shaking her head, staring at Kealana. 'There must be a mistake. You're in it with him, aren't you? You set this up for me to find. That's why you gave me the password. You want me out.'

Kealana was silent.

'I'm going to tell Alex about this.' She picked up her phone from the desk. Her hands trembled as she dialled. She got his voicemail. 'Call me back, now,' she cried into the device before she disconnected.

'Think about this.'

'There is nothing to think about.'

'Your husband is very influential in Hong Kong and the Renshaws have money. Money equals power and Hong Kong can be lawless at times.'

Celeste folded her arms. 'Get out,' she commanded.

Kealana stood up and took the orange post-it note from the desk. Then she bowed her head before leaving the room, closing the door behind her.

Celeste sat back down in front of the computer and double clicked on the folder titled *Ultimate Stock*.

60

6th August 2012
Mid-Levels, Central and Western District, Hong Kong

'It has to be all right,' Celeste reassured herself as the first document opened. It was titled *Preferred Stock*. Another trading term that she saw through. She glanced at the spread-sheet containing a list of dates. It looked like an itinerary for travel spanning at least a year.

The first destination she spotted at the end of last year was Vienna. She had always wanted to go to Austria but she and Alex never seemed to find the time to make the trip. Plus, Alex had rightly said that it was a long way from Hong Kong for a city break. Last year had been busy – it was the year the boat had arrived at Aberdeen Marina; the year Alex had been flying to Shanghai frequently and she had taken to drinking champagne in excess to combat her loneliness, but she didn't remembered Alex saying he had been to Vienna.

But she did remember that at around that time he had given her a box of those little marzipan balls covered in chocolate that she loved. She couldn't remember what he had said at the time. Had a client given them to him? Did he find them in one of the international supermarkets? Or was it just guilt that made him pick them up – a last minute duty-free purchase?

She bit the inside of her cheek accepting that Vienna must have been a trip with one of his many whores. Perhaps he had been with Rachel. Didn't his slut look at his passport and twig that his name was not William? She could picture the scene now. 'Alex is my middle name,' he would have said smiling with those irresistible blue eyes – eyes which could easily make you forget your own name.

Why Vienna? Surely London was easier. Alex had never shown an interest in visiting these European cities brimming with culture. He only ever favoured London, Hong Kong and Paris – and then of course they had Thailand. But even on their last trip out there he complained about the weather and poor mobile reception. She wasn't going to get an answer from the spread-sheet. She looked at the rest of the itinerary. Scotland and Miami stood out in between several trips to Paris and London. There was no mention of Shanghai and there was no Thailand either, but Scotland featured several times on the list since March this year.

The dates didn't make sense if he was taking a lover away. They were for such short periods of time. Thinking that *Preferred Stock* was just a money-making scam like the dawn raid on *Cross* made her feel slightly better. Anything would be better than thinking of Alex flying of with one of his *Low Stock* women. But whom was she trying to kid? Alex was impatient. He never liked staying somewhere too long. He hadn't been like that when they had been travelling but over the years he had changed. Even five nights in Thailand in February had been a struggle for him.

She noticed the last entry on the travel plan. It was for last week. It had the early hours of tomorrow morning as a return date and time. So the delay he had spoken of a couple of days ago had been planned. Of course he had planned it. This was Alex, he planned everything. But his itinerary didn't say 'Shanghai' – where Alex had purported to be and Graham had insisted he wasn't. It said 'Scotland' – the same place his mobile phone tracker application had always placed him. She had been stupid enough to think the application was not working. Alex had nothing in Scotland. She had nothing in Scotland. Just…No. It couldn't be.

She pursed her lips and closed the document and saw the folder she wanted. The folder titled *Bull*. So this was Alex's prize possession. Renshaw, you Bull or Bear? Bill had asked so many times. That day on the *Premier Cru* Alex had said he was definitely Bull. She felt sick. If Rachel was Bear, someone he had provided with a flat in London and took away with him, who the hell was Bull? She rubbed her temples. The boat had arrived in September last year, which meant the person in this folder had been seeing Alex since then, since before Thailand, before she was pregnant.

When the folder opened she saw at least fifty icons appear – folders, jpegs and word documents. With dread she clicked on the first photo and then instantly she knew.

*

Alex was in love with Bonnie. Two hours later Celeste knew the entire history of their affair. With Bonnie Alex wasn't William Harris, not Bill, not any other name. Of course he couldn't be. Bonnie knew who he was. After all, she had watched her marry the man. From delving into Alex's conveniently labelled emails and various sub folders, Celeste gathered that Bonnie and Alex had met again last year, by chance, through a friend, in London. They had an instant chemistry and spent the first hour talking about their common ground, which was of course, Celeste. They spent the second hour screwing each other in a hotel room in Mayfair. Of course Alex couldn't have used his Mayfair apartment, Celeste thought, he still had poor Rachel stationed there at the time.

She read the details of their sordid affair. She knew that Alex liked the way Bonnie put her makeup on before the rest of her clothes whilst she sat in front of her dresser stark naked. Bonnie on the other had 'absolutely loved' the way he let the stubble on his face grow out when they were together. Alex liked Bonnie in French knickers. Bonnie preferred it when Alex didn't wear any underwear at all. It was all there in black and white – streams of emails and conversations for Celeste to pore over. As with Alex's conversations with Rachel, after their initial common ground had been established, Celeste's name wasn't mentioned. It was as if she never existed. There were no 'How's your wife?' or, 'When are you going to leave her?' pleas from Bonnie. There were no, 'My wife's a bitch,' comments from Alex. Was her existence that insignificant that they failed to even mention it?

Document after document told her that Alex was in love with Bonnie. Unlike Rachel, who had done all the chasing for a man whose real name she didn't even know, Bonnie was the one who had been pursued by Alex. 'Don't be crazy, Alex,' she had written, when he offered to fly down to see her, just for dinner. 'I wouldn't let you come here just for dinner. It's a waste. I have work to get on with.'

'I must see you,' he protested. But Bonnie was firm and Celeste knew she had practice in dating other married men. Alicia had told her about this second married lover. Celeste never for one moment thought it was her own husband.

Alex had been the one to encourage her to cut Bonnie out of her life. Had he fancied her friend then? She remembered the way he had looked at Bonnie when he had first met her. She had been stupid enough to think nothing of it – all men looked at Bonnie that way. But she remembered it now and it made his betrayal hurt all the more. She had tried reaching out to Bonnie when she was in London, but Bonnie had given her the cold shoulder. She thought she had deserved it, but now she could see Bonnie was afraid – afraid she would find out about the affair and her romance would come to an end.

With each new file Celeste opened she felt like she was doing another round in a boxing ring. By the time she closed the last document she felt battered and bruised. She touched her belly. Her eyes were dry. She couldn't cry anymore. She switched off the computer and gazed out of the window watching the smoggy Hong Kong skyline disappearing into darkness.

61

7th August 2012
Mid-Levels, Central and Western District, Hong Kong

The clock flashed 3:05am when Celeste heard the click of the front door. She had drifted in and out of sleep since twelve and her eyes were sore. It hurt to blink. She reached over to the glass on the bedside table and took a sip of water. She turned over and looked towards Alex's side of the bed, the left side. Ruby had diligently placed a tall glass of water by the bed for him. She thought about spitting in his tumbler but she didn't have the energy to move.

She could sense him outside their bedroom door. She turned and closed her eyes because she couldn't face talking to him. Then she heard the door open and close. He was in the room with her. She sensed him walking around the bed then she heard the click of his sidelight being switched on. She imagined him undressing. His familiar scent of sandalwood drifted towards her, and she wanted to forget the last two days, but she couldn't. A tear touched her pillow. When he slipped under the covers and she could feel the heat of his body next to hers, she recoiled.

'Hey,' she heard him whisper. She almost answered, but then realized he was on his phone. 'No, I've just got back… at home…of course I do.'

She stiffened.

'Wait a second,' he was saying. Then he pulled back the covers and got out of their bed. She heard the soft click of the door.

How many times had Alex come home from business trips recently and was too tired talk? Now, she could imagine Bonnie on the other end of the line, running her fingers through her hair, telling someone else's husband how much she loved him.

…you too,' Alex said. He was back in the room.

Celeste clenched her teeth. She wanted to die.

*

The next morning her eyes were still sore as she opened them.

'Hi,' Alex said. 'I'm back.' He was looking directly at her, his face just opposite hers as she lay on her left side.

'You are,' Celeste managed. She closed her eyes. She couldn't bear to look at him.

'Got back early this morning. You looked so peaceful, I didn't want to wake you.' He pushed her hair back from her face and she felt her body tense. Then he sprang to his feet and she could hear him pulling on his jeans.

'Still not feeling well? You look tired.'

'I don't feel great.'

'Gonna pop out and get breakfast. Want anything?' He said, grabbing a white T-Shirt from the drawer.

Celeste heard herself say 'no'.

'Coffee? A croissant?' There was a distinct positivity in his voice. He must have enjoyed screwing Bonnie.

Eventually, she nodded, even though she knew she wouldn't drink it. Alex had forgotten that she had stopped drinking coffee when she found out she was pregnant. But that didn't matter now. She just wanted him to leave the house. She couldn't think straight with him standing over her, looking at her with those big blue eyes. It was making her doubt what she'd seen. It was foolish not to have saved the information. She bit her bottom lip considering what her next move could be.

As soon as Alex had left the apartment, Celeste pulled on her dressing gown and went over to the phone. She picked it up and dialled Graham's number.

62

7th August 2012
Mid-Levels, Central and Western District, Hong Kong

'What the fuck's wrong with you?' Alex screamed, as he entered their apartment.

Celeste swayed slightly. She felt faint. She had hardly eaten anything yesterday. The dull ache had returned. She didn't know if something was wrong with her baby or if it was just stress. She would call the doctor today. She closed her eyes. There was too much to think about. Her mind was shrouded in a thick fog. She opened her eyes and saw Ruby step out of the kitchen. She could sense the poor thing trying to disappear into the walls. Then, like a flash of light, Ruby shot up the stairs with a duster in her hand.

'This pregnancy is making you delusional.' Alex's blue eyes bore into her and immediately she felt guilty, like it was her who had done something wrong. She reminded herself she was not at fault, but that feeling of dread had already made itself known in the pit of her stomach.

She braced herself, putting a protective hand on her belly. 'I just wanted to know where you were last week?'

'You're paranoid. I sent you a picture.'

'You were with her,' she said, finding some strength. Her

fingers trembled and her legs felt weak. She sat down. She had spoken to Graham, confronted him about Alex's affairs, but Graham had denied it. Blood was thicker than water and she had been foolish to think otherwise. It was Graham who had mentioned a pre-nup before they were married. Something Alex insisted she didn't sign. At the time, she had thought it sweet, now she knew why Alex was so nonchalant about the whole matter – the company owned everything.

'What the hell are you on about?'

She watched him, his facial expressions and his hands – the way they moved. She looked for the signs of a liar – a twitching nose, a scratch to the face, a moment's hesitation as he spoke.

Something.

Anything.

Nothing. Alex was a professional. 'It's bad enough that you're fucking her. Do I have to say her name?'

'Is this a joke? I was in Shanghai on business. Graham doesn't know his arse from his elbow when it comes to *Renshaw*. We keep him out of it, like I've told you a million times. That's why he didn't know where I was. That's why he called. Calling my brother and making a scene is ridiculous.' Alex put the cup of coffee on the table along with a grease-stained brown paper bag.' He started to walk towards her.

Don't come near me.' Celeste put her hand out and he stepped back. She looked away. His confidence had made her doubt herself. She still loved him, but she couldn't believe him. She couldn't deny what she had seen yesterday. Had he and Bonnie dined in the same restaurants that were special to her and Alex? He had flown to Scotland several times over the last year, she had seen that in his itinerary. He had taken her to Vienna and Miami too, she was sure of that. Places she had always wanted to go. Had he flown her to Hong Kong to be with her, like he had done with one of his *Low Stock* women? Yes, he had. She was certain now that it was Bonnie she had seen in the *Mont Blanc* store that time. Alex said she was imagining things. Hadn't Alex received a new *Mont Blanc* pen from a 'client' that very week? She had never even thought to question it.

Cheating was on a whole other level when you had money to burn. And all the while he was screwing Bonnie, he had purposefully encouraged the distance in their friendship. Whenever she asked for his advice on trying to make contact with her, he would always say, 'Let her call you.' She had stupidly assumed his father's cheating had turned him against adulterers. Yet he had turned a blind eye to Bill and the expats in Hong Kong and she had accepted that. She had been so naïve, only seeing what she wanted to.

She looked out at the hazy Hong Kong skyline and then up to the oppressive, blood-red, crystal chandelier that hung over their dining table. 'It's hard to leave,' Kealana had said, 'when you are accustomed to this lifestyle.' Now she wondered how she would live if she left Alex with nothing but her dignity? And where did integrity get you when you didn't have money for your next meal?

'Just tell me the truth.'

Alex reached for the brown bag and pulled out a glazed pastry. He bit into it, ignoring her.

'You do want us to get past this, don't you?'

'Your hormones are all over the place. When you've calmed down, we can talk about whatever it is that's bothering you. Something's upset you.' He put his half eaten pastry back in the paper bag and walked towards her. They both sat down on the brown leather sofa. 'What's the matter?' he asked, but she couldn't talk, instead she let him pull her towards him.

They sat in silence until Celeste pulled away. 'You were in Scotland, not Shanghai.'

Alex pulled back just slightly, and she noted a split second of shock in his eyes, before he regained his composure. Her heart sank.

He began to laugh.

'You were with her?'

'What?'

'I'm not talking about Rachel. I met Rachel when I was in London.'

Alex looked nonplussed.

'I'm sure you heard about it from the staff at *The Emerald Rooms*. She knew you as William. It explains why you were so desperate to speak to me that night, when normally you don't give a toss.'

'You told me about that. You found it all very entertaining. It was one of Bill's women – you were laughing about it. Why are you projecting his affairs on me?'

'This isn't about Bill. Was Bill also sleeping with my assistant designer Mo Li? She was one of your conquests as well, wasn't she?'

'Did she say something? She's young. Probably pissed about *Cross* making her redundant. Blames you as her manager.'

'My designers were beneath your standing, I remember you saying that I shouldn't hang out with them. Yet you didn't mind screwing Mo Li, before taking away her job, did you? Taking away all our jobs. I know you own *Cross*.'

'Who've you been talking to? Or did you make it up, like

when you thought Kealana was trying to poison you?'

A shiver ran down her spine, Kealana's warning came back to her. 'The Renshaws are influential.' She had implied that she could be in danger if she rocked the boat, but this was no ordinary boat, this was her marriage. She wouldn't be a martyr like Alex's mother. She was going to fight her corner.

She could feel Alex's hot breath on her face as he leaned towards her. 'Tell me who has been making up these lies,' he whispered with such a chill in his voice that the fine hair on the back of her arms stood up. She dropped her knees and rubbed her belly. 'It's all lies.'

If Alex was having an affair, this was his opportunity to get out of their marriage, so why was he denying it? Was it because he wanted to be the innocent one? Was he that insecure? She took a deep breath. 'You were with Bonnie this past week. I logged on to your computer. I've seen what you've been up to. I know you own *Cross*. I know you've been having affairs.'

Alex stood up and walked towards the stairs. 'I told you categorically not to use my computer. You don't know what you're doing. I have sensitive data on there for *Renshaw*. This isn't a joke.'

'Do you have time to work, juggling all your women? Flying here and there to be with your stock? Graham said you had taken a back seat at *Renshaw* and now I see why. You criticized your brother for all these years but it was just a smoke screen, wasn't it, for your ignorant wife?'

'You don't know what you're saying.'

'You're the one who's broken *my* heart. You can't deny what you've done.'

'How did you access my computer?'

'That's what you're worried about?'

'Tell me.'

'I had a stab at the password. It was pretty simple to guess,' she said, covering up for Kealana.

He stopped in his tracks and turned around. Then he walked up to her and squatted down to where she was sitting. He looked at her with intense eyes. Eyes she didn't recognize.

'I guessed,' she said and then looked away. She did everything in her power to stop herself from bursting into tears. When she looked back at him she could see hatred behind the bright blue of his eyes. Had it always been there, lurking in the shadows of his eyes? Why did he hate her so much? Was it because he had been found out, because the perfect persona he had created for himself was crumbling?

Alex took a deep breath and closed his eyes. Her body tensed. She noticed his fists were clenched. She put a protective hand on her belly. He had never raised a hand to her before, but she had seen him hit a man and she could feel his anger now. It was radiating off him. For the first time in her life she was scared. Would he do something to harm her? Would he do something to hurt their baby? The baby he never wanted.

He opened his eyes. 'It's all lies,' he said calmly, and walked away from her towards his study. Celeste breathed a sigh of relief. Alex would never hurt her, she told herself, but she wasn't quite sure she believed it.

63

20th August 2012
Mid-Levels, Central and Western District, Hong Kong

Two weeks had passed and Alex and Celeste passed each other, like ghosts, in their own home. Alex had moved to the spare room and was out of their apartment most of the time. Celeste had tried getting into his computer again but he had changed the password – of course he had. It was her own fault for telling him how she had found out about his affairs. She knew now that she should have emailed some of the documents to herself if she couldn't save them. She had been foolish not to, but she hadn't been thinking straight.

She had visited the doctor and he had said that the baby was fine. He put her pains down to stress and now when she experienced a dull ache she calmed herself until they passed. She had her doubts about the doctor, on *Renshaw*'s payroll, but she had little choice. And she knew even if Alex had been unfaithful to her he wouldn't harm their child. He wasn't a monster.

Alex wasn't helping. She lay back on the sofa thinking of his increasingly irrational and temperamental behaviour – one minute he was nice, the next he was horrid. Only last week he said he wanted to make things right between them. He had booked a table at one of her favourite restaurants and had sent her flowers that morning. She in turn had chosen a red dress, a dress she knew Alex loved, and one she felt attractive in, although it was difficult these days with her protruding belly. When they got to the restaurant he had ordered, asked her about her day and then indulged her by talking about their days travelling together. Reminiscing about their visit to Monkey Island and reminding her of the snorkelling they had done in Koh Phi Phi. But just half way through their main course she had tensed, knowing that Alex was about to do his *Jekyll and Hyde* act because it wasn't the first time that he had done this to her.

It always started when he mentioned *Cross*, telling her how financially inept Maryanne had been, explaining how he had rescued the brand. Oh all hail Alex the saviour! A lump at the back of her throat would form when he told her that she only got to where she was because of him. 'I told Maryanne to keep you on,' he would say, stinging Celeste, even though she had heard it from his mouth countless times now. 'Maryanne did what she was told. Why do you think she didn't come to our wedding?' If that wasn't enough, he would tell her how fantastically the Paris store was doing and that the designer there was only in her twenties and a size two. He provoked her and she reacted, even though she knew the game he was playing. Each time it hurt afresh, but there was something about Alex that made her stay and listen to everything he had to stay. His tricks had worked and he had what he had wanted all along – full control over her.

Of course the first time he had emotionally attacked her like this she had been angry, she had fought back. But recently she had lost the energy – she found it was better to just listen.

She thought she would be able to block out his harsh words, but after hearing them over and over, she began to believe them. The waiters would see her pain, but they walked past as if it were perfectly ordinary. They wouldn't interfere, not with the kind of tips Alex doled out. It was her fault. She could have said 'no' to the dinner invite, but then it always was difficult to say 'no' to Alex. He would needle and cajole until he got his way and if she held her ground he would turn it around on her.

'You see, Celeste,' he would say. 'I'm trying to make things right between us. You don't seem to care, to want to make an effort.' He always knew what buttons to press.

'The last couple of times we fought. Let's stay in and talk,' she would say.

'I can't think clearly here. And you can't cook. We can make this right. You just have to give us a chance.' He would look at her with those big blue eyes, and eventually she would give in, thinking maybe this time would be different. It never was.

This week Alex had been ignoring her. It was tortuous. But she didn't have a choice. Her due date was in three months, so going back to England was no longer an option. A few weeks ago she had filled her empty days by busying herself with buying things for the baby, organizing the guest room into a nursery and making sure she read up on what being a new mum was like. But her thoughts were always peppered with concerns about Alex. If he wasn't at home she wondered if he was with Bonnie or perhaps someone new. She played tortuous conversations in her mind over and over on what she would say if he asked for a divorce. Would she say she was relieved and walk out or would she break down and beg him to stay like the weakling she had become? Without a single true friend in Hong Kong she thought the latter was most likely to be true. She couldn't cope with the idea of a divorce, let alone Alex asking for one. She prayed it wouldn't come to that.

Lately she had been feeling lethargic. The more Alex ignored her, the less she wanted to move. Most days this week she didn't even want to get out of bed. Her sleeping pattern was erratic. At night she would try and sleep but mostly she was gripped with anxiety – irrational thoughts waking her up. At times she thought she could hear Alex in his bed with another woman. Twice she had crept down to listen at his door – there had been nothing. The mornings were hardest for her. It was when she felt most sleepy, but still she couldn't sleep, and by midday, Kealana would come to her room, draw the curtains and encourage her to get up and brush her teeth. It took her at least half an hour to walk to the bathroom, wash her face and brush her teeth, and although she had nothing but time, she didn't see the point in any of it. She just about managed two meals a day, and that was mostly to stop Kealana and Ruby from hassling her. The baby was about the only thing keeping her going.

The worst days were the days like today when she woke up and felt like there was a ten tonne weight on her chest – a weight comprised of guilt and inadequacy. Alex's words played in her mind – he had saved her, given her a job, without him she was nothing. And she soon believed that there was no way she could care for a baby on her own. It was on days like today that she wanted to die. She ran her fingers through her knotted hair and buried herself further under the blanket on the sofa.

'Talk to someone,' Kealana said, pulling the cover off Celeste and handing her a cup of green tea. Kealana had now made it her duty to visit Celeste as often as she could.

'I have no one.'

'Your friend from the UK.'

'I can't,' she said, thinking of Alicia, her fiery mop of hair and her ready smile. 'I was terrible to her. I cut her out.'

'Your mother?'

Celeste shook her head. She couldn't bear the thought of burdening her poor mother with her news, not when she was so excited about the arrival of their first grandchild.

'Then get out of the house. You sit at home all day in your gown. You keep the television on all night because you are afraid being alone. All you have is Ruby and me, and that is not the way for a young woman to be.'

'I have a husband and I'm pregnant.'

Kealana pursed her lips together. 'Being pregnant is not a disease.'

'Do you know where Alex is today?' Celeste's eyes shone, hungry for more information about Bonnie and Alex. She had asked Kealana what his new password was, but she said she didn't know, and Celeste believed her. Alex was untrusting before, now he was absolutely suspicious of everyone and everything. He had even stopped Kealana from opening his post. But she craved reading his emails. It was the perfect insight into what he was thinking, what he was doing.

'No, I don't. It's not good to dwell on this. Has he apologized?'

She shook her head. Alex had said a lot of things since his return from Shanghai or Scotland or wherever he had been, but he had not yet uttered an apology. He would never admit his guilt. By putting Celeste down all the time he was justifying his infidelity. She didn't need to be a psychologist to see that, yet she couldn't do anything about it. She turned her face away from Kealana.

Ruby entered the lounge and Kealana found an excuse to leave. She watched Kealana move towards the kitchen. She didn't want to admit it, but she enjoyed her company. It was hard to believe that the woman she was once afraid of, was now her closest…closest what? Friend? Probably. She had no one else.

*

'Going out again?' she asked Alex when the sun had set and he appeared wearing dark jeans, a black shirt and a black blazer. Living in a house with the man she loved without being able to touch him or speak to him left her empty.

'I have friends to meet,' he said casually.

'Do I know them?'

'Don't think so.'

'Will you be back late?'

'Don't make a fuss.'

'I could change and come with you?'

'You're not feeling well.'

It was true. Since Alex's return, the nausea had come back with a vengeance. The doctor blamed it on stress and Celeste had to agree with him.

'I have to leave now,' he said, looking at her swollen belly. He had still not shown any love towards the unborn child – no putting his hand on her belly to feel a kick, no talking of possible names. Celeste did all this with Ruby and Kealana.

'Alex,' she said, tears staining her cheeks. 'How did we get here?'

He stopped at the front door, turned around, walked over to her and squatted beside her. 'How long have you been in those pyjamas for?'

She looked at her attire and for the first time in two days she noticed what she was wearing. She touched her greasy hair. 'I've just been so…'

'This isn't healthy for either of us. Look at you. We have staff in the house. Imagine how they must see you.'

She opened her mouth. She wanted to say that Ruby and Kealana understood, but she knew what his response would be. Instead she closed her mouth. Alex was right. What was wrong with her?

He stared at her.

He's going to ask for a divorce.

'I think we…'

'Don't Alex,' she pleaded. 'Don't say it.'

He stood up and put his hand on her neck. She froze under his grip.

'You lose the baby. I have no reason to stay. I can't leave my pregnant wife, can I? What would people say? But, just my wife? I could leave her easily.' The words came to her mind. Had Alex said that or had she imagined it?

He relaxed his grip and started rubbing her neck. Her tears fell onto her clothes. 'I think we should move back into the same bed. I'll move back in tonight.'

She breathed out a sigh of relief then looked up at Alex.

Alex turned and left.

64

Barnet, North London

'He moved back into your room that night?' Elaine asked.

'I had asked Ruby to buy me some hair dye that very evening, despite any worries of how it would affect my unborn baby. I sorted out my hair, dyed it black, just how Alex liked it, thinking it would make things better between us. But Alex moving back into our marital bed was the worst thing that could have happened.' Celeste's fingers trembled as she spoke. 'I see that now.'

'Why was that?'

'He snuck back into our room early the next morning reeking of alcohol. He wanted sex. I wasn't ready for that. But I let him do to me what he wanted. It makes me feel sick now when I think of how weak I was.'

'It wasn't your fault. You wanted your marriage to work.'

'As I lay there, my only thought was that he probably hadn't been with another woman that night because he wanted me. That's how desperate I was.'

'Alex had been drip-feeding you lies for so long. Then suddenly you were struck with deceit, false identities and a string of women that your husband had been having affairs with. It's understandable that you felt that way. Women often feel somehow to blame for their husbands' infidelities. That's what he would have wanted you to believe.'

'He never said "sorry." Not once.'

'Men like Alex have an ego…'

'But I let him become that person. I turned a blind eye to all those business trips and late night meetings. I thought it was the most natural thing in the world to be dropped home after a night out only for Alex to make his excuses and head out again. He usually said he was going to carry on with the *guys*. Of course, now I see, there was no meeting other guys. It was an excuse to call *Asian Escorts* and chat up impressionable young girls. He must have laughed every time he told me he had to fly out on business. All those duty free presents were just to cover up his guilt, and I gladly accepted them without question. I didn't see what Alex was doing because I didn't want to see it. Yet he always wanted to know where I was with that tracking application he installed on my phone so that he could always monitor where I was. Can you believe I was actually flattered by his apparent jealousy? But not once did I cheat, I had the opportunity – even Toby Cain had tried it on – I just never took it. I was too in love. Why did he install it, when he was the one screwing around?'

'To rationalize his behaviour. Because he was being unfaithful he assumed you would be too, and if he had proof of an affair it would have been easier for him to blame you. He couldn't accept culpability himself.'

'He used to take calls in the other room, use the computer in secrecy, claiming it was business – important business stuff that I wouldn't understand.'

Elaine nodded. 'He was belittling you, making you feel

worthless to justify his actions. And of course, to give him the cover he needed to be unfaithful.'

'He was an ass.'

Elaine smiled.

Celeste smiled too. She had to admit it, opening up to Elaine was making her feel better. She could feel herself letting go, gearing up towards the next step. It was a big step, but she had to take it. She paused now, wondering why she had trusted Elaine. She had told her so much. And why? There had been no reason to. But she had started, so she may as well finish. 'I let Alex get away with it for so long. I accepted his behaviour and lies without question, I accepted the late nights at the office, laughed at the incompetence of his brother, Graham, and wore diamond bracelets like shackles around my wrists. I was blinded by material possessions.'

'You didn't see what was happening, because you couldn't cope with what would happen if you confronted him.'

'What hurt the most was that I was the last to know. Even Angela must have known. That's why she met me in London. Maybe she purposely took me to *The Emerald Rooms*. I thought Angela was being naïve about Bill, but really it was me who was the innocent one.'

'People underestimate humiliation. It can cause such pain, and because of that we can often do things we regret. From what you've described, it sounds like you were madly in love and just blind to his faults. No wonder you plunged into depression, especially after what happened.'

Celeste was silent. This is what Elaine had been steering the conversation towards. She should have known that.

'Is that when you picked up the knife?'

Celeste looked at her shoes.

'Violence can often build in failed relationships, both towards the other person or oneself. You said you could see the contempt in Alex's eyes. But how did *you* really feel about Alex?'

Celeste shifted in her chair then looked at the clock. 'You're jumping ahead. I didn't pick up the knife then. I'm ashamed to say that at this point I still loved Alex, despite all the deceit, despite the hurt. Alex and I remained in this state of limbo for another month – fighting, making up, and crying publicly over dinner. Instead of breaking away, I was becoming more and more dependent on him and I was terrified of divorce. I knew I just couldn't cope without him, and Alex began to feed off that.'

'Men who are serial cheaters do that. When they start a relationship with someone else, it isn't that they don't want to be with you, it's just that they want more…'

'They want to have their cake and eat it too. I thought I knew Alex. He was this beautiful man, who had saved me in Thailand and loved me unconditionally. It was all a lie. He certainly knew me – well enough to play me. Even after I found out about his affairs, I still thought there was a chance. In the month that followed, with no access to Alex's computer, the vision of him and Bonnie started to fade from my memory. Alex had never admitted it, so I thought maybe he had seen sense and ended it with her. I should have got out when I had the chance. I would have, if I had known what was coming.' Celeste put a hand on her stomach.

'The man you married was not the man you divorced. People change over the course of a marriage. You must have changed as well during that time. You were independent before you moved to Hong Kong – you had your own job, your own identity. You also refused to be a stay-at-home wife when you married into the *Renshaw* empire. You should be proud of that. It was Alex who slowly took it all away from you.'

'When I lost my job at *Cross*, I thought it pointless getting a new one. I was pregnant and I felt ill all the time. I should have been the trophy wife Alex wanted from the start, then he would have stayed.'

'Few husbands are faithful to trophy wives. And Alex fell in love with the independent Celeste. He wouldn't have wanted you any other way at the time. Don't forget that.'

'In the end he didn't want me, but he didn't want to let me go either,' she said taking a tissue from the box on the desk and dabbing her eyes. 'In the end I had no choice. I had to ask him for a divorce. It all happened so fast after…' she trailed off.

'After what?'

Celeste looked at Elaine. 'He gave me no choice.'

65

15th October 2012
Mid-Levels, Central and Western District, Hong Kong

Celeste pulled back the duvet and padded over to the bathroom. She washed her face, pulled her gown around her and rested her hand on her belly.

Alex was packing for a business trip or he was going to meet Bonnie, she wasn't quite sure, but she hoped it wasn't the latter. Like a switch, Alex's mood had improved a few days ago, and he had even offered to rub her shoulders last night. She walked back into the bedroom, sat down on the bed and watched Alex for a few minutes whilst he sorted out his white shirts from the black ones. Twice he looked up at her and smiled. She wasn't used to him smiling at her of late and she couldn't help thinking that his smile had changed. Before, his smile was broad and genuine, and his eyes had shone at her with a tenderness she could not describe. Now, his smile seemed a little distant and forced. But she couldn't say anything – a smile was better than a scowl.

The house was silent, Ruby was out fetching groceries and Kealana wasn't due for another hour. Celeste savoured moments like this, when she and Alex were alone with no one to interrupt them. Even if they were not on the best of terms with each other they were getting back to some normality. The fear of divorce was starting to fade from her mind, and she felt better in herself since Alex had returned to their bedroom. Waking and getting dressed in the morning was no longer so much of an effort, and her appetite had somewhat returned. But despite her improved mood, she still felt like she was standing on the edge of a deep, black hole and she knew it would only take something small to push her into that dark place again. She shook the feeling off and told Alex she was going to make some tea. She walked towards the bedroom door and stood on the landing. 'Do you want anything?' she asked as she studied the wooden flight of steps in front of her. Alex mumbled something.

'A coffee?'

'Yes,' he said a little louder this time. She could sense him behind her. She took in his fragrance and her body relaxed. When they had first moved into this apartment Alex would come up behind her and wrap his big arms around her, telling her just how much he loved her. She was desperate for him to do that now. She closed her eyes and silently willed him to put an arm around her.

Nothing.

Of course, it was too soon. She attempted a smile. One day, he would love her the way he used to. She opened her eyes and took a step forward.

She felt a hand behind her. Alex was holding her.

No, pushing her.

She was falling.

Seconds later, she opened her eyes. She was at the bottom of the stairs. She felt a sharp stab of pain in her abdomen. Her legs wouldn't move. 'Alex,' she mumbled. She could barely hear her voice, only the blood rushing in her ears. She felt another sharp stabbing pain and a dull ache deep in her belly. 'My baby!' she screamed.

She heard footsteps behind her. 'Alex help me. Our baby,' she said, lifting her head just in time to see him step over her.

'Alex!' she screamed. In her confusion she wondered if he had not seen her. Her vision was blurred but she saw him enter the kitchen before she dropped her head back to the floor.

'My baby,' Celeste groaned as the pain sliced through her.

She heard a key in the door. 'Help,' she heard herself say. She felt numb

'*Aiyaaa*!' she heard Kealana scream, followed by hurried steps from the kitchen.

'What the hell?' It was Alex.

'What's this?' Kealana said, dropping her bag. 'Did you not hear her fall?'

'I had the radio on in the kitchen,' Alex said. Celeste felt her husband squat down and stroke her hair. 'Don't just stand there,' he shouted at Kealana. 'Call a bloody doctor. My wife, my baby!'

Celeste opened her mouth to say something but no words would come. It was the first time Alex had said the words 'my baby'. She cried out in pain just before she passed out.

66

17th October 2012

Aldridge Hospital, Central and Western District, Hong Kong

'Where am I?' she asked, looking around the white and green room. A nurse stood at the end of her bed.

'You're in the hospital now,' the nurse said as she walked over to her side and checked her notes.

'Why? Oh,' Celeste said, remembering. She sat up and touched her belly. It hurt her to move. 'My baby. What happened?'

'You had an accident. Your stomach ulcer medicine didn't help either. Misoprostol can be dangerous. They should have warned you.'

'I don't have a stomach ulcer. Get me the doctor. You don't know. You're confusing me with my husband.'

The nurse looked puzzled. 'You definitely had misoprostol in your system.'

'Who brought me here?' she asked. Memories of the past forty-eight hours started to filter through. She remembered her fall, Alex stepping over her. And then the hospital – the green walls, the smell of bleach. She had given birth. But there had been no crying, had there? Where was her baby? What happened to the child she delivered?

She had used those stairs to their bedroom countless times. It was reckless of her to have fallen. But she hadn't fallen, had she? She had felt something behind her. Someone. She had smelled the sandalwood and citrus of Alex's cologne as she stood on the landing, willing him to hold her. But instead he had pushed her. She recoiled at the thought before she realized it to be true. 'No!' she cried out.

He would never have pushed her. Not kind and gentle Alex. But the Alex she knew now wasn't the same person she had married. He was capable of causing her harm. He was more than capable. She had seen his cold and calculating smile just moments before he pushed her, which she had foolishly mistaken for affection. She had seen the hatred he had for her in his eyes, and she had witnessed him punch a man out cold in Thailand. She couldn't forget his anger then. It had made her blood run cold. Since then Alex had been so calm. Had he hidden his anger from her like he had hidden his whores?

Kealana had been there, she remembered that. She had helped her. What would she have done if she hadn't turned up when she did? Alex had tried to kill both her and the baby. 'My baby?' she asked the nurse. 'Where's my baby?'

'I'll get the doctor now,' the nurse said, walking towards the door.

'Leave,' a man in a white coat said to the nurse as he entered. Alex followed the man into the room.

'You're up Celeste. I'm glad. I'm Doctor Rosenbaum. I was just explaining to your husband…'

'Is my baby okay?' Celeste asked impatiently.

The doctor rubbed his chin. 'I am so very sorry, Mrs Renshaw…'

'No!' Celeste screamed. 'No, this can't be.'

'You're lucky to be here. If it wasn't for your husband bringing you in immediately…'

She narrowed her eyes. 'Alex brought me in?'

'Of course, hon.'

She looked at the doctor and then at her husband.

Alex flashed her a smile. 'The doctor said you didn't lose too much blood. You're going to be okay. Thank God. We can have you out of here in a couple of days.'

'I gave birth. I want to see my baby.'

'I'm sorry to tell you this, but when you arrived at the hospital your baby had already lost its life. We had to induce labour. It was not viable.'

Celeste stared at the doctor and then at Alex. Alex walked over to her side and took her hand. She immediately pulled away. 'It would have been better if I had died.'

'It's natural to grieve after what has happened.'

'He killed my baby,' Celeste said under her breath.

Dr Rosenbaum cleared his throat. 'It's unlikely at this stage in the pregnancy that the fall would cause this. The baby could have already…'

Celeste held her hand out for the doctor to stop talking. 'I want to see my baby.'

Dr Rosenbaum nodded and then looked at Alex. 'It's a distressing time for both of you. Let me give you some space.'

'Don't leave me alone with this man. I don't want him here.'

Dr Rosenbaum looked from Celeste to Alex before making his way towards the door.

Alex stroked Celeste's hair until the door was firmly closed. 'Aldridge Hospital is one of the most prestigious private hospitals in Hong Kong.' He walked over to the window and looked out.

'And your father is a benefactor.'

'We funded the whole Renshaw wing.'

'Are we in it?'

'It's the other side,' Alex said, turning towards her. We funded the heart unit,' he said, as he tapped his chest. 'I explained to Dr Rosenbaum how much we wanted this child. That we had been trying for some time. He said we can try again soon, maybe in four months or so.'

'You're a liar.'

'I also explained your delusions of late.'

Celeste shook her head. Tears fell from her eyes.

'That whole episode when you thought Kealana was trying to poison you was a bit far-fetched. But they have the records. Dr Asthall and Dr Rosenbaum are firm friends. He'll be requesting your file soon.'

'But you can't just do that without my authorization.'

'This isn't England, Celeste. You can do a lot more over here without all that confidentiality business. A quick cremation if required, that kind of thing. All very helpful.'

'You fucking bastard.'

'I didn't want you to get upset by seeing the baby. I think the doctor understood.'

'What about an autopsy.'

'Try and rest.' Alex walked towards the door. 'I'll come and get you tomorrow. But until then...' Alex put his finger to his lips. 'You don't want them to think you need sedating, do you?' With that he left the room and closed the door behind him.

Celeste screamed and banged her fists on the bed until the doctor returned.

'He's lying,' she said. 'He killed my baby! Don't listen to him! He can't just buy his way out of everything.'

Dr Rosenbaum gave her a reassuring look. Celeste didn't feel the pinprick in her arm but in less than a minute her eyelids closed and she was fast asleep.

67

24th November 2012
Mid-Levels, Central and Western District, Hong Kong

'He's moved out and asked for a divorce, but I don't see any papers. I've tried speaking to Bill, but he's no help,' Celeste said into the receiver. It had been difficult relaying the story to her mother, who was about as far removed from the situation as possible. But she didn't have anyone else to talk to.

'Call her,' Kealana had said.

'I can't speak to her, not after what's happened. How do you tell your mother her grandchild is dead? How do you tell her that you tried to kill yourself?' Celeste's eyes had been red raw from crying.

'Mr Alex has told your mother everything,' Kealana had said. Celeste's jaw dropped open. She was sure that Alex had lied to her mother, made it out like it was all her fault. That's what he believed, that's what he wanted everyone to believe. Jackie and Melanie had called on her yesterday, but she had turned them away. She didn't know what lies Alex had been feeding them, but she could imagine. 'She fell down the stairs. She's always so clumsy, and I told her to be careful,' he must have said, and Jackie would have held her hand to her mouth and shaken her head as pity leaked out of her. She couldn't handle them right now. She could barely handle herself.

In just two weeks she had gone from a healthy mother-to-be to an emaciated wreck. Her sleep was broken, punctuated with nightmares of delivering a dead baby whilst Bonnie and Alex looked on and laughed. The dark hole had lured her in – a place where she didn't have to think of divorce, dead babies or being poisoned by her husband. When the fog had lifted she remembered what the nurse had said about the misoprostol harming her baby and she had looked up his ulcer medicine on-line. It clearly said that the drug could cause miscarriage. The sickness she had felt through her pregnancy and the pain in her abdomen, she knew, was more than a urinary tract infection. It was because of Alex: he had been trying to make her miscarry. She remembered after the nurse had let slip about the misoprostol that she felt at her worst only when Alex had been in the house. The thought of that alone had plunged her deep into depression. Her supposed soulmate had killed their baby. If it wasn't the fall that killed their baby it must have been the misoprostol. She had asked Alex why, but he had ignored her question.

She realized that once the darkness had swallowed her, she couldn't get out of it. Her appetite disappeared. This time she had no reason to eat, and her legs refused to work. She slept during the day, barely managing to wash her face when she did rise. Kealana had tried making her favourite foods and had encouraged her to take a shower, but all these activities, tasks she would normally do without even thinking, now just seemed like pointless endeavours. In those early days, Alex had looked in on her occasionally, but she sensed that he was enjoying her deterioration. His charming blue eyes had vanished. The loving looks and the affectionate squeeze of her hand that he had once given her had been replaced with nonchalance and the occasional push.

When she felt like she couldn't cope any longer, she had taken a knife from the kitchen, sat on the bottom stair that led to their bedroom, the place she had lost her baby, and slashed her wrists. As the knife pierced her skin the pain began to subside along with the anger and the guilt. The pain and the grief were finally being released. She smiled as the blood seeped out of her left wrist, staining the wooden floor that had only recently been polished. The next thing she knew she was lying in a bed, once again in the Aldridge Hospital, her wrists bandaged. Ruby had found her, Alex had said in front of the nurse. As soon as they were out of earshot, he had said, 'Your own death – you couldn't even get that right.'

Alex had told her to leave, and still she stayed. He had sat on the edge of her bed and said, 'Paranoia and attempted suicide is not going to do you any favours. You're unstable and delusional. I suggest you get out of my life quickly so we can both move on.' She didn't move. She didn't have anywhere to go. So eventually, he left. 'Temporarily,' he said. Yet it seemed he didn't want her out of his life. Weeks had passed, and each day she waited to be served divorce papers, but they never arrived.

She shook the memory from her mind as she paced the living room. 'I think he wants to marry Bonnie,' she said into the receiver.

'Have you thought about coming home, pet,' her mother said. 'It's not healthy, Celeste, being there, in that apartment. Where it all happened like. It's like yer punishing yerself.'

Celeste stopped pacing. She looked at the stairs that led to their bedroom, touching her empty belly and felt a shiver run down her spine. Today was her due date. She hated Alex. But for some reason, she couldn't leave. She had tried the only way she knew, but that had failed too, she had not slashed her wrists deep enough. Alex was right, she was a failure.

'Celeste? You there?' her mother said.

'I need to check my account. See how much money I've got.' Now she wished she had taken better care of her finances. Since they married she had left all that to Alex. 'You won't get a penny out of me,' he had said, as he left their apartment that final time. 'How will I survive?' she had asked. When he shrugged she had said she was entitled to half of what he had, but he had just laughed then and told her that he didn't own anything.

'He'd give yer money to get home surely?' her mother said. 'B-but don't worry if he won't. Don't you worry 'bout a thing, we can send you some money.'

Celeste could hear her mother's voice catching and she swallowed the lump at the back of her throat. 'I have to go.'

'Don't go, pet. Not just yet. Are yer alone?'

'I'm not going to do anything stupid. Kealana's here,' she lied.

'Come home, sweetheart. Just come home. Yer don't need him.'

'You don't know what I need.'

'I didn't mean it like that.'

Celeste heard a key in the door. Her heartbeat quickened. She said goodbye to her mother and disconnected the call. She looked apprehensively at the door. She was afraid it would be Alex. She looked down at her clothes and couldn't remember when she had put her pyjamas on. She wished she didn't feel so useless, so weak. If it were Alex at the door, he would mock and ridicule her. She couldn't handle it. Not today. She had not seen him since last week, but he had called her a few times since, in the dead of night. Depending on his mood he would either verbally assault her or tell her she was the only woman he had ever loved. She found his behaviour erratic and confusing but she remembered the little bags of cocaine he had in his wardrobe. It was slowly falling into place.

She had asked him about the coke but he had laughed. 'You clearly don't know anything about me,' he had said in response, and so she had dropped it. It wasn't worth another fight. So when he called she would listen to whatever he had to say and cry until the sun rose and her eyes closed. She loved him, but she hated him more. What he had done to her, what he had done to their baby, was ruthless. There was no remorse. No matter how many times he told her that she had tripped and fallen, it would never be true.

As the door creaked, her heartbeat quickened.

The door opened. Celeste breathed a sigh of relief. 'It's you.'

'Mr Alex is in London. But we need to get you sorted before he comes back.'

'I spoke to Bill. Alex thinks Bill can use his charm to get me out. But I've seen how the two have collaborated before. He can't get his friends to do his dirty work.'

'Mr Bill only wants to help. He is your friend too.'

'Warwick sent you to clear up his mess.'

'I came because I care for you.'

Celeste nodded. 'Sorry, I know that.'

'But it won't be long before they want you out.'

'What will they do?'

'You know the power they have here. They can make life difficult. Do you know that Alex has already cancelled your cards?'

'I've not been out of the house. I haven't used them.'

'We need to get you a plan. You can't carry on like this, indefinitely.'

'I don't know where to start.' Just the thought of having to make a decision left Celeste with a feeling of dread in the pit of her stomach.

'First, I'm going to make you breakfast. Poached eggs on toast, yes.' Kealana took the brown paper bag she was carrying into the kitchen. 'Why don't you take a bath?'

Celeste made a face. 'I can't face doing anything today.'

'Nonsense,' Kealana said. She made her way upstairs. Celeste could hear her bath being filled. She buried her face in her hands. Minutes later Kealana was at her side. 'Today we make a plan. Then I promise you, you'll feel better.' She put her arm around Celeste and encouraged her to stand up.

*

'Thank you,' Celeste said to Kealana. She stood in the doorway of the kitchen dressed in the jeans and jumper Kealana had laid out for her.

'Go sit at the table. I'll bring this out.'

She did as she was told and saw that her address book was on the table. It was open. 'What's this?'

Kealana appeared with a plate of eggs. 'You must call her.'

Celeste studied the open page. She shook her head. 'I can't.'

'You need to talk to someone. Since you found out about Alex's affairs you've not seen or spoken to a single friend. Not even those British ones that live here.'

'They don't really care.'

'Who's your real friend?'

'I don't have any real friends anymore.'

'The girl with the red hair – she is real. I saw photos of you together. You used to speak on the phone all the time. In London, she used to visit nearly every day when Alex was away.'

'She lied to me and the last time I spoke to her I said some terrible things to her. Plus, she's friends with Bonnie. If Alex is in London now, he's probably with her. They might all be together.'

'You won't know if you don't call her.'

'I'll just stay put for a while.'

'Staying here is not good for you. It's eating away at your soul. Mr Alex will do what is best for him. You have to do what's right for you. Buddha says that it is better to conquer yourself than to win a thousand battles. Because then the victory is yours. It cannot be taken from you. Not by angels or demons, heaven or hell.'

'You're wasted working for the Renshaws.'

'Call the woman with the fire-red hair and tell her to come for you. You need to get out now Mrs Celeste, whilst you still can.'

68

Barnet, North London

'So that's why you took a knife to your wrists. That's why your mother wanted you to come here.'

Celeste looked away. It was a reason, but not the only reason.

'It makes sense. I remember when you first came here. You looked so lost. You don't look lost any more. You look quite determined.'

'I've realised I have a purpose.'

'You're still angry?'

'Alex killed my baby, I'll never forgive him for that.'

'The anger balances out the grief.'

'I loved Alex, even after he left. I thought he would come back and save me, but he didn't. You can't just stop loving someone overnight. It's not like there is a switch in your brain you can just turn off and on. I now know why some people stay with people who have done terrible things.'

'How do you feel now?'

Celeste shrugged. She hated him with every fibre of her being, but she wasn't going to tell Elaine that. That wouldn't help her in the long run. 'That picture you have there,' Celeste pointed to the picture lying on the desk. 'Alex took that on his phone when I was in hospital. I had lost my baby and tried to take my own life and he took a picture of my misery. He sent it to me not long after. I almost picked up the knife again when I saw it.'

'You didn't though.'

'Alex had someone from his office pick up some of his things while I was supposed to be organising my departure from his life. As his man was carrying a box out of the apartment, a letter slipped to the floor. It must have been picked up with some of Alex's stuff. His office assistant didn't notice the letter fall, and as soon as he left the apartment I closed the door and pounced on it. I thought it would be a love note from Bonnie. I could imagine her writing him soppy love notes.'

'Was it?'

'The letter had been opened, but it was addressed to me. It was from Maryanne.'

'Your old boss.'

'The one who passed away, yes. She had written it to me just before her death. The executor of her will sent it to me when she died. Why she didn't email me I'll never know. Perhaps she was too frail to get to a computer or perhaps she was worried Alex would intercept my emails. The letter never reached me though. Alex had got to it first, read its contents and kept it from me.'

'What did it say?'

'Maryanne had tried to save me. Her letter explained that Alex's offer to buy *Cross* came soon after her second diagnosis of cancer. I never realized she'd had it once already when she was younger. Her health insurance wouldn't cover it the second time as it was a pre-existing condition, and she was desperate for the money, for her treatment. Her bones were too old to withstand the NHS, she had written. Maryanne said that Alex's offer was generous – all done through Mr William Harris, but that she had known he was behind it the whole time. "Alex isn't the only one with contacts," she wrote. She had wanted to tell me of his deception at the time, but she felt she should ask Alex about it first. She approached him before the wedding, but he had charmed his way out of it. "It's a surprise," he had said. "I'm buying the business for Celeste," he assured her. He told her not to breathe a word of what he was doing and Maryanne reluctantly agreed, but she was apprehensive.

'She had once had an affair with Warwick, and it had ended badly. She knew that when the Renshaws wanted something they made sure they got it. She wasn't sure if Alex was cut from the same cloth so she gave him the benefit of the doubt, but it pricked at her conscience. It's why she never came to the wedding in the end. Alex had lied when he said she didn't come because he told her not to. It was only after we married that she realized she had got into bed "with the devil." She apologized for not having told me, but by then too much time had passed and in the small print of her contract Alex had made it a condition of the sale that she never speak to me about his involvement. He pointed it out when she confronted him later. It wasn't until she knew that her time was up that she wrote to me. She asked for my forgiveness.

'She wanted my understanding, yet I had not seen what she had been going through. After I read the letter and dried my eyes, I decided then that I had to help myself if I was going to get out of the mess I was in. Maryanne had told me that a bee had a sting in its tail and I was the bee. I owed it to her to use all my energy to get out of that toxic relationship and make something of my life. That afternoon I took Kealana's advice. I swallowed my pride and called Alicia.

'In the end it was Alicia who saved me. She flew out to Hong Kong immediately. "Nonsense," she said when I apologized for being cruel to her about her affair with Bill. Alicia always had a good heart, it was I who had been so self-absorbed. I didn't see I was pushing away those closest to me. I wasn't even there for Maryanne when she died. She didn't have any family. She needed me, but I wasn't there. In that letter she had asked for my forgiveness. I needed to ask for hers, but it was too late. There was only one thing I could do for her – something I knew she'd be proud of.'

'What was that?'

'To live, of course.'

69

30th November 2012

Mid-Levels, Central and Western District, Hong Kong

'Have you been to the police?' Alicia asked after Celeste had told her the whole story. They were sitting on the floor, their backs against the chocolate brown leather sofas. Darkness had fallen over Hong Kong and the Symphony of Lights had started. One by one in succession each skyscraper took their turn at flashing their lights, in primary colours, over the harbour. They had just finished their Chinese takeaway and were well on their way to finishing their second bottle of red.

'He owns the police.' Celeste said, topping up her glass. 'In Hong Kong everything and everyone can be bought.'

'And this nonsense with Bonnie, is it true? She told me she was in love. I never guessed it would be with Alex.'

'You didn't know about Rachel?'

'Don't you think I'd have told you if I had known?'

'Do you think she knew he was married?'

Alicia shook her head.

Celeste could believe that. In all the conversations she had read on his computer, she hadn't been mentioned once. It stung as much as his betrayal. 'You'll introduce me to her when I'm back in London?'

'If that's what you want.' Alicia leaned over and tucked a lock of hair behind Celeste's ear. 'She's not as pretty as you.'

'I saw pictures of them – Alex and Bonnie.'

'She started asking after you recently and I thought she wanted a reconciliation. Now, I know better.'

'You always think the best of people. Do you think he's with her now?'

Alicia shrugged. 'When did you last speak to him?'

'Yesterday.'

'So you asked him?'

'He never answers any of my questions.' She took a sip of her wine. 'I asked him when I would receive the divorce papers, but he just laughed. He doesn't want me and he doesn't want anyone else to have me. This way I'm still his puppet. Most nights he calls me, either to scream at me or conversely to tell me how much he loves me and no one else will ever take my place. I don't listen anymore.'

'This can't be good for your state of mind.'

'I'm used to it now.'

'Disconnect the phone.'

'If I do that he might turn up here.'

'Change the locks.'

'This building needs the permission of the freeholder before they can authorise a lock change. The apartment is company owned. They need Alex's authority, and that means he'll automatically get a key cut if I change the locks.'

'You can speak to someone and explain the situation.'

'Alex's made sure that the management company know about this rift between us. They're on his side.'

'You can't sit around waiting for him to make the first move. Come back to England with me. We'll get you a top lawyer and you can be the one to serve divorce papers on him. You have to take back some control.'

Celeste picked up her glass. It shook in her hand. 'Maybe I should leave it for a while. Get back on my feet here.'

'Do you really want to be here, after everything? Come back home. As long as you are trapped in this marriage that man will own you. You've got to get out.'

'Alex will go crazy if I serve divorce papers on him. He doesn't expect it of me.'

'Why should you care how he feels? And why should you only do what *he* expects of you?'

'What if he comes after me?'

'You'll be in England, not here. You can get help. If Alex threatens you more than once and you've registered his behaviour with the police each time he has harassed you, you can get a restraining order against him.'

'That would anger him even more.'

Alicia moved closer to Celeste and put her arms around her. 'You'll be okay. You have to do this.'

'It's too much, too soon.'

Alicia took a deep breath. 'Baby steps, then. The first step is to leave this place.' She looked towards the front door. 'You're not safe here.'

70

Barnet, North London

'Is that what you did?'

'I went back to England, but I didn't stay with Alicia for long. I couldn't impose on her and Tom like that. I moved back into the house I grew up in, in Bristol. The house I had been so desperate to leave.'

'It must have been hard for you.'

'I could see how much my parents were hurting, but they didn't mention it. Instead they fed me up and got me through the divorce. I couldn't have done it without them.'

'You worry about what you put your parents through?'

'It was a tough time, that's all. It was hard moving in with my parents after being with Alex for so long and it must have been tough for them – being parents again.'

'Parents never stop being parents. But was it not better being there than to be living a fake life in Hong Kong?'

Celeste smiled. 'My parents supported me but they didn't remind me of it everyday, like Alex would have.'

Elaine twisted one of her curls around her index finger. 'Do you miss your old lifestyle?'

Celeste took a breath then shook her head. 'Don't get me

wrong, having money is not all bad. In fact, it's all I ever dreamed about growing up. I'd be lying to you if I said otherwise. Of course, I miss the expensive meals at high-end restaurants and buying designer clothes, but I've learnt that it's not everything. Now I don't have cash at my disposal but I look forward to things more. I'm learning to appreciate the little things in life again – a meal out is a treat, not a regular Monday night.

'I served Alex with divorce papers three months after I returned to England. He tried contacting me several times, rolled up to my parent's house in a flashy new *Maserati* and made a scene. Every time I spoke to him, it would set me three steps back. Eventually, my solicitor threatened him with an occupation order. He hasn't contacted me since, but I did hear from Bill.'

'What did he want?'

'He said that Alex wanted to talk, sort it out amicably. It was tough saying "no" to Bill.'

'Even after he helped Alex deceive you?'

'He was Alex's best mate, and Bill was the sort of friend that would do anything for a good mate. We ended up going for a coffee – against Alicia's advice. I wanted to know what Alex was up to. I wanted to catch up on his news too.'

'And?'

'He didn't give me the insight that I wanted into Alex's life. But he told me Bill was still in Hong Kong, still with Angela *and* Anya and that he was there if I ever wanted to talk. I wanted to know what was happening with Alex, but he never told me anything Alex didn't want me to know. Eventually, I got the message and stopped calling.'

'You came out of the divorce stronger.'

She nodded. She was strong now. She had a plan.

'And you're financially stable?'

'No matter how hard my lawyers tried to unravel the intricacies of the Renshaws' finances, they couldn't get to the bottom of things. I told them specifically to look into *Heavenly Limited*. I knew that Alex had owned that company in its entirety, but by the time I served those divorce papers nothing was solely in his name. My solicitors fought my corner and the judge was pretty favourable in the end.'

'That's why they call London the divorce capital of the world.'

'As part of the settlement I managed to keep our house in central London. My solicitors argued that I needed a home. The house is mortgage free and I rent it out. I can't afford to live there, but it gives me a good income. I'm renting a small house here in Barnet in the meantime. I also received a small amount of cash, which I paid my parents back with. They pretty much funded my divorce.'

'And did you ever meet Rachel Blake?'

'I suppose that's the main reason why I'm here.'

'I thought it was because of the loss of your baby, and because you tried to kill yourself?'

'When I returned to London I tried calling Bonnie, but she wouldn't take my calls. Rachel was my next best alternative. I was desperate to meet her. I thought that by asking her about her relationship with Alex I would understand him better, but I left that meeting distraught.'

'Why, what did she say?'

'She told me that towards the end of her relationship with Alex they had bumped into Bonnie. Rachel knew her, but the way in which Alex looked at her unnerved her. At the time she put it behind her, but after her break up with Alex she kept tabs on Bonnie through social media. She showed me a picture that Bonnie had recently put up on her profile.'

'You and Alicia were not friends with Bonnie on social media?'

'Didn't even know she had a profile. Alicia and I later realised she had blocked her profile from us so we couldn't even see that it existed.'

'The picture upset you?'

'It was a picture of Bonnie and Alex.'

'I can imagine that would hurt.'

'Alex was holding their newborn.'

Elaine put her hand to her mouth.

'They looked like the perfect family.'

'So, nothing good came from your meeting?'

Celeste shrugged. 'I spoke to Rachel for quite a while. She had her faults but underneath it all she really had loved Alex. I was jealous of her though, because by the time I met her she had already met someone else, online. She said after Alex – or William as she knew him – she had a better chance of meeting a complete stranger who was genuine than a love rat in places like *The Emerald Rooms*.

'After seeing that picture of Alex, Bonnie and the baby I was just days away from wanting to end my life again. Then my mother turned up at my door. She suggested this place, and I, for a change, listened. After all they had done for me I had to listen. I'm glad I did. So my mother is the main reason why I am here.'

'Do you still think of Alex?'

Celeste pursed her lips. She wasn't sure how to answer. She could have told Elaine the truth – that she had started tracking

Alex on the long forgotten application he had installed on their phones to keep tabs on each other. Perhaps, Alex had forgotten he had installed it on his phone or maybe he wanted her to know where he was. Either way, she often pulled up the data because it was comforting knowing where in the world he was.

'It's completely understandable if you still think about him,' Elaine said as if reading her mind. 'He was a big part of your life and you met him when you were so young. When we meet people who form impressions on us at such a young age we find it difficult to let go of them.'

Celeste attempted a smile, but her hands were entwined tightly in her lap. 'I do think of Alex – not the person he turned out to be, but the person he was when we first met.'

'Sometimes that's the hardest part – wondering if they still remember you.' Elaine looked into the distance. It was bright outside now and light was streaming into the office.

Celeste knew Elaine's story. Everyone did. She had lost a loved one, that's why she had first come here to this cognitive behavioural therapy unit in Barnet – couldn't cope with the loss.

The door opened behind Celeste. She expected to feel anxiety, but she felt calm. She turned in her seat.

'Elaine, Celeste, what are you doing in here? How did you get in here? My files!'

Hilary walked into her office and examined her locked filing cabinet. 'So you haven't broken into the filing cabinet as well then.' She stared at them.

'The door was unlocked,' Elaine said.

'Was it?' Hilary asked, arching an eyebrow.

'It was,' Celeste confirmed. No one needed to know that

Elaine had a key. It wouldn't be very generous of her if she told.

Celeste followed Hilary's eyes towards the photo on the desk. She picked it up and slipped it in her pocket.

'Patients are not allowed in here. Celeste, you're due to leave,' Hilary looked at her watch, 'today, in the next half hour.' She shook her head, although her thick brown bushy hair stayed motionless. 'Celeste, I expected better from you. What were you doing?'

'Just having a chat.'

Hilary sighed. 'I hope this hasn't hindered your progress.'

Celeste looked at Elaine and smiled. 'Actually, I think it's helped.'

Hilary cleared her throat. 'Elaine, we've been through this before. You're no longer practicing as a counsellor. And you certainly can't use my office as your own. We'll discuss it in our session later.'

Elaine winked at Celeste.

Epilogue

Celeste signed the necessary paperwork and waited in the reception area for her taxi. Pouring her heart out to Elaine had felt cathartic, now she was ready to move on with her life. She held the gold bumblebee pendant in her hand and squeezed it before she let it swing free around her waist. *Remember if a bumblebee ever feels under attack it has a nice sting in its tail.*

The therapists had said that when she was ready she should draw a line under this episode in her life and move on, and that was exactly what she had planned. There was just one last thing she needed to do. A couple of minutes later, her taxi pulled up.

'Where to, luv?' The cab driver asked her.

Celeste accessed her phone. In less than a minute she found the e-ticket she had booked yesterday. 'Heathrow, terminal five.'

'No problem. Going anywhere nice? You don't have much luggage.'

Celeste looked at her red carry-on and smiled.

*

Twenty hours later, she was in Hong Kong. The one thing she had realised during her time at the centre was that she needed closure. After speaking to Elaine, this was the final part of her therapy. She had to face her demons before she could move on. Hong Kong was where it all ended. A place she thought she would never return to. But why not? Hong Kong had been her home as much as it had been Alex's. She checked into her hotel, slept for a few hours and as the sun set, she showered and changed before taking a taxi to Causeway Bay. *Cross* was no longer there. The fuchsia and gold now replaced by the blue and coral of a Spanish designer brand. She walked in the shop and ran her fingers across the fine silks and wool the store offered, then she took a deep breath and as she exhaled she felt a weight lift off her shoulders. *Cross* was the past now. She had let go.

At ten that evening she found herself at the IFC Mall. She realised she hadn't eaten much all day and so she stopped at one of the restaurants she and Alex used to frequent for a plate of duck and rice. Her stomach churched as she thought of him entering the restaurant and she felt in her pocket for the vial to steady her nerves. After a cup of green tea she took out her phone and thought about calling Ben. Ben had been the attractive passenger sitting next to her on the flight over. Ben, a soft-spoken English teacher, had given her his number and she had felt her cheeks colour for the first time in a long while. Then she slipped her phone back into her bag. Tomorrow. She would call him tomorrow. Today she had one more demon to face.

At midnight she arrived at her old apartment building. She waited outside till the porter at the reception desk went into the back room. Then she adjusted her wig and tried her key card – the unregistered spare she had got in a hurry from good old Charlie – the one she had promised to return to register on their system, but never did. She rode the elevator up to the thirty-ninth floor.

Exiting the lift, she carefully tried her keys on the front door. They worked, of course they did. Alex would never have expected her to come back, he would have thought her too scared to do that. A smile touched her lips.

As she walked into the dark apartment she held her breath. She had forgotten the extravagance of the mahogany table and the ornate red chandelier that hung in the main atrium. She glanced over at Ruby's door. It was closed. She padded over to the staircase and carefully took one step at a time, but with each step she took a sliver of doubt for what she was about to do crept into her mind.

At the top of the stairs she stopped. Her heart leapt as she heard Ruby's door open. She waited and watched as the maid entered the kitchen and then a minute later returned to her room. When she heard her door close, Celeste allowed herself to breathe. She looked around the apartment and remembered the moment Alex first showed her their new home in Hong Kong; his brilliant blue eyes had delighted in her enthusiasm. Those eyes had made her feel like she was the luckiest woman in the world. She almost had second thoughts for what she was about to do. But then she remembered the doctor telling her that the baby she had lost was a little girl. She looked back down the steps and then up towards Alex's bedroom door. Just a couple of steps further and she would be inside his room. But now her legs were rooted to the spot. They trembled as she commanded them to do as she wished.

She made her way to his door and then gently turned the handle, holding her breath as the door creaked open. She knew Bonnie and their new baby were in England. Kealana hadn't considered the consequences of telling her when they had spoken two days ago. She gambled on the fact that Alex would be sleeping alone. She didn't think he would cheat on Bonnie. After sleeping next to Alex for years, she knew that he wouldn't register the sound of her entering his room like this.

She walked into the room and breathed a sigh of relief – there was only one person in the bed and she could tell by the shape it was Alex. She looked for the tall glass of water on his bedside table, the one she was certain would be there. Old habits were hard to change. The white light from the skyscrapers outside lit up his face and body. He looked so peaceful in sleep.

She squeezed the vial tightly in her gloved hand. This was what she had planned, what she wanted to do. But now, looking at Alex, asleep and vulnerable, she wondered whether poisoning him would really help. Even with the wig and the unregistered key card, Alex's death would be traced to her. And killing him would make her no better than him. Did she really want to give up the rest of her life for him? She had already lost years trapped in a false marriage.

She had to look forward now, not back. She was in Hong Kong, a place she thought she would never return to. She had been to the places that had haunted her. She had overcome her fears. Even now, standing in her old apartment, she expected to feel anger, but she didn't. She felt alive. And Ben had given her his number and she actually wanted to call him. She hadn't felt that way about someone since… she couldn't even remember. That was a sign, wasn't it? A sign that her future was in front of her. It was her chance to start again, not spend the rest of her life in a prison cell repenting for what she had done. Alex had taken too much from her already. She took one last look at Alex, pocketed the vial, and made her way out of the room.

Outside, she pulled her wig off and quickly walked away from the apartment building. She didn't look back.

Did you like this book?

Let us know and leave your review!

Acknowledgements

I would like to thank my friends, family and work colleagues for their help and encouragement. A huge thank you to Abingdon Writers for their continual support and critique.

10665530R00213

Printed in Great Britain
by Amazon